PRAIRIE SCHOONER BOOK PRIZE IN FICTION

Editor Kwame Dawes

If the Body Allows It

Stories　　　　MEGAN CUMMINS

University of Nebraska Press　LINCOLN

The following chapters were previously published, some
in different forms: "Aerosol" in *One Teen Story*; "We Are
Holding Our Own" in *A Public Space*; "That Was Me Once"
in the *Masters Review*; "Water Burial" in *Hobart*; "The
Beast" in *Ninth Letter*; "*Heart*" as "Wild Beating Hearts" in
Okey-Panky; "*Eyes*" as "Engine" in *Phoebe*; and "*Skeleton*" as
"Q&A" in *Joyland*.

Library of Congress Cataloging-in-Publication Data

Names: Cummins, Megan, author.
Title: If the body allows it: stories / Megan Cummins.
Description: Lincoln: University of Nebraska Press, [2020] |
Series: Prairie schooner book prize in fiction
Identifiers: LCCN 2019054553
ISBN 9781496222831 (paperback)
ISBN 9781496223050 (epub)
ISBN 9781496223067 (mobi)
ISBN 9781496223074 (pdf)
Classification: LCC PS3603.U66333 A6 2020 | DDC 813/.6—
dc23
LC record available at https://lccn.loc.gov/2019054553

Set in Adobe Caslon Pro by Laura Buis.
Designed by L. Auten.

For Mark Cummins
who was my father

CONTENTS

If the Body Allows It

I

Heart

The doctor looks at me and says—no fuss, no apology—that someone like me should never be pregnant. This medication, that complication: they keep on doing card tricks with your life, even when you're doing better. I can't decide whether to be relieved or devastated. What's gone is not only the chance to have a baby but also the chance to decide whether or not I want a baby. So I say to my doctor, "Huh, that's interesting." Afterward the room is silent except for the crinkling of the exam table paper and the bubbling of the keyboard as the doctor finishes her notes.

I make my next appointment on my way out—*Marie, M-a-r-i-e*, I spell for the receptionist when she doesn't hear me. I sit alone in my car and glide through New Jersey toward the Newark brownstone where I live.

I think of the time I lied and told a cashier at Meijer that I had a daughter. This was in Ann Arbor, during college, years ago. The years since seem to have come and gone without even taking off their coats. The cashier asked me if I had a sick kid at home when the ten bottles of Pedialyte I was buying wobbled down the conveyor belt, fluorescent against the night outside, little lies themselves. I said yes, and the cashier—I remember her hair was the color of the inside of an almond—asked how old and I said eleven.

The lie emerged from my mouth sure of itself. But it was a ridiculous lie, the type of lie that would capsize you, the type of lie that makes people believe they know everything about you. I was only twenty-one, after all.

I was buying the Pedialyte for Octavia, who was my roommate, not my child, and her colon was full of bleeding ulcers. The Meijer was familiar to us, we'd been shopping there for years, but now Octavia was bedridden and in many ways I'd gotten used to doing everything with her, so it felt strange to wander the bright empty aisles alone.

Only one month earlier we'd decided, she and I, that it would be wise to go grocery shopping in a blizzard. This was before she got sick, before I got sick, before her father died and before mine did too. Before we both left Michigan and lost each other in the world, and back when writing was easier because I didn't have anything to write about. Maybe the blizzard was telling us: Stay home, girls, and let the world do its worst, but not to you, not yet. Instead we flew through the aisles, staticky with excitement because we loved this kind of daily danger back then, and beckoned it. By the time we were outside the wind was busy rearranging the world. The wheels of the cart tried to trample the snowdrifts, those piles of uncarved marble looking bright and starved on the asphalt. She pulled the cart and I pushed. Our laughter was crinkle cut and captured by the wind, carried to the stars, which I seem to recall shining brightly, which is impossible, but still, that's how I remember it: the constellations looking down on us through the white silk of the storm as though we were their only constituents, the two of us and our plastic bags that flapped in the wind like wild beating hearts.

Then we drove home on the icy roads and we were completely fine.

As I angle my car into its spot in Newark, a light precipitation falls. Somewhere between snow and rain. I kill the engine and sit in the car, which ticks as it cools, surrounded by the quiet midday street. Ralph, my boyfriend, is gone for the day, and when he gets home we'll pick up where we left off in our daily arguing. I should get on the train and go to work for the afternoon like I said I would, but I might call in. I want to call Octavia but she and I lost touch years ago. I've heard she's better. I've heard she has a baby. I'll probably cry in the shower later. There's nothing wrong with crying in the shower sometimes, even when you're in your thirties. Especially when you're in your thirties.

Back then I'd been embarrassed by the lie. Now I think that it might have felt good to shock someone, to have, if only briefly, a secret life. The cashier had stared at me when I said the made-up age—eleven—and the look in her eyes had said she could do nothing for me but tell me how much I owed.

The Beast

Twenty years had passed since I'd last seen the Beast. We were seventeen and embarrassed by each other back then. I'd asked him to prom. He'd agreed on the conditions that I would cover expenses and that we would have sex. I'd accepted the terms, so we had shared one night together, me in an aqua spaghetti-strap dress and him in a cheap rented tux. We both seemed to think we could have done better as we lay together in the motel bed, a foot of space between us.

On a Sunday morning at my kitchen table all those years later, I turned a page in the *New Plains Record*, and there he was. He'd become famous without my knowing it. His real name was Hadrian, and it was strange to see it in print. He and his band—a heavy metal group called Beastific—were doing what they called a Rural Terror Tour. They played small venues outside of cities, or they rented barns far out in the country.

I know we've played much bigger venues, noted Hadrian in the article, *but we like the intimacy of a small place off the beaten track. Our fans do, too. Beastific is about the people.*

"Beast. Ific," I said. "Be-ah-stific."

"What are you saying?" my husband asked.

I hadn't heard him walk into the kitchen. He wore a bathrobe, though it was nearly noon. We slept like teenagers on weekends, throwing off our REM cycles and making Monday mornings hellish. Our jobs at offices eroded the idea that living a long life was a good thing. We just wanted to sleep and never wake up.

The terms of our marriage also included a no-children clause, a stipulation that remained uncontested by either of us, even though boredom had come to our hearth like a sleeping dog. I'd assumed one of us would have a change of heart, or that we'd make a mistake: an insurgent zygote would hold us at gunpoint and make us *really* decide if we meant it.

But that never happened, and I told myself I didn't want children. What if I couldn't love them? Worse, what if they couldn't love me?

"Beverly, what are you thinking so hard about?" Robert asked. "Yoo-hoo. You look like you want to kill someone."

"If you were going to name your band with a pun on the word *beatific*, by spelling it like this"—I held up the paper and pointed to the name in the headline—"would you expect people to pronounce the first part normally, like *beast*, or the way you pronounce *beatific*, like *be-ahst* . . ."

"I'm not sure I follow," he said.

"I just think it's asking a lot of people."

"Hmm." Robert sat down across from me and tugged at the Financial section until it came loose.

"We should unsubscribe from the paper," I said.

"Does this beast thing really upset you that much?"

"It's not that," I said. "It's just garbage. They just write garbage. We can't afford to pay for garbage."

"We're actually doing okay right now, money-wise," Robert said. "So we can buy garbage if we want it. Do you know their music?"

"No."

"Do you want to go see them play?" Robert asked.

"Not really," I said quickly, folding the page and tucking it beneath the Sports section. "I'm making an Eggo. Want one?"

"Two," Robert said.

I took the box from the freezer and shook out a handful of waffles. Did the band's name mean Hadrian remembered me? The Beast had been my nickname for him. When he transferred to my school in the eleventh grade, he had long, chestnut-brown hair and a chiseled-looking face. He looked like the Beast from *Beauty and the Beast* after he turned back into a prince. A trace of rage shimmered around him, but for the most part the Beast was a quiet person.

I meant to taunt him with the nickname, because everyone else sought to make his life miserable, but then I grew fond of him. I thought of myself then as having one shy foot in the popular circle, so it was important to me that no one find out about my crush. I was mortified, of course, to realize I was in love with him—but this was before I knew I was neither popular nor unpopular, utterly nondescript. No one cared what I did or who I liked.

Then he found out about the nickname. I told too many people, thought myself too clever. One day he came to school with a close-cropped haircut, and the sudden transformation made me love him even more. I wondered if I'd had an effect on him, if he cared what I thought. The next day, I asked him to prom, jumping at his stipulations because I didn't know enough then to know I was acting cowardly. I told my friends I was doing it as a joke.

The ringing phone brought me back to our kitchen in New Plains, Nebraska. I answered.

"I'm calling about an overdue balance on an American Express card," said the woman on the other end. She'd asked for me by name. She had a pleasant voice, but cool and firm.

"I know this is a scam," I said. "I've never had an American Express card in my life. Goodbye."

"Again?" Robert asked.

"Again. On a Sunday, too. I looked it up on the internet. Apparently, these scammers convince people to mail checks to them."

"I just checked your credit score last week," Robert said. "You're looking good."

He put down the paper and grinned. "Definitely looking good from here."

From here was about as close as we came to each other these days.

I worked at an insurance brokerage firm as something called a marketing specialist, but I mostly answered phones and forwarded emails and acted as a personal assistant and, sometimes, partner in crime to my boss, Cal Nevins.

Once, without discomfort, Cal handed me a pair of women's glasses and a disk of birth control pills along with an address written on a scrap of paper. I wrapped the glasses in paper towels from the bathroom and slipped everything into a manila envelope, sticking a generic return label to its corner. I thought about adding a note, warning the woman she could get pregnant on the pill if she chronically missed days, but no one needs a stranger to patronize her.

One time I walked to the liquor store on my lunch break and bought him a fifth of Grey Goose with the company card. I didn't mind, I told him. I needed to buy a lottery ticket anyway, and a tube of Pringles for my lunch. I used my own cash for the lottery ticket, not his card, and I saved the receipt. I didn't want any trouble if I won, but I didn't end up winning.

Cal often went out for long lunches at the bar in the hotel next door to our building, then called me from the parking lot and asked me to bring him his car keys. I always did, no matter how strongly he smelled of booze or how red his eyes were.

I commuted forty minutes from New Plains to Omaha each day to do these things. Taking care of Cal's twin daughters, I liked best. They could be spoiled, grumbling girls, but they were sweethearts more than anything.

I found them both sitting in my desk chair when I arrived at work on Monday morning. The office was empty except for them. They'd taken ice cream from the freezer and were sucking chocolate off of flimsy plastic spoons. The lights were off, and cartoons playing on my computer blew moonlight over the girls' faces.

"Dad told us to wait here for you, Bevie." Caroline looked up at me.

"Is that so?" I leaned over them and nudged down the volume on the computer. "Are these cartoons pirated?"

"No." Maggie giggled. "You don't have to pirate anymore, Bev, you *stream*."

"Let's go." I frowned. "I'll take you to school."

Maggie cried in the car, while Caroline stared pensively out the window.

"I've just about had enough of the second grade." Maggie hiccupped.

"I know," I said. "It's a hard life. Here's a wet wipe. Clean that chocolate off your face."

"I didn't do my homework," Caroline said. "I was supposed to make bookmarks."

I sighed. Caroline's poor performance in school meant Cal had to go to conferences with his loathed ex-wife. "Tell your teacher you left them at home, but that someone's bringing them later. Okay?"

"Which home?" Caroline asked. "Mom's or Dad's?"

"Well, that's up to you. Actually, say it was your dad's."

"I did my homework," mumbled Maggie.

I finished Caroline's bookmarks when I returned to the office, which was now alive with ringing phones and the rushing sound of the copier. The lights were on in Cal's office, but the blinds were drawn and the door closed. Caroline's smile, reflected in the rearview mirror, had harpooned me. I felt elated from having spent a little time with her and Maggie. Sometimes I wondered what I wouldn't do for those girls.

The assignment was to illustrate bookmarks with depictions from *The Trumpet of the Swan*. I wasn't a good artist, and my thoughts wandered from the girls to Hadrian. The night before had brought a burgeoning fantasy of the two of us together and young. I'd imagined we'd done things we hadn't, normal things like driving around in his car or eating at a restaurant. As quickly as the fantasy brought joy, it brought unhappiness, a reminder I was no longer very young.

Our old selves, or what could have been our old selves, filled me with sadness, the striking type of sadness that demands to be remedied someway, somehow, and immediately. I put Caroline's bookmarks aside and clicked through the internet until I had two tickets to the Beastific show in my basket. Luckily they were cheap; my credit card was nearly maxed out. I paid for the tickets before I could change my mind.

I bought two tickets because one seemed desperate. I didn't want to take Robert with me, but who else was there? The show was the next day, a Tuesday night in New Plains, when everything was so dead we sometimes wondered if the sun would overlook us in the morning.

The phone rang. I answered.

"How did you get this number?" I said. "Stop harassing me."

The caller was a man this time, from the same supposed collection agency, and he recited with confidence my full name and my Social Security number. He gave the balance on the credit card, an astronomical amount I wasn't sure I'd heard correctly.

"I've told you that I know this is a scam. If you were a real collection agency you'd send me something in the mail."

"We have. Several times."

I listened to his breathing as he waited for me to respond. Then I hung up. I pulled up the number for Amex's customer service and was ready to call them—to complain, to ease my worries—when Cal emerged from his office, wearing a white shirt with thin silky pinstripes running up and down the fabric. His always bleary eyes made him look some combination of tired and high. Sometimes I thought he was the wrong sort of person to have money; other times I believed the money had made him the way he was. I often felt protective of him, or maybe I was only protective of myself: I helped him with so many of the things he did wrong.

"Beautiful," he said, picking up a bookmark. "You made it look like a child drew these."

I wanted to ask him for gas money for this morning and for the trip I would be making later to drop off the bookmarks. The girls went to a private school thirty minutes away. But I felt too ashamed. Asking for money reminded me I had no real claim to their love.

But Cal would pay anything to show his two daughters he loved them, especially after he and his wife had dragged each other through that nasty divorce. I sent the girls presents to her house using Cal's credit card. I made their lunches for the next day in the office kitchen before I left on the afternoons Cal had the girls. I spread mayonnaise on turkey sandwiches, peeled carrots, and filled tiny containers with ranch dressing, and tied neat baggies of chocolate with ribbon.

Other people would quit or at least find the work demeaning. I hadn't gotten a promotion in the five years I'd worked for Cal, and I could be making more money somewhere else—money Robert and I could put toward a down payment. But this job made me comfortable, as though I'd found a knot of people who understood and appreciated me. Their dilemmas were mine to solve, and I solved them better than I did my own.

Robert and I had met ten years ago when we both worked for a labor union, he as the bookkeeper and I as the office manager. We worked for activists, which we felt good about, but we didn't have to be activists ourselves, which made us feel even better.

Then a new president and financial secretary were elected. The financial secretary would keep the books and do the taxes herself, so Robert lost his job. I was let go because the new administration was suspicious of the old. The former president had been ousted for using union funds to visit, repeatedly, a psychic who charged a hundred dollars an hour. He'd gone crazy, but he was my friend.

Why hadn't anything concerned me back then? Even when the

president was charged with embezzlement, the idea that I might face my own consequences for my choices someday never seemed real to me.

Robert and I fell in love in our waning days at the union. We whispered in the break room about our futures and complained that it wasn't fair that we were suspected of complicity. Integrity, trust, honor: those things had been important to us back then. Robert said he hadn't known about the president's secret debit card until it was too late, and as soon as he found out, he told a trustee. I believed him at the time, and now I didn't care.

Robert and I were less in love now but we were still friends. There wasn't any ill will between us, only boredom, and, on my part, occasional weeping in the shower. All that life, six years of marriage plus two years of dating, had passed serenely, without excitement or tragedy. We could have done with more money, but we always made rent, even if it meant putting groceries on credit. If only one of us had been mentally ill, or an alcoholic. If only I'd won the lottery one of those times I'd put a five-dollar bill down on the counter and asked for five easy picks.

I stood over the stove that night, stirring ramen noodles for our dinner. The collection calls had distracted me. I'd looked through Robert's spreadsheets of our finances when I'd gotten home, but nothing seemed strange to me. The usual expenses, the usual low balance left over at the end.

"Robert?" I called. "I need the computer. I want to look at my credit score. Did you use the website that aggregates all the different reports out there?"

Robert didn't seem to hear me. His office popped with the sound of music and gunfire. He was playing his computer game in which he was a spy on the *Titanic*. The objective wasn't to stop the ship from sinking, that happened regardless, but rather to stop World War I and the Russian Revolution from happening. I didn't get the connection but trusted it was there.

I turned the burner off and poured the noodles and their packets of salty powder into bowls.

"What's this?" I set his bowl down on a pile of papers, picking up a book that lay open, pages down, on the desk.

Robert snatched it away. "Don't," he said.

But I'd seen the title. "*Cheater's Guide to 'Titanic: Adventure out of Time'!*" I exclaimed. "You're cheating at the game?"

"Oh, come on, Beverly," he said. "It's a game."

"But you've been telling me about the complicated puzzles as though you'd figured them all out yourself."

Robert turned the computer off the way you weren't supposed to, with one push of one button, and left the room. The book, with its answers and shortcuts, was small and depressing. We didn't even have anything interesting to hide. Better not to fight at all.

"You didn't save your game," I said quietly.

He didn't hear me.

"I don't care how you play the game!" I said loudly.

Steam spiraled from the bowl of noodles, but even the steam looked pitiful, as though it could barely bring itself to rise.

Robert returned, a sheepish smile on his face. Our fights never lasted long.

"I'm sorry," he said.

"Me too."

He took the pair of chopsticks I'd set on his desk and clacked them together, then used them to pick up a strand of my hair and put it in his mouth. I smiled; he smiled. I put the book down on the desk but picked it up again. It had been covering an American Express bill with my name on it, addressed to Robert's office.

"Bev, don't. That's a mistake."

The bill unfurled in my hands, revealing a long list of charges. Gas, groceries, but also large amounts spent at Best Buy and on Amazon, and then other websites I didn't recognize.

"I was going to pay it all off. I just needed more time." Robert's face looked alien: his small mouth was open wide and red splotches appeared on his neck and cheeks as though he'd been hexed.

Until he spoke, a part of me—a desperate, hopeful part—believed this to be part of the scam. Then it was as though I'd been sleeping on a plane, and I was thrown awake by the thump of wheels on the tarmac.

"How much?"

Robert hesitated. I stared him down.

"Twenty thousand," he said.

A voice came back to me, one of the debt collectors on the phone. The number, so high, had made me completely sure it was a scam. But now Robert was standing there with his lie breaking apart between us, and I could hear myself snapping at the man on the phone. In my own memory I now sounded like the one who was wrong, a belligerent woman trying to get out of paying her bills.

I let the bill fall to the floor and sat heavily in the office chair. It twirled vaguely beneath my weight. Robert stood before me, admitting to what he'd done, but I felt guilty, like a criminal surprised at having been caught. There was the bill with my name on it. It said I had spent that money; it said those numbers belonged to me.

I asked Robert what he'd spent the money on, but he didn't answer me, and I didn't really want to know. Not tonight at least. I was just dumbstruck, and tired, and wanted to eat my pathetic dinner alone. I told Robert so, and he went into the bedroom and closed the door.

The noodles had gone gummy. Moonlight shifted through the curtains and I listened to the night birds making a cacophony outside. To soothe myself, I thought of the motel room where the Beast and I had spent our night. I remembered the stained red carpeting and an electrical outlet dangling from the wall by its wires. I'd stood on the balcony in my ridiculous dress, watching a girl—my age, or a little older—swim the length of the pool in slow strokes. I could see her whole body: long legs shimmering in the pool lights, the wavy white of her bathing suit, her hair moving like a jellyfish as she swam.

I'd turned to see Hadrian, his jacket removed, his tie undone and hanging from his neck. Had I gone to him or waited for him to come to me? Had he torn my dress off with the curtains wide open? No. I went inside and closed the door and the blinds. I think I might have tried to talk about poetry with him. I liked to write poetry back then, but mostly my poems were full of questions that made no sense, questions only a deranged person would ask. *Oh, and didn't we love to go into the river?*

I was glad to find Cal full of anxious energy the next day at work. I needed a distraction. Robert and I had woken to our alarms and readied ourselves without speaking. Why hadn't I thrown him out? Because I didn't want him to put a motel on credit? Because I didn't want to be alone? I had thought the two of us had been bearing our boredom silently, bravely, but Robert had been buying things to make himself happy. And what had he been buying? Only a horrible habit could require that amount of money. I wondered if it was gambling or pornography, or hookers or drugs. I almost missed my exit, so caught up was I in Robert's imagined transgressions.

I parked my car and was waiting for the weather report to come on the radio—my signal that it was time to walk the two minutes from the car to the office so I could clock in by eight—when Robert called. I ignored it. He texted me a photo of the Amex cut in half, a gesture that annoyed me since it seemed he'd done most of his shopping online, where he probably had the number saved.

The morning brought a problem with one of the clients, a parking service called Safely Park. Cal had brokered the policy but now the carrier had canceled the general liability insurance because, when the policy was initially signed, Cal had forged the loss runs to make it appear as though Safely Park had never had an accident or filed a claim. But Safely Park crashed cars all the time.

Cal was furious when the notice of cancellation was faxed over. He snapped at the sales staff and the customer service reps. The general liability specialist emerged from Cal's office with her head hung. I caught her blotting tears in the kitchen. Somehow, this was everyone's fault but Cal's and mine, though I'd used Photoshop to make the loss runs look clean. "I'll end up in the slammer right next to Cal," I'd joked back then, but I grew nervous as the day went on. What if the carrier reported the fraudulent loss runs to the department of insurance? What if I did go to prison?

Cal was on the phone all afternoon, calling in favors, saying he didn't know how the mistake had happened. Finally, he slapped the phone into its cradle, which I heard from my desk outside of his office. I turned to see him take the bottle of Grey Goose from his desk, and he called out, "All clear! Get out of here, you scoundrels."

Everyone in the office clapped. I did too. We hated Cal when he yelled and we loved him when he let us leave at 3:00 p.m., even if we'd almost gotten arrested earlier that day.

I lingered, and when everyone except Cal had left, I checked my credit rating. There was the American Express card, the balance glowering at me, and beneath it a Visa I didn't recognize. I began weeping. I'd gotten pregnant on prom night, the night I'd spent with Hadrian. I stayed pregnant for twelve weeks, until I turned eighteen and didn't need my parents' permission. Getting rid of the baby then had been the right choice, but now, having a baby would never be an option, would never be feasible. I wondered if I could sue Robert, or put him in jail. But the truth was I was either bound to Robert, bound to the debt, or free of it but on my own.

I put my head in my hands.

"Beverly? You okay?"

Cal had come out of his office.

I swiped tears from my eyes and slowly gathered my things. Cal stood in his doorway, clutching the bottle of Grey Goose by his side. I avoided his eyes as I slipped my arms into my jacket. "Yeah. Yep. Just worried about today. I didn't mean to do anything wrong."

"You didn't do anything wrong."

"Everything's really okay?" I said.

"Oh, Bevie," he said. "I would never throw you under the bus. If the DOI came for you they'd have to go through me first."

"Of course," I said.

"What a day," he said as he swung the bottle of vodka to his mouth. "I need to go get a drink."

I looked at him closely and saw tears brimming in his eyes.

"I'm going to a concert tonight." I didn't know why I was telling him but I knew I didn't want to see him cry. I hadn't told Robert about the show, and as I spoke I knew I wasn't going to.

"What band?"

"Someone's I knew a long time ago. I don't think the music will be very good."

"Sounds fun."

"I have an extra ticket. It's all the way in New Plains, though."

Sunlight pierced the window behind Cal's head. He appeared to be thinking. We didn't want each other. If we did, something would have happened by now. We just wanted to be a little less lonely; we wanted something different than what we had.

Cal and I ate dinner at the hotel bar, Cal guzzling vodka sodas, and then I drove us to the venue, a barn just outside of New Plains. I parked in a roped-off grass lot that spread away from the barn. Clusters of wild violets sprouted in the fields surrounding. Teenagers in heavy black boots stomped over them. Cal had fallen asleep on the way, and I sat in the car with the engine clicking, embarrassed that I'd cried, and surprised that I'd felt so strongly that I'd lost someone upon seeing my ruined credit, the rating persistently red on the screen. In a life of blind, vague longings, I'd seen clearly something I wanted, only to have it taken away.

I nudged Cal awake. "Ready, or would you rather stay here?"

"Ready."

The barn teemed with teenagers wearing black. They'd painted their faces to look like skulls, and some wore devil's horns like I'd seen Hadrian wearing in the paper. I trudged in my pumps and nylons toward the door. Cal trailed behind, looking ill. The last of the sun fell on a boy selling T-shirts adorned with the band name. The *t* in Beastific was an upside-down Gothic cross.

"Twenty bucks," the kid said. He looked gaunt but his teeth had been straightened with braces.

"No thanks," I said.

"These kids are fucked up," Cal said. He pointed to a group of girls staring ghoulishly from within the hoods of their sweatshirts, their eyes rimmed with heavy black eyeliner. "What parents would let their kids dress like this?"

I thought of Cal's girls and wondered what their futures would bring. Now they wore matching sapphire rings, Christmas gifts from Cal. What would they trade those rings for, when the time came?

"They probably think we're parents who wouldn't let our kids go alone," I said. "They're probably wondering who here is the loser who came with their parents."

I warmed at the thought that one of these kids could be my own. I'd noticed a few women in parked cars, piles of coats in the back seats.

"I'm going to find the bar," Cal said.

One long note resounded from inside the barn. The show had begun.

I stood in the back and watched Hadrian sing into a microphone swinging from the ceiling. His face was the same face: strong chin and sunken eyes, high cheekbones. He was wearing his hair long again. He still looked boyish. I became, once again, the girl who wanted him, the girl who had teased him out of love, but standing there, I also felt the presence of all the time we'd been apart. We'd never even known each other in the first place. I'd had nothing to do with his angst. I was not the wicked bitch he sang about. Our lives had briefly overlapped, and that was it. These two feelings—I loved him, and we meant nothing to each other—combined to make me brazen.

The crowd of teenagers moved chaotically, but I tried to shoulder my way into the mosh pit. I lost my breath quickly; my jostled bones felt like rattling tin cans. I was knocked to my knees, and a group of hands pulled me up and pushed me toward the back wall—the safe haven of the few adults who had chosen to come inside. I felt stupid, but no one seemed to notice me.

Hadrian sang one song, then another. They all sounded the same to me. But I couldn't take my eyes off of him. I wanted to talk to him, touch him. Above me the packed beams of the roof seemed to clasp their hands in prayer.

The show ended, and my keys were in my hands but I didn't go to my car. I milled around outside with the rest of the people finishing their drinks or buying T-shirts and waiting for a chance to get an autograph. I didn't see Cal. I put my keys back in my purse. And then a swell of sound rose from the crowd as the band emerged from the barn, their long hair flying in the breeze. Hadrian was close enough I could see the closed smile that shaped his jaw. And I knew, upon seeing it, that I wanted to know if he would recognize me. I thought of Robert as I shouldered through the crowd, nudging aside the girls who lingered around Hadrian. I pictured Robert at home, nosing around the *Titanic*, flipping through his book for clues.

Then I was in front of Hadrian, and his eyes met mine with the blankness of a stranger's.

"Do you want me to sign something?" he asked, looking down at my hands, which weren't holding a T-shirt.

"I'm sorry," I said, fumbling through my purse. "I'm here to get something signed for my daughter. She couldn't make it—she really wanted to come, but she had to work."

The lie came out like a ball of light: enthusiastic and with a true-ness of spirit that even my truths didn't always possess. I thought he might recognize my voice, but he didn't seem to.

"I was going to say," Hadrian said, and his smile opened up a little, "that you don't look like our typical fan."

I gave him a twenty, and he pulled a T-shirt from a box near his feet and signed his name to it. He handed it to me along with a flyer for an after party.

"Bring your daughter if she gets off work," he said. "We'll take a photo."

And without saying anything else, he handed his attention over to the group of kids standing behind me, smoking impatiently.

A photo. A family photo. I almost said the words aloud.

I was overjoyed, my heart punching my chest, but as I walked away the joy grew damp with dread. I looked for Cal, hoping he needed me for something. I wanted to go to the party but hoped to have a reason not to. I was afraid of what I would do, and I was afraid I wouldn't do anything at all.

I found Cal making out with a woman. She looked like some-one's mother, and also a businesswoman. I wondered what I'd be mailing back to her the next day. I called Cal's name, and he broke away from her.

"Bevie!" He sounded delighted. "Look, you go home. I've got a ride."

"Do you need me to pick up the girls? I could stay with them."

The girls. As though they were mine, too.

"No," Cal said. "The bitch on wheels has them tonight."

I walked away, but slowly. What if earlier, when we were walking from the car, I'd reached out and held his hand? What if we'd played the role of parents, even if only for one night?

But one thing in my life I was realistic about was this: I couldn't make a move on Cal. I would have to quit a job I badly needed. I knew, too, that Cal was self-centered, had been a bad husband,

and wasn't that good of a father. And, no matter how dysfunctional our relationship already was, neither of us had anything else that was stable.

So I left Cal with the woman and went to the party.

The after party was at a motel off I-80. Beastific had booked a few rooms on the top floor. People wound their way in and out of rooms with doors propped open. Music blared and people mingled close to one another. I picked my way through plastic cups and wafting cigarette smoke, looking for Hadrian. I was curious to know how much the motel would charge their credit card for damages when all was said and done.

I went out on one of the balconies and watched cars go by, their headlights straining to cut through the dark. I swayed against the railing, suddenly dizzy from the height and from the beer I'd been handed upon entry.

I felt a gust of air behind me. Someone had slid open the glass door. I turned to see Hadrian, who was flanked by two girls who looked to be in their twenties. I looked at the blond one with her lips near Hadrian's earlobe and saw Caroline. The sulking one behind her could be Maggie in ten years. What I felt when I looked at them wasn't rivalry but a hope that Hadrian wouldn't use them—and in that sense I wanted to take him from them, because I'd already been used, and when one got to be my age, being used was at least a little bit of excitement.

"Hey," Hadrian said, unsnaking his arm from the brunette's waist so he could snap a lighter beneath the cigarette that dangled from his lips. "Did your daughter make it?"

"She isn't coming." I looked away as I said it, into the distance, as though I might recognize her in a car speeding by on the highway.

I turned back toward him. Beyond his shoulder I could see my coat on the bed where I'd left it. I could grab it and flee. My eyes lingered on it: a camel coat, made from a nice buttery fabric, a

Christmas gift from Cal the year before. I'd found it tucked under my desk in a ribbon-tied box while the rest of the office received a bottle of cheap red wine.

But I couldn't leave without talking to Hadrian, without bringing him to recognize me. I wanted to stop thinking of each day as something to be gotten out of the way, and this night was one of the most important of my life so far, a night I would remember forever, and I didn't want to have to revise the memory later on, to scratch out the silence and write in words I hadn't said.

"We need to talk alone."

In a moment of boldness I looked pointedly at the girls, who raised their eyebrows but complied because I was old enough to be their mother. They slid shut the door, muffling the sounds of the party.

Hadrian was uncomfortable, I could tell. He looked at the retreating backs of the girls regretfully, and I knew he'd only come out here to look for a younger version of me. He flicked ash from his cigarette and gestured toward the cars as though I'd only told him to stay with me so I could show him the view.

"So," he said, "what's up?"

I didn't say anything more, not right away. I put my hand on his arm, though, to keep him from going inside. What if I hadn't asked him to prom, hadn't gotten pregnant? How much of my life had been shaped by the decisions I had made with this man years ago? Here with me seemed to be not all the people I could've been, but all the people I hadn't been. Hadrian probably wasn't worth my obsession—as I wasn't worth his—but I wanted to be sure so I backed him against the railing and kissed him.

His lips didn't feel familiar. I didn't recall their shape from years ago, but I wanted more of them all the same. My nerves leaped, fiery, when he returned the kiss and touched my neck. He dropped his beer on the ground—I felt it splash my leg—so he could grab my ass.

He put his mouth on my neck. "You might be older than those two girls combined," he said, laughing.

I pulled away. "We're the same age, you asshole," I said.

He looked surprised. Maybe he thought he looked younger. Maybe his career depended on it. The shows, the parties, the angst of his music. I laughed at him. He laughed, too, except he had no clue why we were laughing.

He took my hand. I was so close to getting what I'd come for, which if not his recognition was his attention, but I caught sight of a red windbreaker I recognized. A man was wandering the lot below with his phone in his palm, its rectangle screen glowing in the dark.

It was Robert. Robert had found me.

My stare drew his attention. He looked up at me and waved.

I could turn my back on him, pull Hadrian into the party and through the crowd until we found a quiet corner, but the sight of my husband brought me, just by an inch, back to the reality of my life. The uncertainty of it. An urge to confront Robert, as I hadn't the night before, swelled in me.

"Do you know him?" Hadrian asked.

"I do," I said. "I have to go talk to him."

I paused.

"Come with me."

Hadrian looked down at the parking lot, at Robert looking up at us, and then back at me and I saw in his eyes that the spell, whatever it had been, was broken.

"No," he said. "You do your thing. Come and find me after."

I looked at him. I smiled. "I'm not going to find you after," I said. "But will you do me one favor first?"

Before he agreed I kissed him again so Robert could see.

When we parted, I cupped his cheek in my palm. "Goodbye, Beast," I said. "Do you remember prom night?"

Hadrian stepped away from me, leaving my hand to cup the air. His eyes searched my face, and I smiled. I was leaving a piece of myself with him; maybe now he would remember me. The baby, though—my baby was my secret, and I would never tell anyone.

In the moonlight these two men looked at me. I knew that using Hadrian wouldn't make me feel less used myself. It wouldn't make me any younger, and it wouldn't make Robert feel ashamed. Still, I would have liked to sleep with him again. I would've liked to send Robert home knowing Hadrian would be good in bed, better than before, and that morning was far away. But part of being an adult was letting passing fantasies blow away, wasn't it, even if I'd already taken the first step toward making a mistake?

The motel doors slid open and Robert stood looking stricken. I closed the distance between us.

"How'd you find me?" I asked.

Robert looked at the balcony, but Hadrian had gone. Slowly, Robert turned his phone around to show me the screen. A map with a pulsing blue dot stared back at me. I looked closer. The dot was in the parking lot of the motel.

I was the dot.

"I installed this app on our phones," Robert said. "GPS tracker. You can track me too—here, give me your phone, I'll show you . . ."

But I held up my hand.

My person, my money, my privacy: my husband had manipulated all of it. Maybe he thought the app was harmless, but he hadn't bothered to tell me about it. As with the credit card, I hadn't bothered to look. But I was waking up.

Robert brought his phone to his chest. "Beverly," he asked. "Who was that?"

"It doesn't matter," I said.

"It *matters*," Robert said.

"No. It would've at one time. But not anymore. I'm sorry, Robert, but I can't trust you."

My car was parked in the back of the lot, and I said nothing more as I walked away. My heels clacked on the concrete, I fished for my keys, and when I was in the car with the engine roaring, I opened the window and flung my phone from it so Robert couldn't track me. I cherished the feeling of being free.

I was surprised to find Cal at the hotel bar where hours earlier we'd shared a meal. I'd planned to go alone for a drink and then sleep on the couch by the receptionist's desk at my office. I thought Cal would be with the woman from the show, but he sat hunched over a vodka on the rocks. The TV stared down at him, beaming a basketball game over the bar, to which Cal paid no attention.

I'd lost my beautiful camel coat, and there wouldn't be another one.

"Your night didn't work out the way you'd hoped either?" I said.

He looked up at me and I saw relief seep into his face, as though it were a spill he'd sopped up with a napkin. "Oh, Bev," he said. "I'm happy to see you."

He hugged me, still holding his glass, which sweated on my back. I ordered a drink over his shoulder, and we sat on the high stools, embracing, surrounded by empty tables and plastic plants. Cal began to shake with silent sobs, and this time, instead of pulling him away from his tears, I ran my hands in circles over his back and let him cry.

"Starting tomorrow," he said, "things will change. No more forged loss runs, no more lies."

"Okay," I said.

"No more close calls with the DOI. We'll do things right going forward."

"I'm going to hold you to that," I said. "Or I'm leaving."

I meant it, too. I didn't want to commit fraud anymore. I wanted to be proud of what I did for a living.

Countergirls

Karen shoveled the dead cat from the road and carried it, balanced on the spade, down the hill to the dock. Beneath the slatted wood, the river ran smoothly. She tilted the cat inside a canvas shopping bag she'd filled with rocks and, with a heave to give the bundle some air, tossed it into the river. The cat sank. In the distance, the dam hummed.

The cat had been one of twelve or so, although Karen could no longer remember which ones had come from which litters. Her older daughter, Venus, had fed them all the first year they appeared under the deck and then waited through winter to see the next batches of bleary eyed little things. Karen eventually foreclosed on this joy: she spent an entire summer capturing each and every one and taking it to the shelter to be fixed. The vet tech came to recognize her.

If Venus had been upset then about her truncated lineage of cats, she would certainly be devastated over Pie à la Mode—her favorite of them all and, even Karen had to admit, the friendliest. It was the only one that would poke its head past a door left ajar, nearly open to the idea of being domesticated.

But Venus lived in a women's shelter now and wouldn't be home until the weekend, an agreement they'd all worked out with Karen's husband, Warren, whom Venus called Fake Dad. Karen's younger daughter, Maille, seemed to like Warren just fine, though she saw him less frequently than Venus did. Maille was six when her father died of a hospital infection after heart surgery. She claimed not to remember much about him. In fact, Maille started calling Warren

Dad (showing no emotion that indicated either love or sarcasm) so soon after Karen's remarriage that it had made even Karen uncomfortable.

Warren reciprocated both girls' feelings: he liked Maille all right but didn't seem interested in treating Venus like family. Soon after he and Karen married, Venus had shown up in California, a bedraggled grad school dropout whose scoliosis kept her taking pills. With nowhere to live, she took the basement bedroom that had once been Warren's son's. Warren had put up with her for two years, but a few weeks ago he'd reached the end of his patience. Venus had to go, he said.

The shelter was her only option. Now Venus called Karen every evening, asking when she could come home.

Tonight, Karen decided, she would say nothing about the cat. But she would have to keep the phone away from Warren, who would definitely blab. He liked to rattle the chain link that separated Karen from Venus, a usually voiceless tension that indicated they each disapproved of the way the other was living her life.

Karen took the broom that was propped against the dock railing and swept some leaves into the water. The dam's sloped wall was brushed with pink evening light. The first mosquitoes popped out of nowhere. All of this was Warren's: the house on the Stanislaus River not far from Yosemite, the cell phone plan, the rickety motorboat they took downriver where Warren would try to show off and run the boat into the churning water beneath the dam. Every time, the boat was battered back to calmer waters. Whenever the battery died, which it did often because Warren was always burning it out this way, Warren claimed it was Karen's job to change it.

She hated the boat. Her first husband, Charlie, would never have asked her to be responsible for his hobbies in her old life, the one in Michigan that seemed about to dissolve like tissue paper stirred up in water. Seventeen years had passed since Charlie died, and Karen was forgetting things about him, as though her memories were coins, and she stood tossing them into a fountain. He was there in her children, of course, but they had been alive for many years without him. Although the two girls had followed Karen to California after college, Venus then Maille, they weren't hers and Charlie's, not anymore. Venus, lost to the endless refills the doctors gave her. And Maille, to the internet.

More specifically, to a man on the internet. Her lovely daughter, who'd never had trouble finding boys, had done the exact thing Karen had: met a man online, then gone and married him. In Karen's own case, she felt she'd done right. She'd been fifty-two, with dwindling options. At least she and Warren had gone to Las Vegas. Maille called her mother from Reno.

Pie à la Mode had sunk from sight. The boat creaked in the water. The river smelled of mud and algae. The first fat drops of rain splattered on Karen's arm as she walked back up the hill to the house. The other cats had all scattered. The four hummingbird feeders were empty—although they usually were now, one bully hummingbird having scared the rest off.

Right inside the house was a small den, cozy, with too much furniture. Warren had lit the potbellied stove. Karen went to the kitchen and prodded slices of candied orange rind from a sheet of wax paper on the counter where they'd been drying all day. Not just Venus would be home that weekend but Maille, too, and a few of her friends. An informal celebration of her marriage, though her new husband, Maille said, could not come. Warren, upon learning this, had asked if he could also skip the dinner.

Warren didn't seem to understand how Karen's old life had worked, its loudness, how for so long it had been full only of girls. Nothing about it particularly agreed with him: the long phone calls, the constant need to see her daughters, her rich cooking. A stick of butter in every meal.

"Venus called," Warren said, walking into the kitchen.

"You didn't!" Karen said.

"Pie à la Road."

"Warren!"

Warren and she got along when it was just the two of them. It was the moment someone else arrived that they became strangers.

Outside, birds swooped into the yard, making big parabolas. The rain had grown hard enough to knock insects from their flight and in the grass was a feast.

Even though Venus was shaken up over the cat and already furious with Karen for having to live in the shelter, she couldn't demand much. She had no car, a flimsy bank account, and a college degree she seemed to have forgotten about. She claimed that the Piercing Pagoda—the last job she'd held, a kiosk in the mall back in Michigan—didn't care how much schooling she had, as long as she could punch holes in girls' ears. (As it turned out, she couldn't: she lost the job after one shift for bringing a baggie of apple slices, a needle, and a lighter, insisting the gun was bad for the cartilage.) But Karen saw her point: Would it be better to meet the expectations for someone who had only finished high school, or fall short of those for a college graduate?

Karen herself had struggled through night classes while working the Clinique counter. She'd been a little glad when Venus lost the Pagoda job, afraid she and her daughters were cursed to work at kiosks. Countergirls. At Clinique, Karen's uniform was a white lab coat, and it had made her feel like a complete fraud. With clients, she overcompensated, rouging the women until they looked like they had rosacea. At least, that was the way one woman had put it, to which Karen had replied, "That, or I just gave you the best orgasm of your life!"

At the end of that shift, Karen was put on probation, under close watch by her manager as she gave women quizzes to determine their nightly moisturizing routines. Still, things more or less worked out for her, even if it had taken longer than she might have liked.

She loved Warren, and their house on the river, and the fact that her daughters lived nearby. She didn't have a job of her own but had stopped feeling disappointed with herself because of it. It was Venus's expiring potential that worried Karen. Karen had spent her own youth being naughty and had avoided ruin, shaping up like most people, but Venus had gone bad late in the game, after a spotless high school and undergraduate record. After college, during her first year at the School of Public Health, she'd dated a heroin addict recently released from two years in Jackson prison, whom Karen loved to blame. Suddenly, it wasn't just him hanging around Venus but all of his friends, too. It shocked Karen, how you couldn't know just one heroin addict. They came in twos, threes. They brought their friends from rehab, and those friends had girl-friends, and those girlfriends had roommates, and so on. They all decided together that it was safe to start drinking again, that they could stick to alcohol and forget the rest. And Venus, with her painkiller buzz, had fit right in.

It seemed unfair that her scoliosis would ruin more than just her spine. Since her diagnosis, her life hadn't been easy; it hadn't even been consistent, full of good years and bad years. Karen's own waffling hadn't helped. For so long, she enabled Venus, and now, at Warren's insistence, she was toughening up. On the phone with Venus after Pie à la Road, Karen almost agreed to pick her up from the shelter in Merced a few days earlier than planned, but there was Warren, sitting in the den, shaking his head.

"You kept him, right? The body?" Venus said. When Karen said nothing, she shouted, "Mom!"

"How about a memorial service?"

"Fine," Venus said. "You know, the social workers think I shouldn't be here."

Karen knew that meant Venus did not think she should be there when the river house had a basement room in which she could languish.

Warren rolled his eyes when Karen hung up. For a psychologist, he did not do very well with people. At least not her people. She regretted that she often felt in his debt, because he paid for everything, even though she cooked and cleaned and kept the house running and had rescued him from loneliness.

But Karen could understand his frustration. It was the same frustration she felt with her daughters, only without the love to alleviate it. Venus could do nothing right; Maille, nothing wrong. In her more honest moments—after a glass of wine or two—Karen admitted to herself that, while she loved them both equally, she preferred Venus to Maille. Maille had a temper when it came to the bad habits of others. Small, meaningless things, such as Karen forgetting to clean out the coffeepot, triggered something borderline venomous in Maille, as though Karen's worth as a person was based on her ability to keep her kitchen clean.

Maille's own indulgences—which she did have, though it might not seem like it—she managed to justify, usually with meticulous research on the internet. The husband wasn't the first time she'd come home with a surprise: a month after she moved to California, she returned from a trip to LA with breasts twice their former size, bought on a payment plan.

When Venus saw them, she accused Maille of stealing her boobs. In the den of the river house she lined her sister up next to her. "See?" she exclaimed, turning Maille by the shoulders so Karen could view the profile. "C cup. Like me. Unfair."

But Maille worked at a café at the time, and the boob job had gotten her the extra shifts she wanted. And bigger tips.

"I can't avoid sexism in the workplace, so I might as well exploit it myself, at least until this country undergoes systemic change," Maille had said.

Karen was dumbstruck. There was something both wrong and right about what her daughter was saying.

In her unkind moments, Karen also indulged the suspicion that the boob job had helped with the husband from the internet, who owned several lucrative avocado farms in San Diego, where he and Maille lived. Maille was soon doing math over the phone with Karen: net income per acre times total acres equaled her newfound fortune. Maille, never one to be an onlooker, kept the books for the business and filed the taxes, putting her accounting degree to use.

The world did right by Maille, who, despite all she required from others, was loyal to the rafters. Friends of Maille's were looked after. She'd convinced Laurel—a frazzled, nervous girl she had lived with in Michigan—to get her PhD in California. Maille claimed Laurel had once been really fun, but now she let her anxiety get the better of her. Laurel was always afraid people wouldn't like her or wouldn't think she was funny. Plus, she dated the wrong men. Maille was hopeful, though, that Laurel could change.

Maille was friendly with each of her ex-boyfriends (except for one, who'd killed himself on Mother's Day a few years back). She'd recently rescued a Chihuahua and nursed the dog through kennel cough. She never used her father's death to receive pity from others. Mortality tested Maille, and Maille usually seemed to win.

Two days later, as Karen packed her purse to go to the shelter, she said to Warren, "You'll be nice, won't you? Don't say anything snide about the cat."

There were more things she wanted to ask of her husband. They played in her mind as she drove: please don't tell me I should stop eating and drinking at dinner, you know it embarrasses me; please don't talk about how the detainees at Guantánamo deserve what they got, you know nobody agrees with you; please don't make anyone go in the boat who doesn't want to, you know that thing should be sunk. But she hadn't said any of it. She drove away from the river and into the hills. The shadows of clouds fell in a patchwork pattern on the tussock grass. She passed into the farmland near Manteca, with its neat rows of grapevines and paddocks of grazing cattle. Of all the parts of California, she'd picked the one that reminded her most of the Midwest.

Later, when Karen returned to the river house with her daughter, Venus retreated to the basement. Karen couldn't tell which Venus wanted more: her family, or, having that, to shun them.

Maille's arrival later than evening couldn't have been more different. She burst through the door. Under one arm was her Chihuahua, quivering, and under the other a crate of avocados. Neither slowed her down. Her friend Laurel followed her in, her arms crossed, and behind her a man whom Karen hadn't met but who was pleasant looking. He had his hand on Laurel's shoulder.

"Mom," Maille said, setting the Chihuahua and the crate down on the floor of the den. "Guess what? I'm pregnant!"

The little dog scurried away. Karen stood and stared at her daughter, who spread her arms wide, though there was nothing to show. Maille was twenty-three years old. Of course she would be the one to have a child first.

"Maille just told me in the car," Laurel said to Karen, leaving her boyfriend unintroduced at the door. "I don't want you to think I knew a long time before you."

Karen's gaze followed Maille, who had gone after the dog. She glanced at Laurel and said, "You look good."

And it was true. At the girls' graduation, Karen had been able to see Laurel's clavicle and sternum under her skin. The cords that hung around her neck—summa cum laude, Maille boasted for Laurel—looked as though they could bring her down. She wasn't anorexic, Maille had insisted on Laurel's behalf, but was sick in some mysterious, undiagnosed way that baffled doctors. Now she was a little fuller, her cheeks rosy.

"The doctor made me gain weight," she said. "Oh, this is Lance."

Lance had moved from the door. He shook Karen's hand and at the same time rubbed Laurel's back in small circular movements.

"Maille said there would be river otters?" Laurel said, moving away from Lance to look out the window. With her back to Karen, she said, "Let me know if you need help with dinner, okay?"

Laurel, Karen thought, was turning out to be sort of boring. Karen had seen her once a year, during visits to Michigan, since the two girls had met. Laurel had always been quick and full of humor, but now she sounded dull, without any of her old enthusiasm. Though Laurel looked better than ever, it seemed as though the weight wasn't so much adding to her as it was diluting what was already there. What had happened to the wry girl? California had been sweet on her; she was a candied rind of what she'd been.

Maille, however, looked radiant. Upon closer look, she had a prenatal glow to her olive skin. She was like a walking blood orange, carrying that surprise inside of her.

From the kitchen, something began to burn. Karen called for Warren, who'd promised to keep an eye on the carrots and brussels sprouts roasting in the oven. But only Venus stood over the stove, staring at the knobs. A thin haze of smoke floated in the air. "Why didn't you turn off the heat?" Karen asked, nudging Venus out of the way. When her daughter said nothing, Karen continued, "Well, go get Warren. He might be changing the battery on the boat."

"I am not going in that boat," Venus said. But she went outside anyway. Karen heard her yell, "Hey, Fake Dad!"

Karen used a spatula to flip the burned vegetables into the sink. She snapped the foil tent off the two roast chickens and carved uneven chunks, plopping them onto the platter. Everything besides the vegetables, she put on the table. When Venus reappeared, she shook her head. "No Fake Dad down there."

"Where's Dad?" Maille asked. "He needs to hear the good news, too."

Karen couldn't imagine how he'd be happy. He'd been against the marriage in the first place. She went to the phone and called him twice, but there was no answer. "Let's just eat," she said, motioning everyone over to the table and sitting down herself. "I'll say grace. Thank you for all this food and family and friends, and for Maille's fetus, and please let the river otters come out tonight so Laurel can see them. Amen."

"Mom," Maille said. "That's not a real grace."

"I liked it," Venus said, reaching over Lance to grab the basket of rolls.

"I do want to see the river otters," Laurel added.

Karen put an artichoke on Maille's plate and removed her wineglass. "If I'd known, I would have gotten some sparkling juice for you."

"I can have a little bit," Maille said, taking back her wineglass. "Don't be so American, Mom."

"I am American," Karen said, frowning.

They all picked at their food. Downriver, the dam's lights popped on—bright and sudden, as though searching for something that shouldn't be there. The neighbors' German shepherds began to bark. Karen went to the phone and dialed her husband's number again.

"Goddamn it, Charlie!" she cried.

The mistake startled her. The whole table looked up, and a pregnant glance passed between Venus and Maille. Karen noticed that poor Lance looked confused. He would get used to them eventually, if he ended up staying around. "I'm sorry," Karen said. Silently, she apologized to her dead husband, who had done nothing wrong but who was still only a slip of the tongue away from blame.

Warren walked in during dinner with a pet carrier, inside of which was a kitten.

"Oh, Warren," Karen said. "We didn't want another one."

Warren seemed not to hear her. Everyone except Karen and Laurel stopped eating and went to the carrier, poking their fingers through the bars. Warren opened the latch and the little animal crawled out, only to be pummeled by the Chihuahua, who was fascinated by the only thing in the world smaller than itself.

"There are stray dogs everywhere in California," Laurel said, rising to join the crowd around the stunned and hissing kitten. "They made you pay an adoption fee, Maille? You could have just gone outside and found one."

"Laurel," Maille said, scowling, "every pet you've ever had has died. Who are you to talk? You thought the hamster I bought you would survive for three days in a hot car while you drove to California."

Laurel grew quiet.

Karen looked over at the two girls. Adults now, they were beginning to do things that couldn't be undone. Maybe they hadn't recognized it yet, hadn't accumulated enough of the briny feeling of guilt, regret. Karen stood and took a few plates with her. In the kitchen, she ran some dishwater.

A pregnant daughter, a homeless one, and Laurel, a girl who wasn't her child but seemed rather lost. Karen had always liked Laurel, had always worried about her. She was smart but now seemed to take direction so easily, and Maille could be so pushy.

And then there was clueless Lance, who stood alone and awkward by the window, drawn to this group of misfits as though by static cling.

"Wash those later, Karen. It's boat time." Warren snapped the door shut on the carrier. "We should go before the mountain lions come out."

Down at the dock, Warren prepped the boat. He'd gutted the inside years ago, when the cushioned seats started to mold. Folding chairs with missing belts had replaced them. The whole thing looked ravaged, already sunk, but Maille climbed in anyway, followed by Venus, despite her earlier promise.

"Charlie, right? I'm Lance." Lance held out his hand. He smiled a big, unknowing smile.

Warren's face locked up.

"Warren, actually," he said, taking Lance's hand and pulling him down into the boat.

Karen sighed, but she couldn't blame Lance, who didn't know any better. She got in the boat herself and sat in the nose, away from her husband, who gave her a look as though this were all somehow her fault: Maille's mopey friend and her know-nothing boyfriend, Venus's homelessness, the fact that Warren resented a dead man for the place he'd had—and still had—in Karen's life.

The boat sputtered to life. Venus turned to Laurel, who was looking up at the hills, and said, "Don't worry about the mountain lions. The neighbors' dogs keep them away. They *can* swim, though." Venus looked away, lost in her own thoughts.

The house next door looked like a fortress. Warren's was a cottage in comparison. A balcony with balustrades swung out over the hill. Two German shepherds sat on cushioned armchairs, looking lazily down at them. The rest of the grounds had been sculpted with cement paths and benches, big urns that held wide-winged ferns.

"They're German, the people who live there, and they have German shepherds," Venus said.

"Germans love concrete," Laurel said.

Lance and Venus laughed, but Maille frowned.

"Laurel, the things you say don't even make sense," she scolded.

Maille had begun to address everyone specifically. Karen couldn't remember when, exactly, this had started, but she had never heard their names said aloud so frequently, never realized they could be so weighty with criticism. Laurel, Venus, *Mom*.

Warren didn't seem to notice any of this. He brooded back by the engine. Lance looked confused. The three girls stared off into the reeds. The boat passed near a clump of cattails, and Venus grabbed one by the spike and pulled.

Warren sped up. "Don't do that," he said. "This is protected wildlife."

"Don't go too fast," Venus said. "Maille's with child."

Warren turned to Maille, his hand still on the tiller. "Glad I paid off those student loans."

Laurel laughed, though no one else did. Karen was starting to see that Laurel had more in common with Venus than Maille. To Venus, her life was like a broken plate: once cracked, it couldn't look the same again, so why bother?

Warren turned the boat sharply toward the mouth of the dam. Water churned at the dam's base, as though it were racking its brain for something. The little boat was pushed back, but Warren kept revving.

"Dad, you're going to burn out the motor again," Maille said.

"There are oars."

"You promised," Karen said, sighing.

"I'd rather swim than row," Venus said.

When the motor sputtered out, and the boat was pushed away from the dam, Venus kept her word: she jumped out and swam. Karen took an oar, and so did Warren. They followed closely behind Venus in case she got too tired.

Venus pulled herself onto the dock and climbed up to the house without waiting for the rest of them. Her wet clothes clung tightly to her body. It had gotten dark. The cats' eyes glowed around the house. Warren tied up the boat, everyone quiet except for Laurel, who said, "That was really fun, actually, even without river otters."

Up at the house, the porch light snapped up insects. Karen felt useless when Venus asked Maille to drop her off at the shelter on her way back to San Diego in the morning, two days earlier than she'd planned.

The next day, with all the shuffling of bags and leftovers, the wrangling of the Chihuahua and the hands on Maille's stomach, no one noticed that Warren's new kitten had slipped out of the house and into the early morning.

It was Maille's mother-in-law who demanded a wedding ceremony. She had not had one herself, and if Maille were going to make the same mistakes she had, then they might as well get a party out of it. Karen liked the idea, and she offered the river house for the ceremony. Her own disapproval stopped far short of Judy's, who called Maille regularly during her first trimester, reminding her the clock was ticking at Planned Parenthood.

Maille, however, was unfazed. "I keep the baby, and Judy pays for the wedding," she told Karen. "It's a win win for me." She invited everyone she liked. The postage alone for the save the dates, invitations, and RSVPs cost nearly $350—the only thing Judy refused to pay for, as though she both wanted a ceremony and desperately abhorred its actually happening.

Karen watched her daughters the day of the wedding. Maille's abdomen was a small hiccup. She ate granola bars as Judy fussed over her. Venus wandered around, smoking cigarettes, which shook in her tremoring hand. The smoke rose and mingled with the white lace and white flowers. She settled in the back row of folding chairs, lying across four of them. Karen wondered what new drug she was taking or what new secret she had. This was Venus's life. She might not ever change.

And then there was Laurel, who joined Venus in the back row of chairs. Maille had given Laurel a bundle of tulle but hadn't told her what to do with it. She didn't really have a need for either Venus or Laurel today.

There was no Lance, which concerned Karen. Or maybe Laurel was better off without him. Karen needed to think of these girls as women, as people on their own in the world, but she worried for them. Or maybe Karen wanted Laurel to be a train wreck. By comparison her own daughters would look better. But thinking so was unkind, and out of guilt Karen felt the need to go to Laurel and say something nice. She even called Laurel's name. Laurel looked up, the bundle of tulle in her arms, and said, "Yes?" But Karen found she couldn't think of anything.

II

Eyes

He sits down next to me at the bar of the sushi restaurant in Newark where I'm waiting for my takeout. With a sideway glance I realize he's old enough to drink but only by a few years. So he's younger than me by almost ten. As soon as he sits down I can tell he wants to talk—and maybe have sex? I seize up, I all but disappear like the new moon: you might be able to see me in the shadow of an eclipse but here at the bar I might as well be the bottle, or the stool, or the little plastic tub of limes.

But those red-rimmed eyes can see me. He tells me that his friend has died. He tosses back a Jack Daniel's and calls for another: a newly minted sad-sack drinker.

I start to shut him out. The dinner I ordered is just for me. It's been two months since my doctor told me I shouldn't have children, and Ralph just moved his things out two weeks ago. At his angriest, he told me to stay in Newark and write my stupid book. He apologized, and on his way out of the house for the last time he took down the Christmas tree and dragged it to the curb. He'd gotten a job in California, and I wasn't following him. It was my choice, but now I'm lonely, and embarrassed to be alone at this restaurant, and I don't want this man to know I'm alone. I turn to my book, place my elbow on the bar, and rest my head in my hand so all he sees is hair.

But maybe I could listen. This man has something to say that might not ever get said if he doesn't say it now. It's safe to talk to strangers about grief. His friend, his stupid goddamn friend, has overdosed and died, and he hates him and loves him and wishes he'd never lived and wishes he would live forever.

I offer a smile. I even touch his shoulder once but pull my hand away in case he is looking for a lover, which I don't want to be. I blunder my way through advice—I lost my father to drugs too, other people won't understand what you're going through—as though I can give him the answer, as though I could be a stranger who leaves an impression on him, but my words appear between us like a worm-eaten rose on a platter.

I should have let him talk longer. His anger had an engine, and he needed to run it out. And I didn't have anywhere to be, or anyone to return home to. Later I would wish I'd asked him what meal they'd last shared together. Tell me everything, I might have said. I want to know about the mayo on your lip, the coffee on your friend's breath. And if he'd asked me—What was your last meal with your father, stranger?—I would have told him it was three years ago that we had blueberry pancakes on the lake with some of the family there, syrup pooling like luck on our plates, luck that would get sopped up and swallowed. Bacon on the side, and sunshine, and the sky a blue ballroom for a few puffy white clouds. The water rippling as though it was running from itself. There's a little love in every meal, I could say.

Instead I mutter, "Well, feel better." Or maybe not even. Maybe when he says, "I'll stop bothering you," I turn back to my book, and when my takeout is ready I leave without a word, still worrying that he probably wants to have sex with me. I'll feel badly later for making it all about me, but for now I go out into the freezing rain, Newark a bright little lymph node clinging to the neck of New York, and I think, My father never knew I would end up living here. He never would have guessed.

Future Breakfasts

In fact Byron and I hadn't seen each other in many years but we found ourselves at the birthday party of an architect whose name I can't remember now. Our greeting was smooth and natural, his hand on my elbow and my lips on his cheek, though when we parted neither of us spoke immediately because it was also a hello between people who no longer know each other well.

A historic blizzard was on its way, but the SoHo loft radiated warmth and light. Tea lights guttered hopefully on coffee tables, illuminating the hand-cupped chins of people deep in conversation. Trays of pale-pink lobster rolls sweated on card tables, and a near-perfect chocolate torte waited on a cake stand in the kitchen to be devoured. I'd had an urge to stick my finger in it when I'd gone for a glass of water because the bandwidth of my self-control had been too low lately. I was just out of a brief and devastating relationship with a poet from the college where I taught. It was the first affair since my divorce. I didn't even want to be at this party, didn't feel ready, but friends urged me to be done wallowing, to get on with my life, and so I went to shut them up.

Before I saw Byron I'd been standing alone against a wall, feeling like an outcast, a feeling I brought on myself often in those days postdivorce, postpoet. I'd had a lot of room-temperature white wine already because when I talked to people I grew distressed and panicky and couldn't stop thinking there might be food in my teeth. Still I craved conversation the way lonely, nervous people do: anxious for another chance to get it right. From the middle of the room Byron gave me a look that said I'd better come and talk to him, that there was no avoiding it.

None of my friends knew what had happened between me, Byron, and my brother, Duck, all those years ago in Florida, where we'd grown up. If they did they might have stopped me from going over there. As it was, one of us, Byron or I, should've left—gently or rudely, whatever it took to get the hell out of there. But neither of us did. I wondered how much Byron remembered from the night everything had gone wrong, also the night things had begun for the two of us. How much was still important to him?

I also wondered if he ever thought of my brother, if he'd forgiven us, or at least forgiven me. In and out of jail in his twenties, Duck was now flying the straight and narrow in Boston. We spoke regularly. We liked each other still; we liked each other even more than we'd liked each other back then.

As we spoke Byron made gestures I recognized—rubbing the back of his neck, leaning his ear toward me to listen better—and sometimes the reason you don't listen to reason is that you're still in love and you won't be able to move past that love until you see it through.

I wasn't exactly sure who I was still in love with. The worse my luck, the more I loved, but I felt something click into place while speaking to Byron, who'd been my very first love. Maybe it was just nostalgia acting as a thickening agent, but I felt something like hope come together in me. This would seem like fate, running into him, except I didn't believe in fate.

We stood surrounded by people beneath a small but baroque chandelier whose crystals clinked in the breeze from an open window, open because the heat was on too high. Byron was dressed perfectly, I thought, in a white T-shirt with a black blazer over it. A pair of jeans with a few holes. A line of sweat shimmered around his hairline. He still wore his hair on the longer side. It fell almost to his shoulders, dirty blond and feathery.

We carried ourselves through the usual small talk. I did fairly well with giving the small, unimportant details of my life. I was clear, didn't embellish. I explained that I taught history at Rutgers in Newark, where I lived, and that was what had brought me to this part of the country. I said this instead of explaining that after my divorce last year moving someplace new became a matter of survival. Involuntarily I looked out at the night, the moon I could see between two big buildings, translucent clouds passing over it, the effulgence of the city piercing the big windows, and I felt special the way people in New York sometimes do.

I was about to ask him for similar details when he shook his head and groaned. The groan, I thought, was unearned, and I felt persecuted. I brought my hand to my face, as though checking for pox. Still shaking his head, Byron took a sip of his drink, an amber liquid with one large melting ice cube. He laughed into his glass; exhaled air from his nose sent ripples across the surface.

"What?" I said finally.

"My therapist will be exasperated when she finds out about this." He pointed at me and then pointed at himself.

It shouldn't have but knowing that he spoke to his therapist about me made me feel intimate with him, as though we still had important places in each other's lives. Sometimes it's nice to know that another person finds you irresistible, even if the feeling you give them, the one they crave, isn't a good one.

"At least you'll get your money's worth," I said.

Laughter passed between us. I had Byron's attention, and I chomped down like a tick into flesh. He motioned to a couch nearby, one tucked away that I hadn't noticed before, and as I sat down with him I saw my friends across the room nodding at me, the drunker ones raising their glasses in support. On the couch I was aware our knees were touching. Maybe Byron was oblivious, or maybe he wanted to touch me, too.

I looked at Byron and had this feeling he knew everything I was thinking. Sometimes words spill out of a person's eyes, and sometimes I'm one of those people. Over the years the agony of the fact he'd never forgiven me had diminished. He'd never responded to the letters I wrote in apology.

"I've thought about looking you up," Byron said. "Every so often I think about it."

He started it. I would remember that later. He was the one who nudged the night toward a place where we could believe there was no danger in being honest.

"Maybe you didn't look me up because you hate me." I brandished my wineglass as I spoke. It was probably not something I would have said if I hadn't been drunk.

"I don't hate you," Byron said quietly.

The urge to say things I felt needed to be said raced through me like a fire up a mine shaft. But I didn't say everything I could have; memories returned to me in a surge, but I couldn't remember what I'd embellished and what was true. I was certain I'd made myself out to be better than I really was and I didn't want Byron to think less of me because I'd held on to a rosy version of what had happened between us.

A tea light on the table burned down to nothing until the flame finally pinched itself out. Byron watched the trail of smoke intently. He looked about to say something more when, from my purse, my phone released a shrill alarm. Then the sound sprang from other pockets and purses throughout the room and all the partygoers looked around, bewildered.

Byron fished his own screaming phone from his pocket. "Blizzard warning," he said. "I'd forgotten. I don't pay attention to the weather these days. Climate change makes it too hard to predict."

I hadn't forgotten. At home I'd checked the batteries in my flashlight and stored bottled water. All night I'd followed New Jersey Transit on social media to see what time they would shut down the trains. Weather was drama I could experience with other people. Even if it became dangerous it was different from the individual struggles of our daily lives. It was an experience to be had together and one local enough to grab our attention unlike other global disasters.

The party began to thin, though no one knew whether or not the storm would deliver its promise of twenty-eight inches, impassable roads, and carbon monoxide poisoning if you weren't careful. The architect's assistant swept away the trays of lobster rolls. Guests slid their arms into coats, everyone suddenly puffy in down jackets. The sleek black dresses covered, all the crisp button-downs obscured. I avoided Byron's eyes; looking at him meant saying goodbye.

"It's a long trip back to New Jersey," I said, as though it were a confession.

"I have a car nearby," he said. "Let me take you home."

I was embarrassed because I thought he'd taken my meaning differently, as though by saying it would be a long trip I was fishing for an offer of a ride. "No," I said. "I wouldn't expect you to do that."

He stood up and extended his hand toward me. I could smell his cologne. I could have pointed out that he would have to drive all the way back to the city, and the storm could start soon, but I was beginning to understand we would spend the night together.

I let him hold my coat as I slipped my arms into its sleeves. We left the warm, gleaming apartment and forced our way through the wind outside. The snow was light, a few flurries getting whipped around. It felt a little old fashioned, rushing to beat the storm, the promise of bare skin, except for me the promise of a night with Byron was cloudy with chalk dust from a story between us that had been started and erased. The story hadn't been good; we were walking into a field land mined with our mistakes. Still, New York magicked away this feeling, the way it does—the way it makes being bad seem like a good thing, an intellectual thing. And an inconsequential thing. We were invisible among the tall buildings, the busy traffic, and the never-ending queue of people making their own decisions, bad or good.

The wind blew and stole our voices. It was too cold to speak anyway, but questions floated between us. And desire. Of course I'd begun to think about sex, the stirring inside when you're almost sure you're going to have it. My own desperation figured into how I thought about that night, but Byron must have been lonely, too, in need of intimacy, and so we were shedding skins, not bothering with formality. It didn't matter that we were staring at each other as we walked, looking like fools as we almost tripped over bags of garbage on the sidewalk.

We came to his car, an old sedan he'd squeezed into a spot on a side street. He opened the door for me, and I lowered myself into its immaculate interior. There wasn't a loose paper or old coffee cup anywhere, which was different from the way I lived, flinging the discards of my life all around me. He slammed the door shut, cutting off the sound of the wind, and I was alone in the car as he circled round front, hands jammed in his pockets. Being alone in someone else's car is a privilege, something not allowed to everyone. As I took in the smell of it, I indulged the fantasy that one day we might look back on this night and consider it the night that brought us together again for good. By then we'd be in a place of togetherness and bliss. I was desperate to see us in those roles. Grocery shopping together, splitting the list down the middle to save time, or else going away for the weekend and having sex in nice hotel rooms. I'd have tenure by then. I still didn't know what he did but he'd have made strides, too. Maybe a child in there somewhere—a baby, we'd be older parents, meticulous and devoted.

But I was always falling in love with a future that required more heart than I had.

Then he opened his car door and the cold air rushed in. The old sputtering engine woke with a little coaxing and choked out the fantasy in my mind. The dash lights glowed blue. A few spins of the wheel and we were on our way to New Jersey. Byron reached out a hand and our icy fingers intertwined. A snap of static passed between us. It was the first time we'd touched in a deliberate way, touching for the sake of touching. We held on to each other for a long time, but our fingers didn't seem to grow much warmer. The heat in the car spilled out in a tepid flow. Feeling tender, I enveloped his right hand with both of mine, brought his hand to my mouth, and let warm air fill the pocket I'd made.

"Cold hands, warm heart," Byron said.

I wondered if he was being ironic. I also wondered if he was being genuine. Maybe we'd both reached a point where we wanted to be gentle with each other.

Of that night in Florida, I remembered humidity, and the moonlight making a mess on the ocean. Waves crashing, too. We lived near the ocean, the four of us—me, my parents, my brother we called Duck. Byron lived with his family not far from us.

I was walking home from a party (I wasn't supposed to have gone), tipsy from a few beers, everything feeling incalculably good the way it does when you first start drinking, before you start drinking too much. I heard Duck's car before I saw it—he had the loudest engine in town—so I stopped and waited to flag him down and fling myself in the back seat and have him drive me home. As he approached I thought I was lucky to be running into him.

The car seemed to pass in slow motion, Duck driving with concentration I didn't usually see from him. He didn't notice me waving, but the road was dark, and I was wearing a tight black dress I'd gotten at the mall and hidden from my parents. Then I noticed Duck wasn't alone. A boy sitting in the back seat locked eyes with me, though I suppose we didn't really lock eyes because he was blindfolded. Still, it felt as though we had. His head snapped my way and I felt attached to his eyes. The world slowed down and all light seemed to disappear except for the car's interior light, which was on, so I could see that boy's face and nothing else.

I would spend many years wondering why I'd stood there entranced instead of doing something. Cleary Duck had done something wrong—clearly Duck had kidnapped this boy—but the mystery of what I'd seen struck me silent. And by the time I'd come to I wasn't sure if what I'd seen was true.

Duck could've gotten away with the kidnapping if he hadn't painted his name on the side of his Mustang in big white letters. Byron had caught a glimpse before Duck slipped the blindfold over his eyes. Some people, people like Duck, become devoted to their nicknames. They put their signature on everything. On various occasions over the years this trait of Duck's would lead the police right to him. He was ostentatious, yet always trying to hide something, my brother.

I'd slipped back through my bedroom window that night, set my alarm for 6:00 so I'd make it to school, and collapsed into bed. Later Duck would be forced to admit what he'd done—it was planned with friends as a mean trick, no doubt, though he claimed to have acted alone—but this would be two days later, after no one had seen Byron since the Blockbuster parking lot where Duck had grabbed him.

But as I fell asleep, all my tired drunk mind had thought at the time was that it was probably only a game. I'd heard about kids at school making teams and dropping off hostages in the middle of nowhere, hostages who called their teammates and tried to describe where they were. I remembered thinking that everyone would be okay.

Every so often I think of the ways his kidnapping might have gone differently, or might not have happened at all. If Byron had had a phone—he'd lost his in the scuffle in the parking lot—or if he'd felt for the handle and jumped out of the car or screamed and kicked until he'd frightened Duck enough to let him go. I knew Duck. Duck would have caved, under the right pressure—but how could Byron have known this? I think these things because even after all of this, I still believe Duck thought he was playing a joke—a cruel trick for which he should have had to atone, but a joke that meant no lasting harm. He couldn't have known what would happen to Byron alone on the roads in the middle of the night. But Byron thought Duck had brought this particular fate to our doorstep and was responsible for all of what happened—and this was where Byron and I had always disagreed.

Byron had gotten lost trying to find his way home and had asked the wrong person for help along the way. He spent three days locked in a basement convinced he wasn't going to live. No food, and though the man who'd taken him hadn't touched him, he'd sat at the top of the stairs and talked low and darkly about what he was going to do when, he said, the time was right. Byron escaped by chance: Carl Sands's uncle had come over unannounced while Sands was out, had gone into the basement looking for the industrial fan he'd loaned his nephew, and found Byron so petrified he was unable to speak. Byron was rescued; the bodies of Sands's past victims were found.

I don't know why I didn't circle the wagons around Duck like my parents had. Instead I started visiting Byron during the day at his house after his rescue. The feeling I'd had on the side of the road, the electric charge at the sight of him, had stayed with me. I brought him books and slices of cake in individual plastic boxes, the folded forks you snapped in place taped to their lids. There was nothing to do but talk and no one was watching us so we got to know each other without awkwardness. I'd visit in the hours after school, before his parents got off work. We fell a little bit in love. He was traumatized, desperate to be loved, as I was but in a different, undamaged way. I was touched that he liked me even though Duck was my brother. Romeo and Juliet—that's who I thought we were.

But he didn't know I'd seen him that night. That I could've ended the trouble with one quick call on my cell phone.

After high school we both went to Florida State where we were free from the town and our parents who said we shouldn't be together, who had kept us apart for the last two years we lived at home. I remember the feeling of finally relaxing in each other's arms. Before I told him the truth. We would have sex in empty basement classrooms if my roommate or his wouldn't leave the room. Dust floated in the columns of light that seeped in through the tilt-turn windows at the top of the walls. Once I pressed a handprint of chalk against the blackboard when we were done, and it was still there when I'd gone back to the classroom for my French class the next day, and seeing it there beneath the conjugations turned me on. Byron, at the time, was in denial about what had happened to him. He'd stopped going to therapy. When I finally told him the truth—it had welled up in me, metastasized, and by that point I'd felt secure enough in Byron's love to anticipate forgiveness—I thought enough time had passed for him to have distanced himself from what had happened. Naively, I thought the fact he'd stopped going to therapy was a sign of his recovery.

He wouldn't look at me while he told me how terrible I was. That was the worst part, that he wouldn't meet my eyes. I'd done nothing the night I'd seen him in Duck's car, nothing the day after, or the following day. I hadn't noticed when he hadn't shown up to school even though we were in the same lab group in biology. It was only after he returned, famous, that I took an interest in him. I tried to tell him that wasn't how it was. He said I was as bad as my brother.

I suppose I assumed that because Byron had spoken to me and was now driving me home, he no longer thought I was a terrible person. I suppose I assumed he'd forgiven me.

The frantic flurries made it seem like we were driving through static, and indeed there was something exciting about impending weather and something very sexy about being together in it. We were partners in a little bit of danger. I gave him directions, but his phone gave him better ones.

Even at the beginning of what they were calling a historic blizzard, the streets of New York were crowded, but then we crossed into New Jersey and the bright buzz of the city thinned as we emerged from the Holland Tunnel into Jersey City and the arteries of freeways that led us to Newark, which spread before us with its empty outstretched palms. We passed city hall and its bright golden dome. I almost pointed it out. There was some story about how the city had gotten that golden dome from someone rich who'd later been indicted for something, but I couldn't remember it. I glanced at Byron. He still held my hand, but limply, and I could see that the quiet and the emptiness unsettled him. We'd been talking cheerfully up until now. In the crowd of people at the party he'd been at ease, as he'd been driving in a sea of other cars, but the sudden aloneness of Newark at night was like going to a beach and finding no water. At least that was how it had felt to me when I first moved there. I wanted to tell him it was a feeling you got used to, living in a big city whose streets emptied of people at night, but his face now looked as stern as the rows of buildings on either side of us.

"I'm surprised you keep a car in the city." I wanted to keep the conversation going. "I don't know many people who drive."

Byron's face darkened. He disentangled his hand from mine and adjusted the vents. He placed both hands on the wheel.

"I drive almost everywhere," he said.

It wouldn't be until later, when a state of emergency was declared and the travel ban put into place, that I realized Byron needed to control his own movements, though it should've been obvious to me. We were in our thirties now; fifteen years had passed, but for Byron the fear of dying had only gotten worse.

We passed the building where I taught, and the café where I got coffee. I wanted to share these small, inconsequential pieces of my life with Byron but worried he wouldn't care. I also had this feeling that because of what I'd done I didn't deserve to do things like teach young people or get takeout coffee. So I just directed him to my street, a row of residential brownstones with a few frat houses mixed in. The frat boys were out and partying; a line of people waited to get inside one of the houses, a tall boy at the door holding out his hand for the five-dollar cover. I lived a few houses down and liked the proximity to these young people and the way the street came alive on weekend nights.

I gestured to the empty side of the street in front of my building, where I rented the first floor. There was nothing but room to park, but even so it was permit parking only, so I fished in my purse for the hanging permit I'd gotten from the city though I didn't have a car myself. I'd given the permit to the poet so he could park his car at my house, and just the other day he'd left it in my mailbox in the History Department.

Byron had relaxed after seeing all the people on the street and the glowing lights in my neighbors' houses. He killed the engine. I lived across the street from a hospital. Lights glowed behind each of its many windows. Byron twisted his neck to look up through the windshield. It was a Catholic hospital, and snow swirled in a frenzy around the cement cross stationed at the top of the hospital's highest gable. I touched his shoulder. He looked down into his lap. We left the car and climbed the porch steps. The things going through my mind were basic: my bathroom wasn't clean enough, and I didn't have anything to eat in the fridge.

Inside, I dropped my purse and coat on a chair by the door and went through the house switching on the lights, as though I needed to reassure Byron I wasn't hiding anything. I never used the overhead lights, they gave me a headache, but I had lamps stationed like sentries in every corner. I caught sight of my reflection in the kitchen window as I tugged the cord to lower the blinds. I was surprised to see I looked happy, that my expression betrayed none of the wild uncertainty I felt. I invited Byron to sit down, gesturing through a pair of pocket doors into the living room, and he loped into it with his hands shoved in his pockets, admiring the marble fireplace while I snapped a lighter, trying to get a few candles lit.

We probably should have had a conversation, but instead we had sex. Byron crossed the room and took the burning candle from my hand, set it on the bookshelf behind me. He dipped his face toward mine and kissed me. The hunger I felt was no longer just hunger for anyone to relieve my loneliness, but hunger for him specifically. The feeling was so strong it made it seem like there was no risk to anything, no risk of waking up tomorrow and wishing we hadn't done this. Everything would be okay if we just kept our bodies close.

Clothes came off. Pressed together, we took big awkward steps toward the armchair. We tripped on my cat who'd slunk in to say hello and who screamed and scattered from underfoot. We laughed into each other's mouths. I pushed him into the chair and slipped off my panties. He pulled me on top of him. We said only dirty, meaningless things. We didn't use protection, as though we were still eighteen and we'd never been with anyone else.

We found our way to the floor. The varnished wood was cold and hard against my bones. For a minute, when we were entangled, I felt that this was everything, that our bodies had fixed everything. Melted the past. Love had come out of something awful.

We were so close I couldn't see his whole face.

The lamps bathed us in yellow light. I liked to get up and clean myself right after sex but I was afraid to disrupt the connection between us.

"Stay here," I whispered finally. Maybe it would be good to give him a minute to collect himself, so we might avoid an awkward conversation that would lead to his leaving. In the bathroom I found my cat on the windowsill, eyeing me as I washed. "Don't judge," I said to him. And then, for no other reason than because I needed the release, I let out one quick dry sob. So much weight had been lifted, and so much love had taken its place. Seeping into my heart was the feeling that Byron wouldn't be here if he didn't want to be, that he'd felt the same dive into rapture I had.

I returned with blankets and pillows. We'd left the party late and it had gotten even later. The storm was picking up but hadn't accumulated much yet. The window for him to leave safely was closing. Still open, but closing. "Stay the night?" I said when I'd sunk to the floor.

Byron lifted his head from the floor and squinted to read the face of the wall clock. His skull met the floor with the sound of a heavy coin dropping.

"I won't go anywhere until the plows come through," he said.

It wasn't quite the answer I was looking for. I could sense Byron drifting into sleep, myself too, but I tried to fight it, knowing we'd have to get reacquainted in the morning. Outside the wind was picking apart the world.

I didn't want to think of the past as I tried to sleep, but it crept in like cold air through the poorly insulated windows. I thought of Byron on the dark country road after Duck had expelled him from the Mustang. Fear dried out Byron's mouth; in the space I occupied, between sleep and wakefulness, my tongue stuck to a dry mouth, too, and plaque crusted my teeth. I kicked the blankets away. The laces on Byron's sneakers were fraying and wouldn't stay tied, so he kept bending to fix them. He felt less lonely and less frightened when he allowed himself to listen to the chorus of insects and birds. In Newark, as I dozed, my cat tracked the progress of the storm in the window, every so often chattering at falling snow. Florida was a loud and lively place at night. A full moon hung low in the sky. A transparent cloud passed over it, like a threadbare towel hung on a knob. The brightness of the moon distracted Byron. He didn't hear the car coming up behind him, and when he finally turned he could feel the heat of its engine.

Outside my window the first plows could be heard waking up the city. Byron weighing options in the glare of one working headlight. Byron getting in the car, the car picking up speed as Byron asked for a ride back to the beach.

I slipped into sleep, and suddenly in the dream I was the one behind the wheel.

I woke up to find Byron looking at me calmly. There's sometimes a loss of meaning when you translate night into morning. He blinked, a small scowl creasing his face.

The room was cold, and my bones felt bruised from sleeping too long on the hard wood without rolling over.

"Is it late?" I asked

"It's not early," Byron said.

I wanted to ask him how long he'd been awake and watching me. I felt ashamed for sleeping late with him here, as though sleeping in was something I should've grown out of.

"Have the plows come through?"

"No," Byron said, "and there's a travel ban. So it looks like you're stuck with me."

He tried to laugh, but the laugh couldn't gain enough momentum to leave his throat, and he choked on it.

"Did you know they would issue a travel ban?" he asked.

"No," I said. "How could I have known that?"

Byron shrugged. "Just—maybe it's something Newark is quick to do, that you might have known could happen."

"This is my first winter here," I said.

There was an accusation hidden in Byron's question, but I didn't address it. I let it turn to ice and break apart in the frigid morning.

"I'll turn up the heat," I said, as though I could warm Byron up that way. "And make some breakfast."

I started to rise, but Byron pulled me back down, kissed me, ran his fingers down my neck. He was hard and I looped my legs around his back and he slipped easily inside of me. We were both trying; maybe this could work.

In the kitchen I rummaged through the fridge and pulled eggs and orange juice from deep inside. As I flipped the eggs in the pan and toasted stale bread I worried he was right, that I must've known that he wouldn't be able to leave. Was that what had driven me to convince him to stay? But now I had to fill the day with conversation and activity, and I worried what he'd felt for me, what had led him to offer me the ride, had crumbled overnight, replaced by cold reality and the knowledge that he was trapped. Spending more time with me was no longer a choice, but rather something the city had mandated.

When we'd eaten we were quiet while we did things like dress and plug in our phones. My phone had died, but when a charge had taken and it came back to life, a few text messages tripped over one another trying to make their presence known. The chiming made Byron look up.

"Who was that?" he asked.

The messages were from my ex-husband, who still worried about me, though he no longer loved me. "Ex-husband," I told Byron. "He lives in California."

"Are you close?"

I shrugged. In truth I didn't know. Some days I still had conversations with him in my mind. Other days I felt free of him. Of course losing the poet had freshened the wound from the loss of my husband, too. Once someone took a place in my life I didn't like to let that person go, even if they'd let me go. As was the case with Byron, who looked at me skeptically, though he'd never met my husband and knew nothing about my divorce. I remembered something about Byron's jealousy. Our relationship, all those years ago, had been about holding each other up, being there for each other. If my attention went somewhere else it meant Byron had less of it.

I pulled the blinds to look at the snow for the first time. The wind moved big drifts of it around. Snow crawled halfway up Byron's car. It gathered on the side-view mirrors into little peaks, cascaded to the ground, repeated.

Byron said, "It has to stop snowing soon, right?"

"Well. I don't know about soon. But eventually."

Byron squinted into the storm. He looked far away. I thought the best way to recover the easiness of the night before was to start drinking. I wanted us to get comfortable again; there'd been space between us all morning and we'd have to close it. So without asking him what he wanted I mixed us drinks in the kitchen and returned with the glasses. The room was cold still, the heat in my apartment poor, and I sat on top of the heating grate. "There's room on the grate," I said to him, hoping to draw him close, and after a moment of hesitation Byron sat down next to me.

It turned out Byron had gotten rich in television. He'd produced a popular show I'd never heard of. He'd just moved from LA to New York a year ago, and now he owned a company that made political videos, social awareness videos, the kind you might see in your news feed as you scrolled. I told him about the class I taught, the shiftless undergraduates, but the conversation halted and the awkwardness, I felt, came from the urge to talk of deeper things, so I asked him about love, I wanted to know how many times he'd fallen into it, and he laughed at me.

"That's quite a question."

"But just a question." I picked up his fingers and squeezed them.

I thought I saw a trace of a grimace shade Byron's face, but it left as quickly as it had come. He pushed hair away from his eyes. "Three," he said. "I was with someone for eight years in my twenties, and then we broke up." He added this last part as though to explain why he hadn't fallen in love with more people, as though loving sparely indicated a lack of conviviality or gameness, but the number sounded reasonable to me, and I told him so. I'd only ever loved three people, too, I said. I didn't tell him that he was one of my three, and I didn't ask if I was one of his, though I felt it must have been true, and I hoped he would tell me so. But he didn't.

"Eight years is a long time to be with someone and not get married," I said.

"That was just it," he said. "We didn't want to be together anymore but spent a long time denying that fact."

"Do you feel like you wasted time?" I asked.

Byron shifted uncomfortably. "I don't go down that road," he said.

I nodded enthusiastically. Sometimes I got caught on a gust of feeling that told me I had something important to say.

"That's good," I said. "My mom doesn't say it, but I know she thinks me and Duck have wasted our time, that we should be farther along in our careers or at least have families, and maybe it's true that Duck's wasted time, God help him, but not me, I don't think. I think people who believe in wasted time also usually believe in destiny or a set path or something, as though they think they had someplace to be and they didn't get there soon enough. It's dangerous to think that way. It makes you feel badly about yourself."

Byron's eyes were still wide, but they weren't looking at me anymore. I wondered what I'd said. For me, the conversation was energizing, and I felt I'd spoken well, that what I'd said about myself and my brother was true.

My brother. I'd mentioned Duck, and for the first time he was here in the room with us.

Wind was caught in the chimney; it sounded fierce. The heat vent had gone cold. The snow still purled outside, falling silently except when it was picked up by the wind. Duck had chosen not to play by the rules that night but as the years between then and now had piled up the rules had started to seem less important to me. I still wouldn't have done what Duck had done, but I almost understood the recklessness that had carried him away and made him play the trick. But maybe for Byron the rules had only become more important, and with each year that passed Duck's actions had become more and more senseless—so perhaps the love I couldn't keep out of my voice when I spoke about my brother bothered Byron.

"I'm sorry," I said. "I didn't mean to mention my brother."

"It's okay." Byron barely moved his mouth when he said the words. "You don't believe in fate?"

I didn't, not really, but because of the way Byron asked I assumed he did, at least a little bit, and I didn't want to alienate him so I said I wasn't sure. I added that a lot of things seemed to happen by accident, and that I didn't like thinking that terrible things were meant to be.

"What about the two of us meeting again?" he said.

"I don't know," I said. "There was a lengthy series of choices that made it so we lived in the same place and were acquainted with some of the same people. You see it on the train all the time, you know. People saying, 'Oh my God, hi!' One thing done differently and we wouldn't have met again."

The silence that followed chewed me up. I felt suddenly as though he was interviewing me, and I was giving all of the wrong answers. Byron looked as though he would prefer for us to sit in silence—he didn't meet my gaze, though I searched for his—but for me the silence was unbearable. The way your body fills a silent space is very personal. I tried to bear the silence but I hurried again to break it. I asked Byron what he was thinking, and he whispered that he was thinking about nothing. I felt it was dangerous for us if his mind was empty.

"I'm tired," he said. "Maybe we should go back to sleep."

I felt if he fell asleep I would lose him completely, as though sleep would cement his misgivings.

"You seem unhappy," I blurted out. "What made you so unhappy?"

Byron released a shuddering sigh. He'd made himself very small next to me. He shivered, though when I threw some of my blanket over him he didn't receive it; it slipped from his knees and he let it fall. I remembered all the times we'd grazed the surface of this same tension between us, how we'd relied on our bodies to diffuse it, how eventually our bodies couldn't keep up. I hoped Byron would take me in his arms but the old traditions we'd had didn't hold up anymore.

Why didn't I just let him sleep?

My phone vibrated from near Byron's elbow, where it was plugged into the wall, and I would've ignored it but Byron pinched it free from its charger and extended it toward me, saying, as he did, "Your brother texted you."

I looked at my phone. Illuminated on the screen was a simple note from my brother, asking if I was okay in the storm. Similar to the one I'd gotten from my ex-husband, notes that had taken ten seconds to compose and send but that made Byron's face harden.

"He's just checking in," I said.

Byron closed his eyes. His mouth was a thin, stern line. Had his anger really not diminished? What was it about my brother's grip on him that couldn't be loosened, that still held him so tightly? Sitting there, mostly naked, I felt stupid for trusting and loving my brother, and maybe it was because I felt attacked, too, that I started to defend Duck. Not just attacked, but cheated—as though by coming to my house Byron had implied he'd forgiven us.

"He's not evil. He wasn't evil then. Just young and stupid." I swallowed tears.

"I don't really want to talk about your brother," Byron said quietly.

"Duck has suffered, too," I said, carried away with my argument. "He may have gotten off easy then but he's paid for it every day since. I had to forgive him. I worried what would happen to him if no one forgave him."

Byron looked at me squarely. After a long silence he said, "There's just something so sinister about what he did. The nature of it."

"It only seems so sinister because of what happened after. Which Duck didn't intend and didn't play any part in."

"You're letting him off too easy." Byron shook his head as he spoke.

Because he wouldn't look at me I looked at the side of his face. The color had drained even from his acne scars. I loved my brother and Byron both. I believed they'd both been through something awful—were both, in a way, victims of Carl Sands's, though it was becoming clear that I couldn't tell Byron this, as Byron thought there'd been two bad guys that night in Florida, three if you count me. There would be no changing his mind.

The more adamant he seemed, the less I agreed with him. I thought it was important that I not condemn Duck, who was often depressed and almost always lonely. If I stopped having hope for him there would be no one left in the world who did—and I worried sometimes that Duck would kill himself.

I felt, and still feel, that I meant what I said next earnestly, but I said the thing no person seeking forgiveness should ever say: "I don't see why this is so hard for you after all this time."

Byron launched himself to his feet. He stood by my books; he looked like he wanted to tear them from the shelves. He rubbed the back of his neck so hard his skin turned red. "If I were meant to forgive him, I would have felt forgiveness by now. I haven't."

I saw then that I was in a position to end the conversation. I could've deleted Duck's text, tossed my phone aside, and if not agreed with Byron then at least accepted that his inability to forgive came from an honest place inside him. I could've offered him my body again, a language we'd always spoken well, and at least I could've made an attempt to be close with him. But I couldn't. I felt Byron was fooling himself. He was being too harsh. I drained my drink. I stood and grabbed the bottle of bourbon from the buffet where I kept my liquor and filled my glass with a few healthy splashes.

"Look at you," I said. "You're hiding behind this idea that everything is meant to be. Some things just happen, and it's shitty, but they do."

Byron rubbed his fists into his eyes and blinked away stars, as though trying to make my living room disappear. "Oh my God," he said. "Oh my God, oh my God."

He was panicking, but I was so caught up in myself I barely registered it.

"It makes you feel important," I went on glibly. The blanket was still wrapped around me. I would've dropped it, almost had, except beneath it I wore only a thigh-length robe, a robe meant to be worn around someone you have sex with, and I had a hard time keeping my confidence while wearing so little. "You like feeling like you're off the hook, like you don't have to work to forgive people. You've made no room in your heart for anyone else. You kicked me out as soon as things got hard, as soon as—"

"As soon as I found out you'd lied? You'd let it happen, you let him take me?" Byron shook with anger, or maybe fear.

"I was a kid!" I said, close to tears now. I couldn't stop talking, though I should've stopped and listened to him, agreed with him, because we had to spend the next however many hours together until the roads were cleared. Since he was my guest, I was the one who should have conceded. I still felt, though, that I could turn things around, that if I just kept talking he would admit to loving and forgiving me. This hadn't worked with my husband, it hadn't worked with the poet, and I didn't know why I thought it would work with him—but we were so deeply connected, he and I. We were so, dare I say it, meant to be.

I spoke quickly: "I would just think that fate and forgiveness would go hand in hand. If things are meant to happen for a reason and the force behind that is a force of good, then why not forgive the people who have apologized? I'm not saying forgive Carl Sands. I'm saying it might be good for you—and me and Duck—if you forgave my brother, who played a dumb trick on you, whose trick by chance spiraled out of his control, and who has regretted it ever since."

Byron's eyes kept flitting toward the door. He pulled at the joints in his fingers. They popped one by one. "Okay," he said, breathing with loud inhales and exhales. "Okay."

He was going through exercises, methods of calming himself, and this bewildered me because there was no danger here, no danger with me. Still, I immediately felt like backing down. I could see I'd taken it too far again—where had the feelings of love and connection from the previous night gone, and why had I replaced them with a need to be right and to have Byron agree with me? The unhappiest people are the ones who need to have everyone agree with them, and that was me right then. I went to Byron, reached out a hand to touch his shoulder. He let it rest there for a minute, he looked at it and blinked, and then, as though waking from a paralysis, he twisted away from my touch.

"Jesus," he muttered.

His rebuke made me feel like I was floating, like sadness had just lifted me away, so when my phone rang and I saw my brother's name on the screen, I answered without thinking, as though a ghost had slid the answer icon across the screen instead of me.

The call connected and Duck began speaking—asking if I was there, if I could hear him. Byron sighed—a loud, windy sound. I had brought Duck into the room with us.

"Duck," I said.

Byron turned from me. He positioned himself squarely in the window, his head tilted back, his gaze fixed on some point in the sky.

"Frances." Duck said my name again. "Calling to make sure you're alive. How much snow have you seen so far?"

I could hear him moving through his apartment, which I'd only visited once; usually he came to see me. He'd visited when I first moved here, and we'd gone to a play. Duck had grown to like musicals. I could hear the low chatter of his television, the rattle of glass bottles in his fridge as he opened the door and peered in. Standing in the light of the fridge as Byron stood in the blinding white light of the blizzard.

"Almost a foot already," I said, "and it's still coming down."

"Are you by yourself? Do you have, you know, water, flashlights?"

"No," I said. "I'm not alone."

Byron turned to me. He raised both hands, palms up. He shook his head slowly, looked around as though Duck was in the room once again, approaching him with the blindfold. *Calm down*, I wanted to say. I was the lightning rod between my brother and Byron, and part of me wanted to step aside and allow the past to strike them.

I knew that with a few words over the phone I could bring them into the same space, they would exist for each other through me, but neither of them wanted that. It would destroy Duck to know Byron was here, unless I had news of forgiveness, which I didn't and wouldn't. And Byron felt, would maybe always feel, that Duck didn't have a right to know anything about his life.

"A new guy?" Duck asked.

"Yeah," I said. "A new one. Got stranded here, poor thing."

"Well I hope he knows he couldn't get stranded with anyone better."

Duck had turned so soft, he could melt me with his kindness. I don't know how deeply he meant it, but he always remembered to fill me up with compliments like this, trying to boost my self-esteem, and sometimes I thought that if we both ended up alone—Duck didn't date much, he was too nervous for it—we'd move to the same city and meet every day for breakfast so we wouldn't start our days alone.

"I'm not sure he feels that way, but it's complicated," I said.

Byron rolled his eyes. His frustration pulled me away from my brother but not closer to him. It pulled me from my own life, the one I sometimes felt proud for having built after my divorce. My things, all the floor lamps and the world map and the painting of a Newark cemetery I'd bought from my neighbor, now seemed silly and shabby. I felt completely alone and out of place, though I was in my own house with my own cat tracing figure eights around our legs. My heart dipped deeper into my chest like a hammock into whose sling somebody had suddenly dropped a heavy weight.

Duck took me rapidly through the past week of his life. He never talked in depth about a subject, didn't like to linger on the details of his life, though in my imagined breakfasts with him we spoke honestly and without fear. Soon I could tell Duck was getting tired of talking. He wasn't good at being on the phone. I didn't want to let him go because having him on the phone gave me an ally in the room, but Duck was impatient, and Byron was still staring me down from his station near the window. Behind him, snow obscured the hospital and the street. The streetlight offered one fist of light that revealed details of the storm, individual flakes, wind whipped. Everything else was a blur.

I clutched my phone tighter while Duck's voice inched away from me. I finally let him go. He was alone with his television, and though I knew Duck craved solitude, I wished we could pass long hours on the phone. There was no one, really, who wanted to spend that long talking to me. I felt almost desperate to sink into the couch cushions and indulge in self-pity, a feeling I enjoyed very much, but Byron's anger pounced the second I pressed the button on my phone that ended the call.

"Unbelievable," Byron said. "God, this fucking storm is never going to end."

"Sorry. I'm sorry. Turning my phone off, see?" I held the power button, dangled the dark phone between my fingers, let it fall to the floor.

Byron snatched his sweater from the floor, pulled it over his head, swore when he couldn't find the armholes. He ferreted around the room, finally retrieved his watch from the corner where it had ended up, but his fingers were shaking and he couldn't clasp the strap.

"Don't you get it? What you're doing here?" he said, but I didn't know what there was to get.

"You were right," I said desperately. "Let's just go to sleep, start over. I'll make lunch, or more coffee. Maybe we drank too much."

Byron didn't answer. As I stood with him, as he finished dressing, he looked less clear to me than he'd been in my memory, and I was struck by panic, as though by being with him I'd made him disappear. The peace was evaporating, lost in the white of the blizzard. I thought if I cried he might stay, at least for a little longer, as my ex-husband had stayed with me longer than he meant to because I was so sad, and because he hadn't meant to fall in love with someone else, and anyway, what had one more night been in the grand scheme of divorce?

"I know what I did to hurt you back then," I said. "I don't know what I did to hurt you today."

He didn't say anything, and his silence made me hopeful, because it wasn't a rebuttal. The hopeful silence before someone makes a decision about you. I'd felt it with the poet, with my husband. I wondered if I'd ever made anyone feel that way. Probably I had, but it's not something you notice about yourself, is it?

"I need some space," he said suddenly. "Do you have a shovel? I'll start digging my car out."

"It will just get covered again."

"You can't keep me here," Byron said, his voice the loudest it had been all day. "If you don't have a shovel I'll ask one of your neighbors."

"It's under the porch stairs," I said, and as I spoke I reached for him again. There was so much that needed to be said still, so much I needed to fix. I needed for him to see I was trying to fix things.

He pulled away. "Don't touch me."

He left. I watched him reappear outside, emerge from beneath the porch steps with a shovel in hand. He began to dig his car out, working in a frenzy. Down the street one of the fraternity houses was carrying on with its partying; as Byron worked, people spilled out onto the porch. They tossed red Solo cups in the air, maybe to see if the beer would freeze before it hit the ground, and the cups landed lightly in the big piles of snow. I drank. I filled my glass again, threw it back, and again, and with renewed energy I put on my long down jacket and my boots, underneath which I still only wore a robe, and stormed outside.

"I wish we could talk," I said, joining Byron by his car. He didn't answer so I yelled, "Why won't you talk?"

"We've been talking all fucking day," Byron said.

"Then why did you come?" I said, my voice a thick loud sob.

The frat boys were looking at us while trying not to seem like they were looking at us. We were making a scene, and it was probably time to go inside. But I was a little crazed, and more than a little drunk, and maybe I wanted the frat boys to be afraid of me. They felt they owned the neighborhood sometimes, with their parties and shenanigans, like Halloween last year when they'd smashed dozens of pumpkins in the middle of the street. I had this urge to rattle them, I wanted to show them how much baggage one can accumulate in fifteen years—behold your future, boys—so I kept going, kept yelling at Byron. I told Byron he had to tell me why he'd come home with me. Why he'd fucked me, and when I said the word it came out viciously, in an unfair way, as though I hadn't fucked him, too. My voice, a hoarse scream, brought neighbors to their windows. I was even louder than the wind.

Byron stood completely still, unmelted snowflakes intact in his hair, his face frozen in an emotion I couldn't discern, and I realized then we'd never been able to read each other. It was how we'd managed to keep secrets for so long and why we'd caused each other so much pain. I didn't know if I was trying to get him to admit that he loved me or to admit that he forgave me. Maybe, for me, the two were the same. But it didn't matter what I felt, what I wanted. I'd trapped him here. I'd known he would get stuck. And whether or not he'd offered the ride, it had been my responsibility to turn it down.

"I'm sorry," I said, feeling foolish. "I'll help you with the car."

It was important that he know I was willing to help him escape me.

The work was never finished because the snow never stopped falling. When the plows did come, they would bury his car again with an icy wall of snow. The intersection up ahead was impassable. Byron craned his neck, looking for a way out, and though there was none, he kept shoveling.

"This is all such a mess," I said, "and it's all because I love you. You know that, right? All the things I said—I said because I love you."

Had I expected him to return my love just because the day was so dramatic? He didn't. He rolled his eyes. He said, "Jesus fucking Christ." He pierced the snow with his shovel and left it sticking up that way; he shoved his hands in his pockets and went inside. I stood there next to the car for a while. A frat boy inched toward me. "Are you okay?" he asked, and though it would have felt good to share my emotions, I knew it wasn't what this boy wanted, so I nodded and smiled, and felt embarrassed because a child had witnessed me arguing. These frat boys might be obnoxious but they were my frat boys.

In any other situation, this would have been the end of things. But neither of us could go anywhere. The streets were choked with snow. I went after Byron, in some ways feeling like I shouldn't, though it was my house, and where else did I have to go?

No matter who loved whom, we were tired of each other. Byron sighed, restless. I went into my room and, finally, got dressed.

I hated that he was bored and anxious. I hated that I had to leave him alone. I typed in the password to my laptop and handed it to him—not because I didn't trust him enough to give him the password but because it was a complicated string of letters and numbers and it was easier just to do it myself.

The light outside faded. I made soup for no reason other than it was a time of day one might eat a meal. By made soup, I meant that I opened cans and heated their contents on the stove. The flames beneath the pot glowed bright blue.

In a way I felt closer to Byron when were in separate rooms, as though we were close enough emotionally to spend time apart while under the same roof. As though we lived together. A peaceful feeling pulled up behind me, its headlights on, but then the headlights snapped off and I knew what I was feeling wasn't true. But I was good at pretending so I called Byron to the table when the soup was hot—offering him the option to decline, of course, I said he was welcome to anything in the fridge if he wanted to eat alone.

"My grandma used to say something at dinner," I said.

"What's that?" Byron said into his soup.

"There's a little love in every meal."

"I don't think that's true."

He saw my face.

"I'm sorry," he added. "I don't mean to be hurtful."

I didn't know what to say so I didn't say anything. I felt he did mean to be hurtful, and in a way so did I, or at least I'd meant to make him feel guilty for not forgiving me and Duck—which is hurtful in its own way.

"This was a bad idea," he said. "I mean, how many more ways can the universe tell us it's not meant to be."

He gestured outside at the still falling snow. I knew he was right that it wasn't going to work between us. Maybe after this I would believe it for good. How quickly things had turned sour—one name mentioned, one phone call had completely destroyed the closeness we'd felt the night before. But I wished he would stop saying we weren't meant to be. I was being stubborn about it, but it made me feel despised by fate, because if fate existed, he was clearly the good guy, and me the bad.

"I mean, Jesus," Byron said. "All those cell phone alarms? Warning! Danger! Telling me to go home, that the storm was going to be bad."

He let his spoon slip silently into the soup.

"Could I have been dumber?" He started laughing.

Someone new to the room might think he was truly joyful, but I knew he was a little delirious, we both were after the long day and the drinking and then the yelling and the past pounding on the door, demanding to be let in, claiming it had us surrounded. The more he laughed, the stronger the sting behind my eyes. I no longer cared if I cried in front of him. It seemed right to weep. I dropped my spoon, beads of soup went flying, and between sobs I told Byron not to tell me to stop crying. When I'd gathered myself a little I said, "Don't you see? It was just us here today. No bigger plan. We made the decision, and it was the wrong one, but we got to decide."

"Maybe you did." Byron's mouth shrunk into a lopsided frown. "But not me."

We were at odds. We'd probably always be at odds, until we found a way to forget about each other completely. He believed in destiny and he thought Duck was meant to be one of the guilty ones, an enduring villain in the story of his life. While I thought nothing was meant to be at all, that we just were and we lived with our decisions and life became much more pleasant if we could . . . if not forgive, at least move on. But I'd never been through anything close to the pain Byron had experienced. That big heart I lacked. I couldn't muster the empathy to understand why he couldn't forgive us.

We ate more soup. Byron told me he liked it. There remained the fact that we were stuck together until the storm let up.

"Is there a way we can turn this around?" I asked.

"Don't start," Byron said sharply.

"No," I said. "I just don't want to be devastated by this weekend. We can't undo it, we can agree not to be friends, not to speak, but while we're stuck here can we agree on something, anything, just to make life after this a little easier? Can we watch a movie or something?"

Byron reached across the table and squeezed my hand. That hope again, inside me, a bird raising its wings. He looked at me almost tenderly. "I think we should stop talking," he said, "so we don't kill each other."

In the morning the snow had stopped but the streets still hadn't been plowed. There was a car blocking the intersection ahead, someone who'd tried to go somewhere during the travel ban. The trains were running, though, and Byron said he would take one of them and return for his car another day. I didn't think we'd ever be at peace, and we could agree that we both wanted peace. That would have to be enough because we had to leave each other alone now.

I still thought, though, that the weekend could have gone differently. If only I'd let him go back to sleep.

I wrote out my phone number and asked him to text me when he got home so I'd know he was safe. It was genuine, my request, something my mother asked me to do all the time, even in my thirties. Something I'd started asking people I cared about because so much could go wrong during one trip home. Byron agreed, and he seemed to appreciate that I'd asked him, and it took me the rest of the day to stop checking my phone, to realize he wasn't going to text me.

He waited a few days before picking up his car. It was there one morning when I left to teach and gone when I returned home for lunch. For a minute I felt something of mine had gone missing and I had the urge to call the police to report the car stolen, but of course it had just been Byron taking back what was his. I wondered if he'd knocked on my door and I'd missed him. Probably not. I think he would have texted me.

I talked to Duck later that week and the urge to tell him everything was strong, but I felt I'd done enough damage for one week. Maybe one day, when we moved to the same city, we could talk about it. During the future breakfasts I imagined for us. During those breakfasts we were always happy, and when the past came up we would recall our former selves with love and forgiveness. That was the thing—there was always the option of forgiving yourself if you could just ignore the fact the people you'd hurt had never forgiven you.

I stayed home the next weekend and watched sad movies to let my feelings run their course. My cat curled up on my lap and looked at me with his head tilted as I cried. I imagined myself finding and losing love like the people in the movies, but it wasn't the same because I wasn't as beautiful as the actors, plus the thought of going out and finding someone to take me home reminded me I'd never gotten the parking permit back from Byron. I wondered if the city of Newark would give me another one, or if they would think I was trying to trick them into giving me two. I didn't find out because on Monday an envelope with no return address arrived in my mailbox. Byron had returned the permit, though he hadn't included a note.

We Are Holding Our Own

Opal was a town of passing through. On Lake Huron, freighters hauled their cargo, and in the warm months tourists chopped through the waves on their Jet Skis. Between holidays, the out-of-towners beetled downstate, leaving their boats to slumber in the marina, where gulls screamed above the water. Those who stayed, the locals, kept up shop, many days the same, but every so often there was a really good storm, and big waves toppled over one another on their way to the shore. Alex had not been born in Opal but he counted himself one of them. He was a barfly at the Evergreen Tavern and a fry cook at the Big Boy in Tawas, and he worked a second job taking care of one of the second homes.

Both jobs Alex had held since he was nineteen, more than a dozen years now, and all that vanished time rattled around inside him like engine knock. He couldn't account for much of it, and when things had changed, they'd done so in expected ways. He married a woman he worked with named Dolores. His mom passed, and so did Jack Leland, the owner of the cottage on the lake that Alex patched up and battened down. Jack left the property to his son, Peter, who was not very well liked. But Alex had known that day would come and was not surprised when it did.

Peter Leland's drinking had thinned his hair and made his skin sallow, something his money could have fixed if he'd chosen, but he chose not to. Everyone except Alex had liked Jack better. Jack never sidestepped from what he thought was right; he had an uncompromising morality admired by some but which Alex found boring. Nothing was so simple to him as it had been to Jack. Peter, however, concerned himself only with having fun. He often drank to tee-tering and said whatever his mind loosed, but none of it offended Alex. Of all his problems (money, boredom, sexual frustration), Alex considered the way Peter acted in Opal the least of them, and Peter left him unperturbed, though that began to change in the summer of 1994.

The night Alex first slept with Beau, he watched Dolores slip into Peter Leland's car like a kerchief caught by a gust. She had squeezed into candy-red shorts, and the tattered ends of her hair flitted around her waist like a crowd of moths. Their laughter when they turned around and saw Alex run after the car and kick its bumper filled him with shame. Her heart was as small as a postage stamp.

Down the way Lake Huron threw itself against the shore and retreated, and Alex went back into the Evergreen. The Fourth of July had just passed. Up and down the beach, the air popped and fizzled with leftover illegal fireworks bought in Ohio and sold out of the back room of the bait shop. Alex hoisted himself back onto his stool and talked to Beau, the owner of the bar. Her voice had a rasp Alex liked and she used it to gossip and laugh into the night. She was nearly forty, about Peter's age, and rumored by some to be a lesbian. She provided the town with most of its gossip, and Alex was attracted to her.

Alex didn't find many people interesting enough to think about for long, his mind moving like a swarm migration, but Beau was different. Beau was able to wrangle Alex's ego, and he even felt shy around her, until he'd had a few. She had full lips and long fingers. Her hair, dark yellow, looked windswept. Beau, his gaze lingered on.

That night, he drank until his reflection above the bathroom sink was fluid. Only a few regulars hung around the bar, so Beau let Alex buy her a drink, then a few more. Alex could feel the two or three other patrons look up from their pool-shooting camaraderie at them—Beau laughing loudly, Alex guzzling booze—but Alex let their attention amble by. The night—the alcohol, the attraction—orbited its own sun. When the bar closed and Beau locked the door behind her, Alex said, "You want me to take you home or something?"

Alex listened to Beau's breathing slow into sleep and thought about Dolores in Peter's bed. He would have to see them both eventually, a notion that numbed the night. To himself he hurled insults at Peter, and to Dolores, he said this was all her fault, that she had pulled the trigger, but he knew that wasn't true. When Alex and Beau had sat in his car, a thrill had gone through his body, and what they were about to do had crackled before them like a downed power line, and there was Alex, stepping forward but somehow invincible.

But while Beau was affectionate with Alex that night, she didn't entertain much conversation. Her job was to talk, she said, and she talked constantly. It was the Evergreen that made her voice hoarse. Beau fell asleep early, leaving Alex awake and alone in her wood-paneled cottage on the Au Sable River, sketches of owls eyeing him from the wall while the current moved silently outside, the water headed for the lake. Beau had laughed once at something Alex had said, a single short chuckle that made his chest rise like a flock of cranes, but come midmorning, Beau wanted him gone, and she answered vaguely when Alex asked what she had planned for the next evening.

He returned home to find Dolores still away.

Their house, a rental on one of Pearl Street's small lots, had the same wood walls as Beau's. A lithograph of a sinking ship that had belonged to Alex's mother hung on one wall. He stared at the print and thought of taking it down and throwing it away, punching the glass into the trash can.

He knew Dolores was scheduled to waitress at the Big Boy that afternoon, and he had heard Peter say he wanted to drive to Champagne Hill. The Leland beach house would be empty, so Alex showered and dressed and went to Peter's, where the garden needed weeding and the snake grass that grew in the sand, throttling. The work was quicker and easier without Peter there—Peter always wanted to talk and always had a drink in his hand—and though Alex had been sure he would be alone today, he arrived to find Dolores and Peter on the beach together, lounging on folding chairs.

When Peter saw Alex, he stood and spread his arms wide in greeting. The jealousy that had beset Alex the night before subsided, and he was not angry with Peter, a lack of feeling that troubled him. Kicking Peter's bumper had been a drunken, meaningless act, and all the things Alex had thought to say to Peter and Dolores floundered at the sight of them. Their figures against the sand were almost unrecognizable, two people Alex did not know.

Dolores only looked at her husband over the rim of her sunglasses before turning back to the water, but Peter moved toward Alex, who started for the garage to get the push mower. Peter stepped quickly through the sand, calling out for Alex to wait.

"Hot, hot, hot," Peter said, shaking sand from his bare feet. He wore swim trunks and an unbuttoned shirt. The ice in his drink chimed, and Alex noticed that Peter's hand shook, almost imperceptibly, but Alex knew to look for it.

"I'm starting with the lawn," Alex said, but Peter waved the thought away.

"No," he said. "No, Alex, come to the water. Don't worry, I'll pay you still!"

Alex watched Peter's retreating back and thought of ignoring him, but soon his feet carried him to the beach. The wind was picking up, and sand stung Alex's legs as he walked. The lake thrashed a canoe that Peter had tied to his dock, and his American flag rattled against its pole. Dolores, upon seeing Alex approach, dragged her chair closer to the water, away from the men. She released the lounger's joints so she could lie down. Her face shone with sweat.

"Look at her," Peter said under his breath as Dolores stretched out her arms to bake them in the sun. Alex braced himself for Peter to say something cruel, but instead he just said, "She looks happy."

Alex inspected his wife from the distance that separated them. Her eyes were closed, her face expressionless, but perhaps Peter was right. She did look serene. Was it possible that Peter, the devil who tore through the town, was the one who could make his wife happy, peaceful?

Alex, startled by this thought, began to laugh. The laughter replenished him. "She does," he said. "Doesn't she?"

A hope rose inside Alex as the day went on that the arrangement might work, that he and Beau could go on with their affair, and so could Dolores with Peter. The next night, Alex drank at the Evergreen until close, and once again went home with Beau. The next one, too, and after a few weeks, Alex waited nightly at the bar for closing time, and the end of every evening approached like a hot-air balloon headed for a tree. Slow, disastrous, exciting. Beau was eight years older than Alex, and he felt like a teenager around her, reckless and wild and uncertain.

At the same time, however, Alex feared the excitement would fade, as it had with Dolores and as it naturally would with Beau, and they wouldn't find anything to replace it with.

One day, they found a quiet place to talk. They rowed a hundred yards out onto Lake Huron in one of Peter's rowboats and the lake heaved them up and down. Instead of not finding anything to talk about, as Alex had feared, they found themselves offering conversation so readily it was as though they were rolling dice. The wind threw pillows of air in their faces, and it helped, maybe, that they didn't have to look at each other as they spoke, as busy as they were fluttering sunlight away from their eyes and Beau pulling strands of her hair from her mouth.

Alex told Beau about his parents, and how they'd moved here when his dad was in the air force, and how they might have left Opal eventually if his father had lived past his station at Winder AFB, where Alex had spent most of his childhood. His father deployed in '67 and never came back, though a buddy brought home his jungle jacket. On the back, his father had written the words "I will surely go to heaven because I've already been to hell." Alex's mother worked a civilian job at the base but had a heart attack when Alex was only twenty-two.

"Do you believe it?" Beau asked.

"Believe what?"

"What the jacket says. That if you endure something terrible you're automatically granted something great."

Alex had never given it much thought. His dad's jacket had been simply that, something his father had worn in the war. The blue waves undulated beneath the boat. Alex had rowed out past the breaking point, and as each wave rolled beneath them to the shore it rolled over itself and dissolved into a frothy puddle.

"Heaven seems convenient," Alex said.

"Maybe," Beau said. "As I've gotten older, I find myself wanting to believe more and more, but believing less and less."

Alex shifted on his wood-plank seat. He didn't like being reminded Beau was older than he was—it made his footing in her life feel tenuous. But Beau didn't seem to be thinking the same thing. She smiled and stretched her feet out so they landed in Alex's lap. The sun veiled her face. She squinted her eyes shut. Alex discreetly checked his watch and was dismayed to find he was due at work in an hour and would soon have to grasp the oars and return to shore. He could hardly believe the conversation he was having. For so long he and Dolores had lived in separate silences, broken only by the chatter of the local news, but here with Beau, Alex felt he was talking about important things. Life-changing things. What had he and Dolores been holding on to? Maybe it was time to divorce.

With eyes closed, Beau mumbled, "This is very nice."

Alex was about to respond eagerly that today had been one of his best days, but Beau wasn't finished.

"With you I feel like I have privacy. I don't usually feel that way around other people, but I crave the feeling."

"I guess the bar doesn't offer much privacy," Alex said.

"That's different," Beau replied. "That's a crowd. I'm talking about the way I feel around one person."

Alex made a noise to show he understood, though he didn't, not really, but that didn't seem to matter because as best as he could tell, Beau was talking about love.

Dolores and Peter continued to see each other. Most nights Dolores stayed on the lake, even during the week when Peter went downstate to go to work, and Alex cherished having their house to himself during the day, and he cherished even more the nights he spent with Beau at her cottage. He would meet her at the bar; on her breaks they would walk to the beach and watch freighters grind past. The lake often faded into the background of Alex's life but with Beau it all looked—not new exactly, but different, bluer, more expansive. When Beau returned to the bar Alex would go with her, unless he had to work, but they'd always find each other when the night had ended and the streets emptied and the lake got dark and quiet.

When Alex and Dolores were together, they didn't feel the need to explain themselves to each other anymore, and they were the happiest they'd ever been. Alex even thought that if the affairs did fall apart, maybe it wouldn't be so bad to go back to the way things were, maybe he and Dolores could have a fresh start. Or they could divorce at some point, which would be fine, too.

There were times in the past when all four of them would sit together at the Evergreen, Beau on their side of the bar until a new customer came in or one of the regulars raised his beer to indicate it was empty, and she went back to serve them. Once the affairs began that camaraderie stopped, with Alex seeking time alone with Beau, and Dolores with Peter.

But one evening in August the door to the bar swung open and a block of light from the streetlight fell on Alex and Beau. The air was cool and lake scented, and a glimpse of the outdoors showed that night had fallen earlier than it had been falling recently, the first signs of summer fizzling into fall. Peter had his arm around Dolores, who'd braided her hair into two long plaits over her shoulders, and they settled onto their usual stools near Alex. Alex clutched his beer in surprise because he hadn't expected to see his wife tonight. She and Peter had been keeping to themselves on the lake. It was one thing for Alex to waste hours with Beau, and for him to be seen leaving with her—they were longtime friends—but gossip had begun to spread about the four of them; they were either swingers or sinners, depending on whom you asked.

Peter and Beau ignored the gossip, but Alex could see flashes of pain in Dolores's eyes when talk reached her. He felt it, too. They were not immune to ridicule as Beau and Peter, who held stations in town, were.

Beau filled their drinks.

"What a lovely evening," Dolores said, and she rubbed Beau's shoulder in greeting. "Hey, you."

Someone put a song on the jukebox, Johnny Cash, and Dolores swayed to the music. Her sandal had fallen from her foot and she squeezed the leg of Peter's barstool with her toes—a gesture Alex found strangely intimate, her bare toes on the same cool metal where Peter's feet rested, and it wasn't jealousy this time that crawled through him when he witnessed them sharing the same space, but worry, because although Peter had had his arm around Dolores when they walked in, he now stared deeply into his beer and didn't react when Dolores tried to take his hand and swing it to the rhythm of the music. They'd both been drinking already, Alex realized. Dolores, just enough to make her cheerful; and Peter, more than enough to have already made him sad.

Beau gave Alex a tight-lipped smile; she didn't like dealing with Peter when he was like this. She slipped down the bar and leaned on her elbows in front of Kevin, one of the town's cops, and Dick, the pharmacist from the Rite Aid.

Alex asked Peter if he'd been out sailing today, the weather had been good for sailing.

Peter rubbed his chin against his shoulder to scratch an itch. He said, "Not many good days left for it."

Alex looked nervously at Dolores, but she didn't seem to hear Peter. She was absorbed in her wine as she studied a group of pool players in the corner.

"We should talk about closing up the cottage," Peter continued. "I might want to do it early this year. Get a jump on things downstate."

"It's early still," Alex said. "Most of August left. And there's Labor Day still."

"My girls have sports and shit," Peter said. "Games starting the first weekend of September. Wife says I have to go to their stuff this year."

As though drawn to the word *wife* like a bug to light, Dolores's attention snapped back to the conversation.

"What's your wife doing now?" she asked.

"Nothing." Peter shrugged. "Same old."

Dolores smiled and Alex had the sense she was sipping on what she thought was her own superiority—she was better than Peter's wife, she was the woman Peter really wanted to be with. And maybe that was so. But Alex knew from Peter's voice, from his agitation, that he wasn't planning to leave his wife, that he wasn't going to keep the cottage open all winter, as he'd promised Dolores he would do. He would not go through with the plans they must've concocted during the long drunken summer nights as they lay in bed.

Alex's breath punched his chest at odd angles. He took a sip of his drink and found his hands were shaking. Of course it would be Peter who would be the first to leave what they had because Peter was the one who had somewhere else to go. Peter whose desires only settled here for the warm months.

Peter seemed more cheerful now, as though he'd gotten something off his chest. He raised his glass and called for Beau to refill it, and she did so reluctantly. Alex must have looked stricken because she searched his face for what was wrong—but he couldn't tell her here, and in fact didn't want to tell her at all, that Peter was leaving Dolores, he was leaving their affairs, and soon Alex would have to make a decision of whether or not to leave Dolores, too.

The neon bar sign in the window made a persistent spitting sound and as Alex's temper rose he wanted to tear the plug from the wall. Throw a punch at Peter. Break a glass. But none of this would bring him any pleasure, and Kevin the cop sat nearby, and Beau had no patience for bad tempers, especially not in her bar. So he stayed in his seat and asked for another drink, too.

After that night Alex assumed Peter would soon have a conversation with Dolores and explain himself. He went one day in mid-August to Peter's cottage and drained the pipes and pulled the boats up from the beach to the garage. He brought down the American flag and folded it, making sure no corner touched the ground. Peter followed him, hands in his pockets, helping occasionally, but he mostly just lingered in Alex's shadow.

When Alex had finished his work, Peter took his wallet out and counted out twenties.

"You're really gone until next summer?" Alex said.

"Looks like it."

They stood in the sand. The lake rolled in and out and the light was turning heathery. Peter finally reached out his hand and shook Alex's.

"Hey," he said. "Give Dolores my best."

Alex nodded, knowing that Dolores must be heartbroken. He wouldn't bring up Peter in her presence, not until he saw how badly she was hurting. Not until he decided if he would leave her, too.

But when he arrived home later he found Dolores bustling through the house. She was looking through cassettes on the rack in the living room, and she called hello to Alex and said she was finding music to play at the cottage.

"I'm thinking of a dinner party soon," she said. "Or a barbecue for Labor Day."

Alex looked over his shoulder, looking for someone who might understand what she was saying.

"What dinner party?" he asked.

"Oh, I'm just planning one in my head," Dolores said.

"With Peter?"

"Yep," she said. "He said he liked the idea."

Alex lowered himself onto the couch. He worked for Peter, cleaned up his messes, took care of his house, and now he would have to be the one to end his affair, too.

Alex told Beau everything at the bar that night. She listened with her eyes averted. Dolores had frozen when Alex said Peter was gone, that he wouldn't be back.

"You're wrong," Dolores had said. "He'll be back next weekend."

Alex had shaken his head and told her he'd turned off the gas and the water in the cottage and pulled the boats up from the beach. The storm windows were in place and the shades drawn, and they wouldn't be opened again for months.

Dolores hadn't believed him. That had always been their problem: neither ever believed the other unless it was something they already thought was true. She'd grabbed her keys from the table by the door and had driven away, down the highway to Peter's, and Alex had gone to the bar.

"I'm just picturing her there," Alex said. "Peter's halfway down-state by now and the cottage is dark and the doors are locked. She doesn't even have keys. She's peering in windows and not seeing anything. Peter really screwed us over this time."

Beau rubbed the same spot on the counter with a rag. She looked about to say something, but then held back, and these expressions repeated themselves until Alex told her to spit it out.

"Well, should you be surprised Peter left? He doesn't live here. His life is downstate."

"Things were different this year," Alex said. "With Dolores—he didn't even tell her."

"I'm not surprised about that, either," Beau said. "Peter does what Peter wants. It's always been that way and always will be."

Beau was right, but Alex still believed Peter should've seen how the affairs involved all four of them. And hadn't glum, drunk Peter been as happy as the rest of them the past two months? Hadn't Alex, as always, been the only one to defend Peter when others ridiculed him?

After close, Beau and Alex went home—Alex wanted to give Dolores some time alone and Beau didn't object to his staying with her. After they'd made love, Alex lost and happy against her smooth skin, he said he'd made his decision. He would wait a little while for Dolores to adjust to Peter's absence, but after that he'd leave her. Their lease was almost up. The timing was right. Maybe he could move in here, with Beau.

Beau freed herself from beneath Alex's arm, which he'd thrown over her. Her hair fell over her big, loose breasts, and she brought the sheet up to cover them.

"You don't need to leave your wife," she said with amused exas-peration, as though Alex had told a bad joke.

Alex raised himself up on his elbow. "I'm ready to."

"Alex," she said. "It's time to talk, I think. I've been thinking a lot lately."

Her words made Alex go pale.

"Do you remember how I told you that being with you felt private?" she said. "How I was so happy because I didn't feel the need to explain myself to you. I still felt like my life was my own. You were a part of it, but I was the one driving. I don't feel that anymore."

"What are you saying?" Alex asked.

"Stay with your wife, Alex," Beau said. "She doesn't want to be alone, and I do. It just makes the most sense."

"She doesn't want to be with me, either."

Beau shrugged, as though to indicate that compromises would have to be made—just not by her.

"Beau . . ." Alex's voice dipped so low it reached his heart.

"Alex, please. I think you should go. Leave me be."

Alex got in his car wondering how he hadn't see this coming. Solitary Beau who never dated anyone, who was so secretive about her love life that people spread rumors she was a lesbian, had briefly let her heart settle on him, for reasons he didn't know. But he was asking her to trade in her solitude for his company, and solitude, she'd decided long ago, was already her lifelong companion.

Alex drove south, his headlights slicing open the night and revealing mailboxes and fireworks stands and boats for sale in yards. He stopped at home but Dolores wasn't there, and the only other place he thought she might be was Peter's, so he drove there and joined her on the porch.

She held out a cigarette, which Alex accepted, and when he put out his hand to rub her shoulder she didn't pull away.

"My thing ended, too," he said.

"Well, look at us sad sacks," Dolores said. Smoke left her mouth in a gauzy stream.

They stared at the lake, or rather, where they knew the lake to be. It was completely unseeable on this moonless night. They could hear its waves, though. Maybe the same could be said of their love—it was there still, audible in the distance, even if they couldn't see it.

"Dolores, do you think we could start over?" Alex said. "Make it like it was when we met."

Dolores nodded slowly. She squinted at the stars through the branches of the oak tree that swept over the porch.

"I don't know what else is left for us." She glanced sideway at Alex. "I don't mean that in a bad way."

She moved her chair closer to his and placed her head on his shoulder. Maybe all they'd really needed was a short time apart. He picked up one of her braids and rubbed its spiky end with his thumb. He closed his eyes. They stayed that way until dawn opened in the sky and its light fell on the lake. They both had the opening shift at the restaurant, and they went there together, tired and hungry, but together.

Alex briefly thought his affair with Beau would rekindle when she told him about the baby in September, but she was annoyed when he suggested it.

"Alex," she said. "Stay with your wife like I told you. I'm only telling you about the baby because you'll find out sooner or later. I don't need anything from you. I'm just letting you know."

They sat outside the tobacconist stand off the highway, in the parking lot of the supermarket. The lot was empty except for a few cars. The vacationers had trickled from the town; these days Alex only saw campers and trailers driving south on Route 23, hardly ever north.

"But we were careful, weren't we?" he said.

She shrugged. "I'm not sure what happened."

Alex left her there because she asked him to, and as he drove home he couldn't help thinking he'd made himself a part of her after all. But there was Dolores to think of, too. He had to tell her, she would know the truth herself soon, or gossip would reach her. He could imagine her being happy to hear the news, as though a miracle had come from the affairs that had broken their hearts.

His brief hope that Beau would take him back had been a passing fantasy, nothing more.

But Dolores was crestfallen when he told her.

"I'm the only one left without anything," she said.

She was wearing her waitress uniform. Alex had caught her before work, a decision he now regretted, because tears misted her eyes and soon she had to be on her feet for hours. She smoothed her skirt and adjusted the tag with her name spelled out in uneven letters.

"Dolores, I'm sorry," he said. "Call in to work. Let's talk."

"No, no," she said. "No use in that."

And she left.

Alex thought he would be able to talk with her later after she had time to think about everything. He would explain that he didn't know how involved Beau would let him be in the baby's life. For all he knew nothing would change.

He worked his own shift, overlapping with Dolores, not meeting her eyes. Afterward he went to the Evergreen but Beau bristled when he walked in, so he ordered a drink and sat at a table away from the bar, and left after just the one.

His headlights swept across his house. He killed them and watched Dolores through the living room window. She was bent over, busying herself with something on the couch, folding laundry maybe, but when he went inside he saw she was bent over a suitcase.

"Where are you going?"

"I'm not going to find Peter, if that's your question."

"That wasn't my question."

Dolores sighed. She sat down on the couch next to her neatly folded things, three pairs of shoes lined up on the floor waiting to be fitted into the corners of the suitcase.

"I just wanted to wait to say goodbye to you. I'm sorry for what happened. We should've put a stop to all this after one night, but we didn't. We didn't want to. But Alex, I don't want a baby, especially not one that came from this summer. That makes me cruel, maybe. I'm sorry, but it's the truth."

She said she was going downstate to stay with her father for a time, and then she would figure out where she would go next.

Alex wanted to argue with her, but he couldn't find the words. The next day, she left him.

Alone in the house, he found his thoughts strayed to Peter. He was jealous, after all, that Peter had stolen his wife away—as though all this was Peter's fault, the baby, and Dolores leaving. Or maybe he was just jealous that Peter had gone away from everything, returned to his old life. Alex also missed Peter, even while feeling jealous of him. The only time he felt like the better person in the room was when he was around Peter, and then not by much. Alex might not treat others as badly as Peter did—at least not as often, and not in the same way—but he seemed to understand the things Peter did. The jealousy might not be about Dolores at all; it was about the fact that Peter made the same mistakes as Alex but got away with them.

Then, appearing like a ghost when Alex first saw him, Peter returned to town in October. He was drunk when Alex found him on a bench outside the Evergreen, jacketless in the middle of the first snow, flurries accumulating on his shoulders and in his hair.

"Thank God it's you," Peter said. "Will you light the pilot light? It's freezing in my house."

Alex took Peter home and told him the gossip on the way. Peter didn't flinch when Alex told him Dolores was gone. He hooted his congratulations when Alex said Beau was pregnant, and Alex mumbled that things were complicated.

His wife had kicked him out, Peter told Alex. He'd lost his job for being drunk in a meeting one too many times. His daughters hated him; their mother had poisoned them against him.

"It's good to see a friendly face," Peter said, squeezing Alex's shoulder. "I knew coming up here was the right decision."

By *friendly*, Alex knew, Peter meant simple—because this place had always been where he'd come to escape the difficulties of his life downstate. He'd never taken seriously the way life in Opal was difficult every day, too.

Alex hadn't yet offered Beau money, hoping she would ask. This was how he had counted on staying near her, and like so much else, it hadn't worked. When he finally walked into the Evergreen around Christmas and handed over part of his paycheck, Beau put down the mug she was drying, took the check, and studied the amount.

"I said not to," she said.

"I know," Alex replied. "But I need to. And now that it looks like Peter's staying around all winter, I've got the extra income, working for him."

Beau sighed. "He's still here?"

Alex shrugged. "He doesn't have anything else to do."

"Well," Beau said, holding up the check. "Thank you for this."

Though Beau warmed a little, there was not even dust of how she'd acted before, when the affair had first begun, but at least Alex was less of an intruder in her day. She told him they were having a girl. He didn't know what sort of father he should be (and Beau wouldn't give him the answer), but Alex noticed the type of father Peter was. Far away, his girls were afterthoughts. Alex knew he had other choices. His own father had been well liked. Alex remembered him as distracted, prickly, but in the end, as his mother had told him, a good man.

Peter could reliably be found at the Evergreen, getting drunk as he talked with Beau about his girls when they were babies. The three of them spent most nights there together, before dispersing. Peter sometimes stayed in town with Alex if he was too drunk to get home.

"Little angels," Peter said of his daughters. "When they were babies, at least, and they didn't ask for anything in exchange for their love."

One night Alex went to the Evergreen hoping to talk to Beau but found her already with Peter, pouring him drinks at the bar. Alex sat down next to Peter, who extended his hand for Alex to shake.

If Dolores hadn't left—if like Alex's, her father were dead and she had no other place but Opal—would she be here with them, too? A shadow of her followed Alex to the bar and sat a short distance away. Alex watched her flip her hair over one shoulder and pinch a bead of sweat from the bridge of her nose.

When Peter handed Alex a drink, Alex blinked a few times, so his eyes could latch on to the image of his wife, but Dolores was gone, and there was only Peter, talking loudly before him.

The three of them had fallen into some sort of life together, while Dolores had escaped. In a way, the relationships made sense to Alex: all their other attempts had failed. Or maybe Alex was making all this up, and Beau was serving Peter as she would any other customer, and Alex was just some man who had gotten her pregnant.

When Peter noticed Beau was making his drinks weaker the drunker he got, he grabbed the whiskey from her and tipped it generously into his glass. "You just can't trust anyone these days, can you, Alex?" His face reddened under the bar light. Alex lit a cigarette. Someone opened the door, and the breeze blew the smoke off its eddy.

A little girl that Beau and Alex named Jan was born in early May, just as the earliest of the tourists were making their way up north to open up their cottages. Peter came to visit them in the hospital, and Alex snapped a Polaroid of him holding Jan in the chair beside the bed. When the fog on the photo cleared they all three huddled together to look at Peter's washed out, overexposed face, smiling a tired and crooked smile, and Jan, looking forlorn to be a part of this world. Peter was drunk, Alex realized, when he inspected the queasy look Peter hadn't been able to hide in the photograph.

Peter stood and stumbled. He doubled over and coughed into his knees; when he straightened his cheeks were dotted with broken blood vessels.

"Are you okay, Peter?" Alex asked. Beau was holding out her arms and Alex brought the baby to her.

"Just fine," Peter said. "Bring her by the lake this week. We'll dip her toes in."

Alex turned to Beau when Peter had swung through the curtain of the shared room. He heard the last echo of Peter clearing his throat before the elevator pinged its arrival and took him away. Beau held the baby, her face gleaming, and with one finger she lifted all of Jan's fingers, which opened and closed like a fan.

Alex brought a chair close to them. He put his hand on his daughter's head. He thought he saw Beau smile. And he smiled, too. "This is something else," he said.

Beau nodded slowly, not taking her eyes away from Jan.

"Beau," Alex said. "This feels right. I want to be with you and Jan."

Beau blinked, looked up—broken away, it seemed, from the private moment she'd been having with Jan. Alex's heart sank.

"Oh, Alex," she said, because they'd been over this before—more than once Alex had tried to hint at the idea of moving in with her, to help take care of the baby. He thought that being together, the three of them, would finally change Beau's mind—but while the tiny, sweet baby was invited into Beau's solitude, Alex was not.

Weeks went by before Beau seemed to trust Alex to be alone with Jan, and if he was being honest with himself, he felt it would take longer than that to grow comfortable with Jan himself. He was an only child; he'd never had anything to do with babies. But eventually Beau couldn't stand it; she needed a break, so Alex took Jan to Peter's to dip her toes in the lake.

She looked up at him with wide eyes while he buckled her into her car seat. Each time she fussed or let out a sob Alex's mind went wild with anxiety because he was driving and could do nothing about it. But once they turned down Peter's driveway, she became entranced by the dark and light pattern of leaves and sky outside the car window.

They walked slowly from the car to the house, Alex stopping to point out squirrels and spiders. Alex knocked on the door and waited, shielding Jan's face from mosquitoes that flew around them, but when the swarm increased he could wait no longer for Peter to answer, and he went inside, brushing bugs from Jan's legs and calling out for Peter.

He went out onto the front porch that faced the lake and searched the beach. He didn't see Peter, and the boats hadn't yet been brought down from the garage. He went back inside and found himself squarely facing Peter's closed bedroom door. The door was never closed during the day. It was nearing noon.

Alex rapped his knuckles on the door. The sound of the fan could be heard through the door; the stale smell of smoke from Peter's clothes reached Alex's nose.

He opened the door and saw Peter lying on his bed, beneath the covers. Alex didn't have to look closely to know he wasn't breathing. The dread that he would find Peter dead had been growing in him as soon as he'd stepped across the threshold and had gotten no eager response from his friend.

"Peter," he said. He leaned over Peter and touched his neck. Jan's head dipped down toward Alex's friend, and she whined, and Alex pulled her up abruptly. He rushed her from the room and stretched the phone cord in the kitchen as far away from the bedroom as it would go.

He held his baby while he waited for the ambulance. He cried silently, but Jan could feel the shaking and cried herself, too.

Peter's body was taken downstate and his brother, a man named Jim, drove north to coordinate the sale of Peter's cottage. Arranging for the exchange of keys and a rundown on the mechanics of the cottage was all Alex had to do with the end of Peter's life. Before Jim drove away, Alex had thought he might tell Jim he'd been Peter's friend, that he missed Peter, but Jim believed so completely that Alex was just a hired hand that Alex was too embarrassed to contradict him.

So with Peter's death there was one fewer person left in Alex's life—but with Jan's birth there was one more.

Beau held a memorial for Peter at the bar. Though he'd frustrated her, he'd been a loyal patron and, she said, raising a glass to Alex, a friend to some.

"Thank you," Alex said afterward.

Beau smiled and handed him their daughter.

There was still one thing weighing heavily on Alex: the question of whether or not Dolores would want to know that Peter had died. Peter's death reminded him of the life they'd had, and lost, and also that they'd never divorced, not formally, and maybe he should talk to her about that, too.

He asked around at the bar, and finally Kevin found someone who was still in touch with her father, and from there Alex found her phone number.

He held Jan while the phone rang. Finally the receiver clicked, and he heard a cough—Dolores's cough, she'd been a heavy smoker since they were teenagers, and he would know that cough anywhere—and then she said hello.

"Wow," she said. "You know, I've been thinking about calling you—I wanted to ask you something."

She launched into her question before Alex could tell her the news, which waited dumbly in his mouth while she recounted their honeymoon. They'd gone to the Upper Peninsula to see the Shipwreck Museum. It was the only place Alex could think to go, and in any case, all they could afford.

"What did that plaque say, the one I loved? About the *Edmund Fitzgerald*."

Alex reminded her. She'd studied each display carefully and lingered on the description of the last radio transmission from the *Edmund Fitzgerald*. "We are holding our own," the captain had said to a nearby ship minutes before the freighter disappeared from the radar.

"Oh right," Dolores said. "I just love that. We think we're doing great right up until the end."

"Dolores," Alex said. "Peter died."

There was silence on the other end of the line. Finally, Dolores said, "Well, damn, he beat me to it. I was planning on haunting him."

Alex laughed. "You're okay? I wasn't sure you'd want to know."

"Alex," Dolores said. "I'm okay with everything these days. And your timing is strange. I wasn't sure you'd want to know. But I guess there's no getting around it. I have lung cancer. Treatment's not taking."

"Dolores," he said. "What do you mean, you weren't sure I'd want to know?"

"You know," Dolores said. "It's a burden, knowing this kind of thing."

"I'll come down," Alex said. "I'll take you to a doctor. We'll find the right treatment. We'll go to the University of Michigan."

At that moment Jan shrieked with laughter. Dolores said, "Is that your baby?" and of course at those words Alex saw how he couldn't go be with Dolores—not anymore.

"I want to help," he said feebly.

"I'm fine," she said. "I had a good year down here. I'm looking forward to seeing what's next."

"Maybe you'll see Peter soon," Alex said quietly, but regretted it, and worried that Dolores would find it morbid or offensive that he spoke so plainly about her death.

But she laughed. "Yeah right. I'll breeze by him on the way to the pearly gates. He's probably still waiting in line, trying to bribe someone to get in."

Alex laughed again. "He wasn't that bad," he said.

"No," Dolores said quietly. "No, I guess not always."

They passed a little more time on the phone, and when they hung up Dolores promised she would call again soon. Alex was reluctant to get off the phone, but he didn't have anything more to say.

Alex had imagined the day Dolores would meet Jan. She'd be Aunt Dolores, and the baby would grow up knowing her. Now he would only have photos to show her, and maybe he wouldn't even want to show those, because the pain would be too great. He could already imagine himself feeling guilty, because he'd survived and Dolores and Peter hadn't. In a single year everything had changed, and just when he was trying to take control—by coming to terms with Peter and calling Dolores to bring her news and arrange a formal divorce—death was swooping in and solving his problems for him. He was alone with Beau and Jan.

His call with Dolores had been pleasant, and when Peter died he and Alex were the closest they'd been in years. So why did Alex feel like he'd gotten away with murder? As though he were a stone that kept skipping on water, while Dolores and Peter had plunged to the bottom. He wondered what everyone in town would say when the news came of Dolores's illness, her death. About Peter, they seemed to remember only the bad things: Peter driving his car into a tree, Peter's divorce, Peter on one of many of his drunken and foolish nights. And what would be remembered of Alex, himself, when his time came? He understood now why Beau never corrected the gossip that she was a lesbian. When the talk was true, there was nothing left but the person Alex was. And what he'd tried to do right, well, none of it had counted.

III

Lungs

It's at the after party of a silent auction in Newark that I see the man from the sushi restaurant again, the one whose friend had just died and for whom I hadn't been able to muster any empathy. He looks the same now as he did then: red spring jacket, tired eyes, neat black hair parted over to one side. Very young.

I've come to the party with my downstairs neighbors, two Danish artists named Per and Thora. Per had a painting on auction that sold for peanuts. Thora is seven months pregnant with twins, and in the evenings, before Per gets home from his art handling job at a warehouse in Newark's South Ward, where one of the big museums in Manhattan stores some of its collections, Thora and I have a glass of wine (I usually finish Thora's for her). She's asked politely what happened between me and Ralph, and I've demurred. I've said the expected things: it wasn't meant to be, it just didn't work out, we were tired of living the way we'd been living. None of these things is untrue, but none of them gives any details, either, and they sound as though I've reflected at least a little bit on the dissolution of my ten-year relationship. So, they do the trick. Per comes home, and sometimes he asks me if I've been writing, and I admit I haven't been writing, and he smiles and says, "Artists need to rest."

"You can say that," I tell him, "because you're prolific."

The party is on Market Street, behind what used to be a storefront that's now an empty event space. The scene could be a disbanded AA meeting: metal folding chairs scattered around, Styrofoam cups (filled with wine instead of coffee), and a general feeling that some people have embraced the party and others would rather be anywhere else. We're the oldest people here. At least Per and Thora look cool. Per's wearing a tailored white button-down, and Thora's draped in loose, flowing linen. I look like what I am: a paralegal for an entertainment lawyer in Manhattan. A cardigan and flats.

Thora and I perch on the circumference of a small number of dancers who move beneath red spotlights strung up in every corner. Thora sips a little wine, and I sip a little more liberally and press the cup to my lips. When Thora puts her hand on her belly I pull it away and smile at her—she asked me to stop her if she ever assumes the "pregnant pose." She doesn't want to look like a Madonna. We sway back and forth to the music, a remix of something I don't know, but our eyes are on Per on the dance floor.

Per is the center of attention, commanding the room with his strange way of dancing. He squats low to the ground and glides around the circle we made for him. He spins on bent ankles, a little like a figure skater, his arms over his head. He stretches his legs in new directions, the rest of his body following. He rises and twirls and shoots out a leg that nearly kicks Thora in the stomach. Thora drops her cup and jumps back. My wine splashes over the top of my cup.

The music falls in a thick layer over the room. Per's dance morphs into a plea as he goes to Thora with his hands outstretched. No one seemed to notice except the three of us.

"I'm sorry," Per says.

"It's okay," Thora whispers, but she looks grave.

Per's fingers touch Thora's elbows, and without saying anything to me they rush to the corner where we piled our coats. I swallow what's left of my wine, most of it spilled on my hands, and follow them, not sure if they want me to walk home with them. When we're outside Thora grasps my hands and says, "I'm sorry, love, we have to go."

The gallery and the party next door are the only places open amid the gated storefronts on Market Street. Down the street, the courthouse blazes, its white facade lit from below with clean white light. It's spring now and strong winds have passed through lately, leaving petals from Newark's blossoming trees, the first trees of spring, scattered on the sidewalk like drops of paint. My hands are sticky, and I dig in my purse where I know there's hand sanitizer.

"Looking for a light?"

I look up. I see him. He has a lighter in his hand and his thumb on the spark wheel. His irises are so dark they look black, and his jacket is zipped up to his neck.

"No," I say. "No, I'm looking for my hand sanitizer."

The difference between what he thought I needed and what I was actually looking for strikes him as funny.

"Hand sanitizer!" he exclaims.

His lips curl into a smile around his cigarette. Dimples appear, half-moon creases around his lips. It's the first time I've seen him smile and, of course, the smile changes his face. He doesn't look like the sad sack shooting Jack Daniel's with his elbows on the bar. I laugh, too, but then guilt nudges my heart because I couldn't be bothered with his pain at the restaurant, or I'd turned his pain into my own pain—which I often do.

I offer an open palm to show I recognize him, and he nods, and at the same time we say our own versions of "Right, yes, we've met."

We exchange facts about our meeting. The month, the weather, the bar. We shake hands and give our names. Patrick is his. We pass through a few moments of silence. Somewhere in the distance a siren wails. I rub my hands together even after the sanitizer has dried.

"I'm sorry about your friend," I say finally. "How are you feeling?"

Patrick shakes his head as he lights another cigarette. "I shouldn't have bothered you with that," he says.

"No, it's okay," I say.

A few people spill from the party. I look over my shoulder, but Per and Thora have disappeared from sight.

"I'll take that cigarette," I say.

He pulls the box from his pocket and holds the lighter near my mouth, cupping it.

"I'm glad I ran into you." I flick ash to the ground. "I felt bad for leaving you at the bar that night."

"God, don't bring it up," he says. "I was a mess."

I shrug. "We all have nights like that."

He nods, but he's looking down the street. Maybe he's tired of talking. "Well," I say.

He looks at me. "Your friends left."

"They had to go."

"Where do you live?" he asks.

"I'm near campus. What about you?"

"The Ironbound." He checks his watch. "I'll walk in your direction."

"That's out of your way."

"It's actually right by the nearest light-rail station."

That's not true, but I start walking without agreeing or disagreeing. I have a feeling I don't often get: that there's something left to excavate in the night, something with more of a payoff than just going to bed.

There's another spill of people from the party on the sidewalk outside the gallery, but when we cross the street to a new block the sidewalk empties. We're downtown, hardly anyone lives downtown, and outside of business hours everything is quiet. The smell of smoke from our cigarettes makes me feel peaceful, it lifts my lungs and leaves me floating on a cloud. My father was a lifelong smoker, and for me the smell of smoke belongs to him alone.

We cut through Military Park, and we don't say anything as we walk past a light-rail station. Soon the park will be full of summer activities: yoga and tai chi; movies on Tuesday nights; plays; and the carousel, which is boarded up right now, undergoing remodeling, but will soon alight and spin. We pass the magnolia tree in the yard of the church on Central Avenue. Its leaves are waxy and its mangled branches make it look fossilized.

"What happened to your dad?" Patrick asks.

"We don't have to talk about that," I say. "Tell me about your friend."

Patrick throws his head back and blows a stream of smoke into the air. "He was just one of those guys you loved even though he was a fuckup."

"You could call my dad a fuckup," I say. My cigarette is down to its filter and I toss it in a puddle.

Even though I said I wasn't going to talk about him, grief is always looking for a mate. I immediately feel badly for calling my dad a fuckup. It's a different thing to call a twenty-year-old a fuckup than it is to say that about someone who was almost sixty when he died. At that age it's not about mistakes anymore. It becomes about who you are rather than the things you did—and that doesn't seem fair, because now my father doesn't have the chance to redeem himself. Patrick's friend, meanwhile, is redeemed merely by the fact of his youth. He didn't have enough time to know better. But I don't feel like explaining this to Patrick. All I manage to say is, "I mean, he was, whatever."

"Yeah," Patrick says, as though I'd actually said something descriptive. I laugh, and when he asks me what's funny, I shake my head. He extends his cigarette toward me, and I take it and take a drag.

We pass through campus, the long brick corridor with Rutgers buildings on either side—the law library, the nursing school. On the next street over there's a row of 150-year-old brick town houses that have been turned into campus buildings. The creative writing program and the Institute on Ethnicity, Culture, and the Modern Experience. We're almost at my apartment. We pass the Catholic hospital, which I've read is near to filing for bankruptcy but for now still blurs with activity. The carriage house of the Ballantine mansion opens up to University Avenue, covered in vines and flowers.

I ask Patrick if he wants a nightcap when we reach the foot of my stoop, and immediately I feel embarrassed. It's not as though we were having a conversation that needed more time to reach its end.

But Patrick agrees, and we go inside and up the stairs. A ribbon of light seeps under the door of Per and Thora's apartment, and I wonder if they take note of the extra pair of footsteps, or if it's only me who thinks the whole world can hear them. It's been a long time since I brought someone home that I didn't know, and it was a lifetime ago that I lived in an apartment I hadn't shared with someone else. With Ralph.

The door to my apartment fits loosely in the jamb, and I unlock the lock that's only a formality. I left the window open earlier, and the glass rattles in the wind, and my tabby sits on the windowsill. He hisses when he sees Patrick. The white lace curtain blows dramatically, getting sucked against the screen and billowing back out into the room as the wind changes. I busy myself pouring wine into glasses, and my heart is an iceberg in my chest. I wonder how long before I can kick him out. We sit across from each other at my table and drink. "Nice apartment," Patrick says, and I can't help but smile. I look lovingly at my high ceilings and big square windowpanes, the cracked wood floors and marble fireplace. I tell Patrick this row of brownstones was built in the 1880s as company housing for the Ballantines, the Newark beer family whose nineteenth-century home is now an annex of the Newark Museum, into whose yard you can see from my fire escape.

"I'll show you," I say, and I lead him into the bathroom and hoist open the window that leads to the fire escape. He holds my wine as I climb out, and then I hold his. There's a wedding tonight in the yard of the museum, inside a white tent, and music billows into the night. The small schoolhouse that's part of the museum yard is dark and empty, the bell still in its belfry. I point to the back of the mansion, tucked between the museum and an office building. Beneath us, Per and Thora's bedroom light glows. They're still awake.

The fire escape is small, and our shoulders touch. Our jackets are inside still, and soon my fingers will lose their color—Reynaud's.

"Were you with friends at the party?" I say. "You left without telling anyone."

"They'll figure it out," he says. "I don't see them much anymore. They don't really understand."

A pang of recognition hits me. It's what I said to him the night we met.

"It's us, too," I say. "Not letting them understand."

He ignores me. I shift on the metal grate, and my arm touches his. It seems to be this soft brush of skin against skin that launches him into an explanation of what happened to his friend. The way one whiff of a certain scent brings back a memory in all of its details.

"We grew up together. Did undergrad together. The first time we did Oxy, I gave it to him. I was supposed to go with him to a meeting the day before he died. But I bailed. I didn't even have a reason. I just didn't feel like it. I was his ride, too."

He looks into his wine. His voice is thick, and he's probably had a lot to drink tonight. I've known addicts like him, ones who think they can keep drinking once they give up drugs. Maybe they can, but for my dad it was always either all or nothing. Patrick tells me how he got clean, how he takes master's classes at the Business School and has a part-time job at the halfway house near Lincoln Park.

I listen. What is it that I want here? Someone to talk to—to understand? Do I just feel bad that he was alone on the night of his friend's funeral, and I brushed him off? And then I see, looking out at my slice of the city and the slow-dancing bride in the wedding tent, that it's already done. I've already brought him here.

"My dad sent me an email a month before he died," I say. "He told me he was lonely and asked that I keep in touch more often. I didn't reply. I didn't call him."

"Why not?" Patrick asks.

"We would go through phases. Talking and not talking. I always thought it was after I didn't write back that he started using again—that he felt betrayed."

"You know that's not the truth," Patrick says. "Or not all of it."

"And you know your friend could've taken an Uber to the meeting. You didn't do anything wrong."

"Okay. You believe that for me, and I'll believe this for you, and one day we'll be ready to swap."

I smile, close my eyes, tap my head lightly against the bricks behind me. I've had enough to drink to tell him about Ralph. I explain that we split up because I couldn't get over my grief. At times I bottled it up and other times I talked about it in a way that accused Ralph of trying to get me to forget about my father when all he wanted was for the two of us to be happy again. I say it with my eyes closed so I don't see Patrick's face. He takes my hand and runs his fingers through mine just as I'm thinking that between the two of us, I'm the bigger fuckup.

"You didn't do anything wrong, either," Patrick says.

"No," I say. "I did."

I open my eyes and look at our clasped hands, suspended between us. The music from the wedding has stopped, and although guests are still lingering in the yard the caterers and museum staff are bustling around, cleaning things up, shooing people away.

He kisses me. Our hands are clasped between our chests.

"Can we go inside?" he asks.

In my bedroom, we get out of our clothes without turning on the light or closing the curtains. Our closeness is a form of silence; it smothers everything we said on the fire escape.

Per and Thora are sleeping beneath us. I saw their light snap off before Patrick and I crawled inside. If I'd left alone earlier, or left with them, Patrick wouldn't be here. Instead I made the guy from the sushi restaurant the keeper of my biggest secret, that I'd ignored my father when he needed me most. I grab the skin on

Patrick's back, pull it taut with my fingers, take his earlobe gently between my teeth.

Patrick keeps his lips close to mine but doesn't kiss me. I try to close the distance but he pulls back. My head falls on the pillow. I wonder if this is a mistake. There's so much I haven't told him. Later on, if we're being kind to ourselves, we can remember: we didn't plan this.

That Was Me Once

Mara and I are trying to do normal things in the time I have left, so on Sunday afternoon we take Brian to lunch in town.

Harper, Michigan, is one of those places that for a long time could have been anywhere. There was a main street with a few dull shops and a Greek diner, but recently people have been trying to make it a more specific place to live. We go to one of the new restaurants that's sprung up in recent years: a tavern with wood booths and bric-a-brac on the walls, twinkle lights strung from the ceiling, a menu full of dishes more expensive than we expected. We have to connive with the waitress to get her to admit the chicken medallions are close enough to chicken fingers, one of the few things Brian will eat, but when his food arrives he tears it apart and not much makes it into his mouth. Mara keeps saying Brian can sense the tension in our lives, that the big approaching changes are bearing down on him. I can never tell with Brian: he's three and a half but doesn't talk much. He's frustrated with the limits being a toddler places on him. I've been with him since he was born but he seems to sense I could depart at any minute. I sometimes have this feeling he can tell when my eye is wandering from our little family, like it has been lately.

Mara sits next to him, across the booth from me, and her hands worry over him: chasing spills and wiping ketchup from his face. I'm supposed to enjoy moments like this, quiet ones, but instead I'm ready to dive into something reckless. For this feeling I blame my moribund chances of avoiding jail time. My hopeless outlook, Mara tries to bulldoze with optimism, but some days, like today, she can't muster it. So she sits and steams frustration—with me, with Brian—and punctuates her scowling with anemic smiles.

It doesn't help that the restaurant is bonfire hot. I twist in my seat to look at the completely still ceiling fan. As I'm about to turn back, my eyes fall on Dani, sitting in a booth by the back window.

She's grown up, though I know that already from the internet, where for years, and lately more often, I've searched her name and lurked on her social media profiles. Reading every post and comment, clicking through every photo. I've seen her here and there over the past three years, rarely speaking, but I feel like I know her still, like we've been circling each other, just waiting to reconnect. I've been hungry for more of her, but online she comes off as cynical.

She was only eighteen when we got married, nineteen when we divorced. I was older, too old: twenty-four when we met.

Now she's twenty-two, and she has a foaming mug of beer in front of her. Her head is bowed toward her phone, and her hair has been electrified with curly blond extensions, new since I last saw a photo of her online. The change rolls me like a whitecap: who knows what else I've missed while I was underwater, out of her real life?

She wears a chunky sweater with elbow patches despite the heat. The sweater blots out her shorts. Only a twig of denim peeks out, and strappy sandals vine up her ankles. It's May and she must be home from school for the summer.

Nostalgia makes quick work of me. It's like I want to ride a motorcycle without a helmet: I forget all the terrible ways hearts and brains can get smashed, all just for a simple feeling. Wind in the hair.

"Is that Dani?" Mara asks.

She knows about Dani, but they haven't met. I've worked hard to make sure of that. I keep my internet sleuthing secret, but Mara's probably done her own. Mara's not a jealous person, but we don't talk much about our pasts. We've made mistakes, accumulated victims. Our biggest transgression: we both disguised ourselves as fun people, people you'd want to hang out with, when we were really just careless and stupid and we brought people down with us. Mara got collared by the world first, in the form of Brian, a baby she wasn't ready for. We were seeing each other when she found out she was pregnant, and we never shared the results of the paternity test. I was willing, and I felt guilty for what happened with Dani. Maybe I thought being his father was a kind of penitence, or that it would bring me reward.

Brian might not be my biological son, but whatever karma I earned from not leaving Mara in favor of a less-complicated paternity situation has dried up. The number of times I've been busted with drugs has surpassed the number of times anyone cares to forgive me.

"Yes, that's her," I say.

"Dani," Mara says, her voice almost a whistle. She looks almost excited as she appraises my ex-wife. I can see her making judgments about Dani's looks. She's critical of people who put in a lot of effort. Her own, which are good, are nonetheless a nuisance to her. She has permanent accessories—tattoos on her shoulders, wrists, and ankles—and she dresses to show them. Otherwise she leaves the house with wet hair, no makeup. She never asks me how she looks. She knows she looks good.

"Would she write you a letter?" Mara asks.

"You're kidding," I say dryly. She knows the marriage ended badly.

Mara's been bugging anyone she thinks will help us, most recently for letters of character to give my lawyer. The two don't speak, Mara and my lawyer. They're similarly obdurate. Mara thinks I should take the case to trial, but the lawyer's saying my best chance is a plea bargain. I haven't decided yet. I've been out on bail for three weeks, and the clock is ticking.

"You always think it hurts to try," Mara says. "That's your number one problem, I'd say."

I'm about to say something mean—You're *my number one problem*,

Mara, which is far from true—when another phantom glides through the door. It's Catherine, who, at least when I knew her, was Dani's best friend. I've seen her posts on Dani's pages, but those, I avoid reading. She was one of the main crusaders against me back when Dani and I were together. Her eyes knock against mine for a second, but they skip right past, and I gather she saw me looking at her but didn't recognize me herself. Enough time has gone by, I guess, and more worthwhile fights have made her raise her banner.

Catherine's swift to cross the room to Dani's booth. The girls exchange a high-voltage greeting, clasping hands over the table as they take seats opposite one another. Dani throws her head back and laughs. I see nothing of the girl I convinced to marry me. She was a senior in high school when we took up together, and I was old enough to know better.

We both worked at the cvs in town. We stole cigarettes and smoked by the dumpsters out back after our shifts. We made out in the boring midwestern evenings. She had homework waiting for her, homework she didn't do. I'd done two years of college, even wrote some poems while I was there that won awards, but I'd dropped out of everything in my life except for cashiering, and then her. I don't know why, really. Just a thing I did. A mistake, I guess.

Brian is growing bored; he arches his back and slides down the booth, a whine like a fly's issuing from his mouth. He hits his head on the table as he tries to slip underneath it, and the whine turns into a sob. He reappears on my side of the table, his eyes trying to press upon me his sudden toddler misery.

"Come up here." I lift him awkwardly by his arms. He doesn't like the way this makes his shirt ride up, and he cries harder. I rub the crown of his head, plant a kiss against the side of his closed eye. "Shh," I whisper, and he starts to quiet. I'm no great consoler, but I can approximate comfort. Eventually his red-washed face breaks into a rare smile. Mara stands up and takes him from me.

Despite myself, I look over at Dani's table. She and Catherine return my gaze. A brief, unsmiling moment passes before I realize they know about the current charges. In a town this size, of course they know.

"I'll go talk to her about the letter," Mara says. She's moving before I can protest.

It's something like a nightmare I've had: all the people I managed to turn joyless in one room, talking to each other. Brian is still in her arms—her empathy card.

The girls stare at Mara and Brian and then trade openly incredulous looks.

Mara doesn't care what anyone thinks of her. She has no ability to estimate how people will receive her, which makes her bold, but also leaves her open to ridicule, which she absorbs like UV rays. You can't see it right away, but it must be working its slow annual damage. I suppose I'm the same way, though. It's part of why we love each other. This thought softens me, and as she walks back across the room toward me I realize what a dick I've been. It's a miracle Mara's with me. I try not to think that it might be because she thinks I'm her only option, the man who accepted her son, lied to her conservative parents, and helped her so she wouldn't have to go to his real dad—a bigger loser, if you can imagine—for support.

I turn away from Dani, but the idea that I would go to her, if beckoned, keeps a steady pace with my love for Mara.

"She says she'll think about it." Mara sets to work eating Brian's uneaten meal, which makes Brian want it again, and the tears begin anew.

"Thank you," I say.

Mara's own eyes mist. I seize up, just like when Brian cries: I feel particularly handicapped when it comes to soothing their emotions. She's holding back tears, and soon she clears her throat.

"Just a little bit of effort goes a long way, Jordan," she says.

We finish eating in silence. Outside of the restaurant we get ready to part ways—me to work down the street, Mara and Brian back to my dad's house, where we live. She rummages my blue CVS polo from her purse, where she bunched it up for me earlier. The afternoon is hot, and the sky looks torn between sun and storm, and we say goodbye beneath it.

I go to work and try to forget about Dani, though it crosses my mind to wait outside for her and Catherine, talk to her again after all these years. Instead I scan and bag the usual drugstore purchases: aspirin and bandages, gum and cold drinks. A shamefaced teenage boy comes up to my register to return a big box of condoms—the biggest quantity one can buy them in—and since the refund amount exceeds ten dollars, I have to call the manager up for approval. The boy looks ready to flee. I try to give him a look that says I'm not passing judgment.

I imagine Dani's left downtown by now, back to her mom's house in the wealthier part of town, or maybe driving the country roads with the music blaring like she and I used to do. But then, a few hours later as I'm paying for a Snickers bar and bottle of ginger ale to take on my break, I hear the bell chime above the door. There's Catherine, with Dani a few paces behind. She's sending quick missives from her phone.

"Jordan," Catherine says.

Dani looks up at me. She blinks and smiles. A year after we split we exchanged perfunctory apology emails, as limp as dissected frogs, and since then it's only been stiff hellos in passing.

Their eyes are guarded but curious, like cats. I expect anger, but I don't receive it, then I feel a sense of opportunity. It's been a long time; maybe I stand a chance to recover a shred of grace with Dani. Things had just gotten too heavy between us. We lived together in a narrow, moldy railroad apartment: no doors, each room leading into the next. We had no money and no way to escape each other.

"I didn't know you were still working here."

This is the first thing Dani says to me. I doubt it's true. From her Facebook I can tell she pretends not to know what's going on in town, as though she's risen above it.

"Yeah. I'm still here," I say. "I was just about to go on my break."

Catherine breaks the silence. "Sell us cigarettes first, and then we'll join you."

I've already clocked out but slip behind the counter, ignored by the other cashier, who's taking a personality test on her iPhone. "Let me use your register," I say to her, and she moves aside without looking up. Catherine points to the kind she wants, and I scan my employee discount for her. Then I hurry them outside, to the back alley where Dani and I used to go, as though they'll change their minds if I'm not fast enough. Once we're outside, the feeling is euphoric. I've just slipped back in with them.

"I guess you only have a few minutes?" Catherine speaks around her cigarette. She snaps her lighter but the alley is a wind tunnel, and a breeze keeps catching the flame.

"Let me do it," Dani says. She cups her hand around her friend's mouth. For some reason they giggle once the cigarette is lit.

I look at my watch. I have fifteen minutes until I should be clocking in.

"I've got some time," I say.

The lie is a foot thrust forward to stop a door from closing. Dani bunches her hair between her hands and looks sideway at Catherine. I used to hate watching Dani defer to Catherine, but now they seem conspiratorial, telepathic. Maybe they were always that way and I just never understood them.

Catherine presses her lips together. She resembles, in personality and physique, an office supply—useful and precise, maybe a ruler.

"Okay," she says. "We're meeting a few friends at Old Harper Village if you want to join for a little bit."

"Haven't been there in ages."

Old Harper Village is a park in town, with a circle of preserved turn-of-the-century buildings: a one-room schoolhouse, a church, a general store, and a blacksmith's. A stream runs behind it; it leads you out into the country if you follow it. I remember school field trips when we were made to dress up as Victorian children and, later, getting into trouble after hours. It's closed Sundays, the buildings locked but unattended.

Dani starts down the alley. "You coming?" she asks.

Dani's simple words beckon me back into her life. Leaving work—just walking away—is everyone's fantasy at some point, and it turns out it's easy to do. Maybe it helps that I'm already outside. I've already given them half my day, I justify. I've already helped them with the after-church crowd.

I follow the girls as they walk single file through the alley, leaving the cool, darkened tunnel with only a small strip of sky overhead. Dani and Catherine don't make room for me to walk beside them once we're on the sidewalk so I walk behind them, feeling the breeze of their quick movements.

My head is somewhere up in the sky—high enough for me not to think about Mara, not to think about work. The clouds are getting dark, but the sun is still bright behind them, turning their image into an x-ray. A bird flies across the storm-ready sky. When I think of Dani, I always think of conflicting things: how it was wrong to be with her in the first place, but how could I have been so stupid as to let her go? She was the biggest mistake of my life, though I can't say which mistake I mean: being with her or losing her.

The confusion sucks me in again, and I look for the easiest answer to it: Here is this girl walking in front of me. She's invited me back into her life again, even if only for an afternoon. She's pretty. Things ended badly, but we'd abandoned a ship that still might be out there somewhere, floating. Dani's texting again, and I imagine it's me she's writing about, me who's making her fingers speed over the keys.

The village is deserted when we arrive. The displaced buildings stand in a horseshoe before us, quiet and dark. A rocking chair, empty, shifts vaguely in the hot breeze on the wood-plank porch of the general store. The iron hitching post outside of the blacksmith's hasn't hitched a horse in nearly a century, but someone keeps giving it a fresh coat of paint.

The first raindrops begin to fall, and soon they quicken into a stream.

Catherine hops up the stairs of the schoolhouse. "If you can believe it, they keep a key underneath the flowerpot," she says, nudging the ceramic pot of petunias aside with her foot. There's a skeleton key beneath it, which fits into the building's original lock. Ill advised, it seems, to keep the key—an antique itself—outside, but this town is backward in more ways than one.

The door swings open with a squeal, and we shuttle inside. Wooden desks with lacy ironwork sides are arranged in neat rows. A half-erased block of cursive script is on the blackboard, a lesson about the Pilgrims. The smell of old wood haunts the place.

"Ballsy," I say, "to come inside the buildings. I always just drank behind them."

"Since when are you afraid of a little danger?" Dani asks.

"I think I'm good on danger. I got myself into some trouble not too long ago. I don't know if you've heard about it."

Dani nods. "I did. My mom told me."

It doesn't surprise me that Dani's mom is still keeping track of my transgressions. When I proposed to Dani, right in front of everyone at Dani's high school graduation, her mom's face looked like a fly on which someone had slammed a dictionary. She did her best to get between us, but Dani was as stubborn then as she seems to be now.

"I think they're bullshit, the charges. Anyway, it's not true, right?"

I shrug. Clouds cover the sky outside and the last of the sun is siphoned away. There's no electricity in the schoolhouse and the room grows dark.

Catherine's been lingering on the periphery of our conversation, but now she says, "Oh my God, it *is* true."

"I only sold to consenting adults. And mostly weed and pills." I'm ready to defend myself. I'm so tired of people looking at me like I was selling fentanyl to toddlers.

"I know that," Dani says. "Pot's going to be legal in a few years anyway." She looks defiant. I remember that look: she gave it to me whenever I underestimated her.

"Are you really going to jail?" Catherine asks.

The door swings opens before I can answer, and standing there is a group of kids, or, rather, the type of young adults who still seem like kids. Six or seven of them, all Dani and Catherine's age. The rain offers them laughing into the schoolhouse. Their shoes leave muddy prints on the old wood floor. I don't know any of them, though I might have met them years ago, when Dani and I were still together.

"Listen." Dani sidles close to me. "I know you're probably flying the straight and narrow, but if you do have any stuff, we'd pay a premium. To help with your legal fees."

I think of what Mara or my father would say. My father is trying hard these days to resist me, but he keeps caving and offering me help. Money for the lawyer, whatever food Mara, Brian, and I want from the fridge. Mara and I don't pay rent, and my dad and I have an unspoken understanding that she and Brian will keep living at his house if I do go away. My transgressions are mounting, though. I'm getting to be beyond help, even beyond the help of my complicit, loving dad.

I do have an eighth in my pocket. I was planning to sell it to a coworker at cvs, who's probably wondering where I am with his weed. My intentions are well meaning if wrongheaded: I want to leave Mara and Brian with as much money as I can. Even with my dad's help, we've been struggling.

Instead, I take the bag out and hand it to Dani. "On the house," I say.

Her fingers graze mine as I hand over the bag, and there's heat in my heart like a beggar's fire burning.

"Awesome," Dani says, but she sounds almost bored. She turns the bag over in her hands, inspecting it. She hands off the baggie and ignores the conversation it produces. She wanders to the corner where there's a stool with a dunce cap perched on it. She knocks off the dunce cap and sits, legs crossed, elbow resting on her thigh, chin resting in her hand, nose back in her phone.

Catherine appears with a backpack from one of the newly arrived guests and tears the zipper open. Inside, it's impossibly full of beer, with a bottle of whiskey perched on top. It's like Mary Poppins's bag: inside is every medicine we need. Watching Dani, trying to analyze her voice and eyes and postures, has made me anxious for an elixir. In other words, ready to get fucked up. I've skipped work, am betraying Mara by being here, and I'd rather delay the regret I know I'll feel.

Rain streams down the windows. I take a swig of whiskey, then a beer, and sit in one of the too-small desks. Time falls away in big chunks, though a small part of me believes I'll be going back to work any second. But the more I drink, the less I entertain the idea.

It stormed on our wedding day. Catherine was there, and my father, because he couldn't stay away. Dani had sewn a short white dress using the fabric from her graduation robe. It had a satiny sheen to it that glinted with light on the courthouse steps even though there were clouds cemented to the sky. When the tornado sirens wailed we had to go inside and crouch in the hallway with the clerks and everyone else waiting to conduct their business.

I bet she's sold the ring I gave her, or tossed it into a lake, but my eyes search her finger anyway. It's bare. She and Catherine are running their tongues up and down rolling papers, pinching the weed into place. I finish my beer quickly and reach for another. I take a puff of a joint that's passed to me. I'm starting to feel the relief I needed, the soothing feeling like a teacher's reassurance I haven't made that big of a mistake. That people will forget about it. That I'll get another chance.

A chill tumbles down my spine. There's a thin song in the air. I look up and see Dani standing above me. She's whistling into my scalp. It's something she used to do at night and now it hangs between us like an invitation. She bites her chapped bottom lip. There's lipstick on her front tooth and I reach up and wipe it away. It doesn't feel like me doing it, not really, though that must be the excuse all cheaters use when they reach out, asking permission to touch someone they shouldn't. The one-room schoolhouse helps along this feeling, as though we've slipped back in time to a completely different past. I remember lining up during school trips here to sit on the corner stool and wear the dunce cap so the teacher could snap a photo. To avoid singling out a dunce, everyone had to be one. Right now we're all dunces. Or none of us is a dunce. Whatever it is, I'm allowed to touch Dani. My thumb lingers on her lip.

"Easy," she says quietly, stepping back. Her tongue licks the spot where my thumb was. She looks around her. People are eavesdropping, and she knows it, and I know it.

"Tell me about Mara," she says. "What's going on with you guys? To be honest I was surprised to learn you were still together."

"There's Brian to think of," I say. To her blank stare I respond, "He's my son."

"Sure. That makes sense. Is that the only reason?"

"No." But I don't offer any others.

"It's easier to just tell people what you really want," she says. "Like with me. You should have just told me you wanted to fuck other women."

It takes me a minute to figure out what she's saying. She's talking about me as though she knows me better than I know myself, better than Mara knows me—but instead of feeling resentful, I'm grateful for the attention. Maybe it's true that people from your past have the right to offer insight based on the differences, or lack of them, they detect between the person you were then and the one you seem to be now.

"What are you trying to say?"

"I'm saying you're a dunce." From behind her back she produces the dunce cap and jams it on my head. Flashes snap around the room as Dani's friends take out their phones, capturing my stunned face, a joint wedged in the crook of my fingers.

"Hey." I tear away the cap.

"Hey, yourself. Don't be so gloomy. We're just having fun."

I expect her to remove herself from my company—I'm the sullen one, sitting by himself, getting too drunk too fast—but instead she sits in the desk in front of me, turns and folds her arms over the back of her chair. She fits her pinky into the groove meant to hold pencils. The wind picks up outside and the eaves utter above us.

"Someone turn on music!" Dani shouts. An iPhone is produced, and speakers, and soon the music gives us some privacy.

She wants to know if I still live with my dad, and what that's like. Does Mara resent me for it? Have I thought about moving someplace else?

Yes. It's awkward. I don't know. Planning is sort of on hold at the moment.

"Oh my gosh. Of course." She brings her palm quickly to her chest—a mea culpa gesture—and in doing so she knocks my bottle of beer to the ground, where it shatters.

"Oops," she says, but she doesn't make a move to clean it up.

Dani and I all but destroyed the apartment where we lived—drinking every night, dishes growing crusty in the sink, a window swollen with humidity, stuck open, so weather, dirt, and pollen blew in. We never cleaned. Once her mom showed up unannounced; we were naked in bed when we heard her on the porch. When we finally let her in, Dani gave her a half-hearted tour. Her mom stopped and stared, aghast, at the still-wet condom in the bedside trash.

"Let's move," Dani says. "These desks are uncomfortable."

She slips from her seat to the floor, slides along the wood until her back's against the wall. When she does this it's all one fluid movement. I follow with two new beers in my hand, and I have to jostle myself until I'm seated next to her. Strands of her hair extend toward my face, touch my cheek.

All these little touches: these are what lead to bigger things. I was also drunk when I first started cheating on Dani. Dani believed whatever story I made up that first time, but then Catherine caught me outside a bar with my tongue in a stranger's mouth.

Things were not going well by then, in a lot of ways. Dani'd started to realize she'd made a mistake. We wore ourselves out with the screaming matches, and I moved back in with my dad, and she went to college the next fall. I found Mara, and things got serious fast, even more so when we found out Brian was on the way—but now when I look at Brian I think all I've done is let him down.

I blink him away, grope about in search of the empty feeling that's allowing me to be here in the schoolhouse in the first place. My gaze settles on Dani. She hasn't even reached the age I was when we met, but being with her brings me back to the person I was then.

"So you haven't lived away from home since you were with me, for not even a year?" She looks concerned for me. A thoughtful frown pulls at her lips. Then lightning shocks the room, slashes Dani's face for a moment, turning the frown into a flat line of ridicule, and I think she's trying to get me to admit I'm a fool. But I also think she might be doing it for my own good, because her posture is soft and easy. Her arm brushes mine.

Still, I start to push back. "There's nothing wrong with living at home. It saves money."

"I can't imagine not being able to take off on an adventure, though," she says. "That's the nice thing about not having anyone tying me down."

"There are nice things about having people," I say.

"Are they really your people, though?" she asks.

My heart stumbles. For a minute I think she might know about Brian and how he's not really my son. But that's impossible—I promised Mara if we ever told anyone, we would tell it together. I broke this promise once already and told my father, who said it didn't matter and he wouldn't tell, and I believe he never has. I've fantasized, though, about telling someone—some shadowy version of Dani—and have that person think of me as a hero.

Dani prods my arm; I've gotten lost in thought. I realize that she isn't implying anything. She's just flirting. She's saying—I think—that she was my people first.

"Sorry," I mumble.

"I've learned a lot since we split up," she goes on. "It was my fault, too, our marriage. But I got back on track pretty quickly."

She looks at me closely as though to indicate I haven't.

"The good girl has never been my natural self," she says. "But not fitting into the good girl mold isn't an excuse for being careless. And we were very careless with each other then."

She speaks matter of factly and as she inspects her nails she opens up a wound in me—a wound that I know I can heal quickly with my desire for her. A desire she knows how to ignite. I want to let her know I made a mistake so she might think of me more kindly.

"It was more my fault than yours," I rush to say.

"Stop trying to take the blame," she says hotly, and I can tell she means it. "I was an adult. We shouldn't have been married, but we had incredible chemistry. You can see how it misled us."

I look at her and try to believe what she's saying, believe it wasn't just me using her back then. The suggestion of forgiveness metastasizes until it's all I can think of, real or not. It swells and collides with the desire I feel for Dani—a new chemistry, a more complicated version of what we had before.

"Is the chemistry gone?" I ask. I smile to show I'm joking, but Dani answers seriously.

"No. It's changed. But still there."

I want to ask her how it's changed, but instead I kiss her, and she returns the kiss. People around us laugh and exclaim, and I hear Catherine say, "What the fuck, Dani?" but Dani doesn't pull away from me. Her lips are thin and smooth and taste like weed and beer. I don't care anymore that the party's not big enough for any real privacy; I just want more of her. Everything she's said today has felt so rational and mature, as though she figured out all the mistakes we made and how to avoid them in the future.

We part but stay close. I swallow. "I'm not happy with where I am," I say.

It's not entirely true—but I think it might, in this moment, bring me closer to her.

"Of course you're not happy." She touches my cheek with her palm. "You might go to prison."

"It's not just that," I say. "It's my life. You're right—living in my dad's basement, my situation with Mara—I blew everything. I blew the best thing in my life years ago."

"Mara seems good," Dani says. "She seems like a good one."

"She is," I say, now regretting bringing her up. "That doesn't have anything to do with it. It's really complicated right now—and I feel sometimes that I can't connect with Brian."

Dani raises her eyebrows. "Can't connect how?" she says.

I think of how she said they might not really be my people. I'll say anything to keep her here with me—anything to try to get her alone. I imagine us leaving together, going somewhere and having sex and smoking after like we used to. I can see a completely different future for myself, and she's holding it, and in it I'm off the hook.

"He's not really my son, my biological son. So there's this feeling that one day he might decide I'm not his father anymore, and it will be true, and I'll be devastated because I really do love him like a son."

Dani flashes her eyes to Catherine, who hasn't heard anything, but in that moment I know she will soon—and I know I've betrayed

Mara. People talk; they've just come to accept us as a family, and now gossip will get built like slipshod houses.

I've fucked up, gone too far, gotten too personal. That was what Dani was saying earlier: we were good at sex and nothing else. She looks uncomfortable, like she's woken up in the middle of an absurd dream and is trying to remember what was in it. She clears her throat. "I don't think we should continue what we're doing here," she says.

I'm reaching for her hand and am about to ask her if we can go outside and talk, when she stands up and shakes herself free from me. She pulls her hair up into a bun and dusts off her shorts. The music rings in my ears, too loud, and Dani whispers something to Catherine and gestures to me. I read her lips: *I'm gonna go.* She waves to her friends, exchanges a few laughs, and I stay on the floor.

Dani opens the schoolhouse door and gasps, her hand flying to her chest. There are two cops walking up the schoolhouse steps, and their car, unheard by us, is parked in the gravel lot.

"All right," one of them says, almost bored. "Party's over."

The cops come in and as we're led out one by one Catherine gives me a look that says this is my fault. Dani's trembling; she's never gotten in trouble like this before. The police radios crackle in the rain and my phone buzzes in my pocket. I know it's Mara. She's just a few blocks away, having come back downtown to pick me up from my shift, except I'm not there—I'm here, ducking my head into the back seat of a cruiser, getting taken in again.

Dani and I don't speak in the holding cell. A fluorescent tube flickers, phones ring, cops shift slowly from one part of the station to the other. One by one the kids get plucked from jail by their parents. They look fearful, but I'm not worried for them. They're first timers; they'll get court dates and pay a fine or maybe do a bit of community service. That was me once.

Dani doesn't look at me when she goes—she's the second to

last to leave, and she says nothing to me. Her mother says she isn't surprised to see me here. I think it might be the last I'll see of Dani. All she wanted today was a little bit of fun; she didn't invite me along to rewrite my life. If the cops hadn't found the drugs I'd brought they might've just let us all go. I hold my face in my hands—ashamed and embarrassed and wishing I'd done things differently, wishing I'd never left work, or if I had left, that I'd just gone somewhere alone with Dani. And then I sense that someone is standing on the other side of the bars.

I look up. It's Mara, but she's not alone. She has Brian on her hip. Brian looks around in fear, his small face twisted with worry, and then his eyes fall on me, and his face wrinkles with the tears that are about to erupt.

Mara stares at me coldly. She holds her sobbing son—the son she could've left at home with my father, who was at the house and who answered the phone when I called. But she didn't. She brought him here to see me like this. She's done hiding the father I really am from her son. She's done hiding the man I really am from herself.

Flour Baby

By the spring of Reggie's junior year, there was only one thing she looked forward to each day: Matt Shames, smiling his lazy smile. Sometimes it was even directed at her, and receiving Matt's smile made Reggie proud of herself.

She and Matt weren't exactly friends, though Reggie was hopeful. Matt was easygoing with everyone, most of all himself. Every so often he caused trouble and got suspended, but a few days later he'd roar up again in the '67 Mustang he'd refurbished himself, flinging the car into its assigned spot, yelling a friendly obscenity to a pal across the parking lot.

He was a junior, too. Reggie longed to have him swear at her like he did his friends. He had beady eyes but Reggie liked his look, which was a little bit punk. He was thin and looked half-starved but he wore it well, like a badge. Rumor had it he did drugs. And a reciprocation of Reggie's feelings wasn't out of the question. Lately he'd been paying her more attention in their sociology class, and Reggie clung to that attention. It helped her get through the day.

She needed a distraction from what was wrong in her life: her mom's new boyfriend (a loser), her father's three-year prison sentence (vehicular manslaughter), her midsemester progress report that showed a 1.7 GPA (for the whole month of February she hadn't been able to find her chemistry book). Unlike these problems, the absence of Matt's affection for her could be remedied. There might be room in his life for her. Often she saw him hanging out with people she wouldn't have expected: the religious kids from the megachurch; the geeky president of the robotics club; or the willowy blond named Arielle, an exchange student from France who—thankfully—would be gone at the end of the school year.

Besides Matt, Reggie had one other sort-of friend, a prickly girl named Jewel with whom having fun was a chore. Jewel and Reggie argued all the time, but no matter how angry they made each other, Jewel always returned to school the next day ready to be friends again. Reggie suspected that Jewel thought she could fix Reggie's life somehow. She was always burdening herself with projects—people, pets—if only to feel the satisfaction of disappointment, it seemed.

Officially, Reggie was getting help from Ms. Thorne, the school guidance counselor. Ms. Thorne was young and had been a cheerleader at Michigan State, a characteristic that in Jewel's mind made her unfit to counsel anyone. Reggie didn't mind Ms. Thorne. She was on the receiving end of no one else's sympathy at the moment. In fact, most people hated her, and in the glare of their derision she was simply shutting down, as though her life were a large switchboard and she was throwing one switch at a time. Her affection for Matt was the only thing she was truly devoted to right now.

One morning in March, Reggie was called out of her life skills class to see Ms. Thorne, who'd heard that Reggie had burst into tears in the cafeteria the previous day.

"I'm worried about you," Ms. Thorne said. She'd braided her mahogany hair into a crown around her head as though she were a princess in a fairy tale. "I'm also worried about your grades. You started the year with a 3.2."

"I know," Reggie said, not wanting to be reminded.

"A lot has happened to you this year," Ms. Thorne went on, "but you do have control of your GPA. What we *might* be able to do is get the school to approve extensions for your work, and maybe some extra credit that you can turn in over the summer."

"Ted Irish got extensions for all his work," Reggie mumbled. "He doesn't even have to come back to school until April."

Ms. Thorne went pale. It was Ted Irish's father that Reggie's dad had hit and killed with his car. Ted Irish had been out of school most of the year; he was only returning because baseball season was starting and he was hoping for a scholarship. Reggie hadn't seen him since early in the fall, before the accident, but he would return in a matter of days.

Reggie lived in a small, conservative town in southeastern Michigan. She'd never really fit in, but now she was a complete outcast. William Irish had been a figure in town. He'd owned an accounting business where everyone got their taxes done. With tax day approaching, his low-budget advertisement still played on the local channels, and when his face appeared on the screen, Reggie's mind tricked her into hoping for a few brief seconds—he's not dead, there he is!—but then Reggie's mom, Carla, would swear and ferret around the couch cushions looking for the remote so she could change the channel.

Reggie wondered why the Irishes didn't stop the ads. Were they doing it on purpose in order to torture Reggie and themselves? Were the remaining Irishes sniveling into tissues while the gray-haired, bespectacled ghost of William Irish pointed at them and said, "It's *your* money, not the government's. We'll help *you* get the big refund *you* deserve."

Ms. Thorne said quietly, "That's true. Ted Irish has been getting homeschooled since the accident. But again, we're talking about you here."

Reggie listened to what Ms. Thorne had to say. Then she agreed to more after-school appointments with Ms. Thorne as well as extra tutoring.

Reggie returned to her desk in Ms. Bird's life skills class. Jewel hissed, "What did Ms. Thorne say?" Reggie didn't respond. She felt tears brimming behind her eyes. She was always almost crying. She tried to think of Matt to make herself feel better. While Reggie backhanded a tear away, Jewel yawned. She would only give someone attention without getting any in return for so long.

Ms. Bird stood in front of the class, holding a bag of flour. "You'll dress up your flour babies, you'll name your flour babies, and your flour babies will go everywhere with you for two weeks."

The flour baby project. Ms. Bird had been talking about it all semester, and finally, it was time. In a way, the project offered Reggie a reprieve: it was worth half her grade and was very easy. She would have to endure a certain amount of embarrassment for pretending a bag of flour was her baby for two weeks, but at least she would be taunted for doing something normal, something other people were doing, too.

The class spent the rest of the period gluing yarn to the scalps of their flour babies and drawing clumsy dresses and overalls on the bags.

"I'll be coming around to sign your bags of flour," chirped Ms. Bird, "so there's no swapping out broken babies for new ones."

On her own bag of flour, Reggie drew plump lips and colored them red. She turned to Jewel. "Do you think it's weird that Ms. Bird is branding our babies?"

Jewel, however, was staring at Reggie's flour baby. "Reggie," she said, "the red lips make her look slutty!"

Later, Reggie slipped into her sociology class just as Mrs. McMahon was closing the door.

"Tardy, Ms. Taylor," Mrs. McMahon said, not without some fondness.

"Sorry," Reggie mumbled. She settled into her desk and stuffed her flour baby into the book tray beneath her seat.

Matt was sitting across from her. She caught his eye; he tapped his wristwatch and wagged one finger back and forth. Reggie tried to smile casually and give a flirtatious half shrug, instead of bursting with the huge, sloppy grin that was welling inside of her.

Reggie wasn't failing sociology but only because Mrs. McMahon never failed anyone. She wasn't doing very well, either. Teachers, students, everyone: they were all siding with Ted Irish. Even Mrs. McMahon had grown cooler—using "Ms. Taylor" or "Regina" in place of "Reggie."

Mrs. McMahon started class, but Reggie's eyes lingered on Matt. He'd been held back in elementary school, whispered the school gossips. Others claimed he'd spent time in rehab. Lately, though, Reggie had eclipsed him in notoriety because of her father, and this formed the basis of Reggie's belief that they were right for each other.

Eventually, Mrs. McMahon set the class to their group work. Reggie focused on the sheet of paper before her. She was supposed to discuss No Child Left Behind with her "quad," what Mrs. McMahon called the groups of four desks she'd pushed together. Reggie's group, however, only had three people, the desk next to hers empty. Next to Matt sat Jewel. Theirs was the loser quad.

"So, what do you think?" Reggie asked the two of them.

"I don't know," Matt said, twirling his pencil in the air. "Seems okay."

"It's like gay marriage," Jewel said. "Everyone deserves to be equal."

"Well, yeah," Reggie said, "but are we going about the school thing right?"

Matt stared furiously at Jewel, and before Jewel could respond to Reggie's question, Matt had pulled out a pocket-size Bible and slapped it on his desk. "The Bible says being gay is wrong."

Reggie frowned at him.

"The Bible is made up," Jewel said.

"The Bible got me through some shit," Matt said. His face lightened. He could change his mood easily, rocketing from bullish to breezy in moments. "Hey, I saw this thing on the History channel about Jesus, and he was totally ripped."

"That's funny," Reggie said with forced conviction.

Jewel straightened the cardigan she had used to swaddle her flour baby, which she'd placed atop the empty desk. "Where's your baby, Reggie?" she asked. "This desk can be day care."

Reggie pointed beneath her desk. "Napping?" she offered.

"Reggie, I'll tell Ms. Bird."

Reggie wanted to strangle Jewel's ugly baby. She needed to succeed on the project, but she hoped to do so clandestinely.

Matt looked curiously between Jewel and Reggie. Reggie sighed and brought up her baby.

"That baby is rad," Matt said, and he reached across the desks to grab Reggie's baby by its face.

"Careful!" Jewel said.

Matt tossed the baby up and down as though it were a football, laughing as he did. Reggie studied him. He could have a good time so easily. Anything he did glimmered.

Rummaging through Carla's closet after school was a catastrophe. Nothing Reggie tried on looked good. Her boobs weren't big enough for Carla's shirts and sweaters. Jewel, meanwhile, sat in the wicker chair by Carla's window, judging as Reggie stood before the full-length mirror. Both flour babies were in Jewel's lap. She looked like a harassed grandmother.

"Where's your mom?" Jewel asked. She looked Reggie's reflection up and down. "That outfit's not . . . you."

"She takes night classes," Reggie said, ignoring Jewel's critique.

Carla attended classes in the evenings after spending all day answering phones for a law office. After class, Carla normally settled in for a few drinks at the pub. She'd also started drinking more at home. She could be heard moving through the house by the chink of ice in her glass, like a cat wearing a bell.

Reggie imagined the new boyfriend sitting with Carla in the wood-paneled bar with the plastic hanging plants. Reggie should've seen him coming, but she hadn't. The only way she'd found to deal with her dad was not to think of him if she could help it—and her mom was doing the same thing. Still, she wished her mom hadn't changed so much in the past few months. The drinking wasn't the only thing. She'd unearthed these new sexy outfits from piles of junk at the Salvation Army, driving all the way to the one in Ann Arbor because Ann Arbor was where the college girls donated their clothes.

Reggie pulled on a red tank top with a padded bra built in. The back was made of two panels of see-through lace that met in a V near Reggie's tailbone. She also found a short jean skirt that fit, mostly.

"Remember to set alarms tonight," Jewel said.

Ms. Bird had told everyone in the class to leave three voice mails (she would turn off her phone's ringer) that night so each of them could feel what it was like to be woken and obligated to take care of something. "I will," Reggie said. "How does this look?"

"I'm not sure why you're dressing up for Matt," Jewel said. "He has no redeeming qualities."

"It's not for him," Reggie said.

"You're lying," Jewel said.

Reggie whirled around and glared at Jewel, who was unimpressed by both the outfit and Reggie's withering stare. "I'm tired," Reggie said through gritted teeth. "I think I'm going to go to bed."

Jewel left and Reggie sat on her bed with her books spread before her. Flour Baby sat on the dresser. Reggie intended to stay awake until Carla came home. She felt secure knowing everyone was in the house. She balanced a few chemical equations, but mostly she thought about Matt. She settled lower and lower against her pillows. Then one of her thoughts caught on a gust of sleep, and she didn't wake up until morning. She had not called Ms. Bird.

"You look different today, Reggie," Ms. Thorne said that afternoon. "Aren't you cold?"

"It's just clothes," Reggie said quietly. Ms. Thorne wasn't the first person to ask her if she felt cold; the question was code for *you look slutty*.

Reggie had worn these clothes for attention, but she was embarrassed that people were noticing and staring. Ted Irish's friend Damien had come up to her in the cafeteria and whispered, "Reggie, with your dad in jail, I guess you'd *have* to become a prostitute to support yourself."

"Go to hell," Reggie had said hotly. Afterward, she cried in the accessible bathroom. She wondered what Ted Irish had heard about her. Stupidly, she'd called his house once, in January, thinking they could talk. Ted's voice, low and bored when he answered, turned brassy when Reggie said her name. "Don't you *dare* call here again," he'd said.

It was strange to imagine Ted Irish's family in a state of collapse. In a way, it made Reggie feel better—they were all miserable because of this—but Ted must have told someone about the call, because later her father's lawyer lectured her. "You may not call the Irish family," he said. "It will look like we're applying pressure."

She'd called Ted to apologize, to share how badly she felt, to say she would have put herself in Mr. Irish's place if she could. No one had cared, though. No one was acting like a human being anymore.

Someone pounded on the bathroom door. The girl in the wheelchair needed it.

Ms. Thorne had heard about the incident in the cafeteria and told Reggie that she understood her anger, but she should do her best to ignore the nastiness of others.

Even worse than all this, Matt was absent from sociology. She'd seen him later on, taking the stairs two at a time, but she hadn't been able to catch up with him.

"Are you trying to get someone's attention with the new look?" Ms. Thorne asked casually. She straightened a porcelain figurine on her desk—an angel with its hands clasped in prayer—and ran her fingers over her perfectly painted nails.

"No," Reggie said quickly.

"I just want you to focus on what's important. Your grades, Reggie, and feeling better."

Reggie wanted to say that what she wore didn't have any effect on her grades—it was all the other stuff that did—but instead she pointed to the clock on Ms. Thorne's wall and reminded her that she had to go to chemistry tutoring.

After an hour of tutoring, Reggie left the chemistry room feeling sad. She'd gotten a D on her last exam. All of her worries grew like an air bubble in her brain, taking up space. She knew she was smart enough to pass, probably even to get a B, but she couldn't focus, couldn't remember anything.

She found Matt sitting outside on a bench by the bike racks, the only bikes left belonging to band kids whose instruments echoed from the football field. With Flour Baby cradled in the crook of her elbow, she went to sit next to him.

He smiled and scooted closer to her, nudged her foot with his.

"What are you still doing here?" he asked.

"I just had some stuff to take care of," she said. "Where's your car?"

"Grounded today. No car." Matt swung his arm and snapped his fingers in mock defeat. "That's why I wasn't in soc. Missed the bus and had to walk."

"It took you three hours to walk here?"

"I may have made a stop or two."

A ray of sun fell on Matt's body. He squinted against the brightness. His brown hair shone. Reggie almost couldn't take it. A gloomy cloud engulfed the sun but to Reggie the world was incandescent at that moment, and the barrage of demons that had plagued her for months vaporized.

"I guess I'm walking home," she said finally, gesturing in the direction where she and her mom lived. She hoped Matt would walk with her but he only held up his hand for a high five. Their palms slapped. As soon as she retreated from him, the cloud gathered around her again.

"Are you staying with your gentleman caller again tonight?" Reggie asked Carla when she got home from school Thursday afternoon. It was near the end of the first week of the flour baby project, and so far Reggie had no clue about her grade. Ms. Bird watched them hawkishly during class. Reportedly, she had spies throughout the school, and she planned to send a questionnaire to parents about the caretaking that had gone on at home. Carla would sign whatever Reggie wrote.

"His name is Jared," Carla said. "I don't know, Reggie. I don't know what this is. I just want to have fun."

They sat together at the kitchen table. Carla smiled at Reggie and squeezed her hand. Reggie couldn't help it; she smiled in return.

Once Carla had gone for her night class, Reggie wrapped herself in her jacket and sat on the splintered porch with a sleeve of rice cakes. Feeling lonely, she went inside for her flour baby, and when she returned, she put her feet up on the railing, the baby in her lap. The night around her was inky, the stars an unfinished mural. Reggie chewed a rice cake slowly.

A car turned onto her street and Reggie moved her wristwatch into the porch light to check the time. Too early for Carla, but the car slowed as it approached and Reggie heard the roar of an old engine, a fast one. It stopped in front of Reggie's house and she looked at it as though it were a mirage. A rust-red Mustang idled, and when the window lowered, she saw Matt behind the wheel.

Reggie rose from her chair and sprang down the porch steps. Her half-eaten rice cake was still between her fingers.

"How'd you know where I live?" she said, leaning inside Matt's window.

"School directory, bitches!" Matt said in a high voice. "Get in."

The headlights pulsed. "Hold on," Reggie said, and she ran back to the porch. Her flour baby was inert in the chair. She scooped up the baby, along with the package of rice cakes, and shivered as she slid into Matt's car.

Matt pulled away from the curb. There was a rosary hanging from his rearview. He drove them down Eight Mile until the road turned to dirt and his car hobbled over potholes. He drove all the way to Walled Lake, where the road was paved again. The lake water trembled in the dark and Reggie rolled down her window so she could listen to the waves lap the shore. Matt rounded the lake swiftly and Reggie leaned her head into the curve. In the moonlight, she could imagine they were driving on the rim of a silver dollar.

The road veered away from the lake and Matt made a left onto another dirt road. His headlights caught a Dead End sign. He killed the lights but left the engine running, the heat blasting. Reggie strained to see his face. He was rummaging in his pockets.

He extended his palm toward Reggie. Two pills sat stark white against his skin, bright as eggs. She pinched one between her fingers, examined it smooth surface. She watched the lump in Matt's throat bob up and down as he swallowed his pill. It was instinct that made Reggie stash hers in her pocket when Matt turned to flick his cigarette out of the cracked window.

He turned back around and started kissing her, pushing her jacket from her shoulders. She'd only kissed one boy before, and now Matt's hands were all over her. This was what she'd wanted but she felt too nervous to close her eyes completely. In her peripheral vision she could see Matt's rosary, swaying a little in the ambient air. Normally this sort of thing would have turned her off. It wasn't that she didn't believe in God. She sort of thought she did. But she didn't like the way the religious kids at her school judged people, as Matt had done in soc the other day. Matt did weird things like this to her—he should have made her crazy and angry but instead she was falling in love with him. It almost wasn't fair, the way he could convince you he deserved to be careless. Like he was just trying on personalities, and Reggie's job was to admire all of them.

There was more to her love for Matt, though. He was the only person who never brought up what her father had done. Maybe it was because he thought about himself too much, but she needed for at least one person in her life not to bring it up. She let herself relax. Matt's hand went under her shirt, under the built-in bra of her tank top. She'd never been kissed like this before and though she had all kinds of ideas about waiting to have sex she could see how she might let him take her clothes off. So she was part relieved and part disappointed when they pulled apart.

"It's getting late," Reggie said, to fill the silence.

Matt held his hands in front of his face, pivoting his wrist. He ran the index finger on his left hand down the index on his right and said, "I can't feel my fingers."

"Maybe it's the cold," Reggie suggested.

"No, it's the pills," he said. He put his finger on her face and traced a line from her ear to her shoulder.

"Stop that," she said, shivering. "What kind of pill was that we took?"

"Never mind," Matt said. "I know you didn't take yours."

Reggie froze. But Matt grinned. He didn't seem to care.

"You can drive stick, right?" he said. "The pills make me light sensitive too."

"I don't have a license," Reggie said, eyeing the keys he dangled before her.

"Who cares?" Matt tossed the keys into her lap.

"Okay," Reggie said. Though her dad had taught her to drive a manual last summer, and though she'd turned sixteen not long ago, she'd never taken the test. It had seemed wrong for her to drive after what happened to William Irish.

Reggie flushed when she pulled up to Matt's house and he brought her hand to his mouth and kissed it. She started walking home, a distance of almost two miles. It was drizzling. She zipped Flour Baby in her jacket and forced herself forward. When she got to her house, she realized she hadn't brought her keys with her. Through the window, she could see the set with its dangling blue flower keychain on the table by the door. Carla was home, her bedroom light on, but when Reggie tried the door it was locked. She rang the bell, pounded the knocker. No one came.

She set Flour Baby down on the porch rail, then hoisted herself up the rain gutter. From the roof of the garage she could climb into her bedroom through the window, which she never locked. She clambered across the shingles and pried up the glass with her fingertips then rolled onto her bed. Her shoes left wet prints on the comforter.

The next morning, Flour Baby had a soggy bottom. Reggie had forgotten it on the porch and rain had soaked the bag.

Her project was falling apart before her eyes. Even with a fake baby that required no real care, she'd ruined everything. Just like her parents before her, she thought miserably.

She plugged in her hair dryer and blew hot air on Flour Baby's yarny scalp. She put tape over its skin to reinforce the structure. Eventually she ziplocked it in a gallon freezer bag, put it in her backpack, and left for school.

Reggie waited for Matt in the parking lot. She went up to his car when he pulled up and said, "Want to skip first period?" She held up her sodden flour baby.

Matt laughed and said, "You bet I do."

They ate hash browns at the McDonald's down the road. Matt

leaned over the table and kissed her with a full mouth. It was gross but still exciting.

"Let's just skip the whole day," Matt said. "We'll go to the movies."

They kissed more in the movie theater; they kissed everywhere. They went back to Reggie's house and ended up in her bedroom. Reggie still wasn't sure what she wanted, but Matt was sure, and the more he touched her, and with each piece of clothing that came off, she became more and more confident that he was worth it. She let him inside of her. She stifled her gasp and gripped his skin. He kissed her as he came.

Afterward, they lay on top of the comforter. "Ted Irish comes back to school on Monday," Reggie said softly. With her hand she explored Matt's curls. Matt said nothing; he'd fallen asleep.

"I don't know how I'll face him," she said.

Reggie felt bulletproof as she walked into school with Matt's arm around her on Monday morning. But then they parted for their separate first periods and Reggie went to her locker to find it graffitied with red marker.

SLUT

A crowd formed behind Reggie. The hall monitor came up behind her. "Oh, jeez," he muttered, and he spit a few words into his walkie-talkie.

Reggie wanted to say something lighthearted, to show she was above all this, but she couldn't find the words. She wasn't above it. She was buried beneath it, and none of the adults seemed to care. She pushed through the people gathered around her and sank with her head down to Ms. Bird's class.

She nearly walked straight into Ted Irish, whose eyes fell so coldly on her that Reggie did an about-face and took the back hallway to class. In the corner of Ms. Bird's room, Arielle, the French girl, was surrounded by a gaggle of girls, the school gossips. In her beautiful accent, the words falling out of her mouth like water, Arielle said, "She thinks she's special because he had sex with her, but he'll have sex with anyone."

Reggie was always astonished by how quickly these girls could call up an invasion of misery.

"Don't listen to them," Jewel said when Reggie sank into her seat. Steadfast Jewel, there by Reggie's side even though Reggie had ignored her calls all weekend.

In sociology, Matt moved to sit next to Reggie instead of across from her. He wound his fingers through her hair until Mrs. McMahon said, "Enough, Matt. Save that for after school."

Everyone laughed, except for Jewel. Reggie saw Ted Irish lean over and whisper something into his girlfriend's ear. Reggie couldn't hear them, but her face burned anyway. She wondered if this day would ever end. She somehow couldn't imagine herself ever making it through.

After school, Ms. Thorne said, "I am very sorry about what they did to your locker. I'm not saying this will be easy. But you're shutting down, Reggie. Skipping school. Not respecting yourself."

Reggie looked at Ms. Thorne. Ms. Thorne was a good person, she cared about Reggie because it was her job, but Reggie couldn't connect with her. She was part of the system that had fallen into place after the accident, where respecting Ted's grief meant sacrificing Reggie. None of the kids who were bullying her had to go to counseling. Reggie was so upset she was shaking.

"I don't drink," Reggie said desperately, "or do drugs."

"Good," Ms. Thorne said, though she looked confused.

"Do you know how drunk my dad was?" Reggie asked.

Ms. Thorne shook her head mournfully.

"0.29," Reggie said. "That's really high. He turned onto a sidewalk."

It was really crucial for Reggie that Ms. Thorne say something—she felt strongly that right at that moment she needed guidance—but Ms. Thorne was silent. Reggie felt like she'd been carrying an armload of bricks these past few months, and the longer the silence lasted the more she felt like letting the bricks fall. She wondered what had been the point of all this talking.

When Matt pulled up that night, Reggie went to his car. She had Flour Baby with her.

"Forget Ted Irish," Matt said through the cranked-down window. "He's a pussy, blaming you."

"Can I drive?" she asked. Matt shrugged and unbuckled his seat belt. Reggie slipped into the driver's seat and Matt shut her door for her. From the passenger side, he told her to go back to Walled Lake, but Reggie turned east instead, toward Detroit, and the night fled from the headlights as she accelerated. She felt the engine ask for a higher gear and she shifted into it.

She'd left Ms. Thorne's office feeling strange, feeling like screaming. Carla had tried to talk to her—"I got a call from the school, sweetie"—but Reggie shrugged her away and phoned Matt.

"Where're you going?" Matt asked.

She turned to look at him, the wheel shaking beneath her fingers. A stoplight turned yellow as they neared it, but Reggie sped up and blew through the intersection in the stolen time between the red light for her and the green light for cross traffic. A cop car pulled out behind her and its flashing lights pivoted in her rearview, casting a pretty glow on Matt's face.

"I'm tired of being a rule follower," she said, and she drove faster. There were tears in her eyes but for the first time they felt cathartic. "Everything's a mess and I haven't even done anything wrong."

The cop sped up too, setting his siren wailing, and Reggie kept going. Her whole life seemed visible on the road before her, ready for ruin, and she thought, get the bad stuff out of the way now. Get it all out. Get arrested now and maybe she wouldn't later; make mistakes with boys now and she'd be too hurt to make them again.

She glanced at Matt as she careened onto the highway entrance ramp. He looked to be teetering between uncertainty and excitement, as though he'd never done anything quite this bad. Then Reggie had an idea. "The flour baby," she said. "Throw it."

A slow smile crept over Matt's face. Whether or not they were right for each other, they could, as Carla said, have fun. He was easygoing, quick to agree, fine with anything, fine with Reggie. And she was desperate to bind herself to him because he was one of the only people who cared about how she felt. And even if he didn't care for long, he did right now.

The cop was close behind them. "Go, go, go!" Matt said. He reached down and pulled Flour Baby from its dark nest in the footwell, tearing away the plastic bag. He cranked down the window and sent the bag of flour soaring toward the cruiser. In the rearview, Reggie watched the baby hit the cop's windshield and explode in a poof of white powder. For a moment, everything behind her was weightless and pure.

IV

Blood

Drinking helps, or at least we think it does. It helps Patrick and me talk, and we do, for hours at my kitchen table or at the cop bar near campus. When we have a conversation there's space for our ghosts to sit between us calmly.

Soon Patrick and I are spending most of our time together, and because we met by chance, something about this time feels as though it doesn't count toward the sum of the season, but the time passes anyway. We take the light rail to Branch Brook Park during the Cherry Blossom Festival in April. Newark has more cherry trees than Washington DC, I tell Patrick. He asks how I know, and I tell him everything I know about Newark I learned from my landlord, Yuejin, a kind man of about sixty who lives across the street from me with his wife and their two teenage children. We circle the lake until we find a spot to lay down a blanket in the grass. I read aloud from the book of poems I have that a friend of mine wrote, and Patrick falls asleep while I read, but I keep reading. His head is in my lap, and I run my fingers through his hair. I like the way the words mingle with the wind, the sounds of geese, and the slap of sneakers from the people who've come to the park to go running.

When Patrick wakes, it's dusk.

"I liked the poems," he says.

"When you meet Aamina, you'll have to tell her which was your favorite and why."

Patrick looks concerned.

"I'm joking," I say.

We go home and make chicken piccata. Even though I curdle

the sauce we clink glasses over what to us is a very special meal. Of course, we keep talking about my father and his friend, but when the conversation gets too heavy, we pour another drink. It's easier to change the subject when your glass is full.

My job as a paralegal started as *for now* and seems to have turned into *forever*. I have a degree in English, but I went back for a paralegal certificate not long after I graduated. I liked my job in Michigan, where Ralph and I met, but we moved here so he could get his master's. He finished. He left. I stayed.

I'm scrolling through my phone while walking home from the train one night and thinking about how the last time I saw the doctor she'd mentioned not to text and walk—it was the latest thing for doctors to remind patients of, the new wearing seat belts. I almost walk into a double-wide stroller carrying two newborns, and Thora, digging in a bag.

"Oh my God," I say. "Babies."

Thora straightens. She looks tired. She comes around to my side of the stroller and hugs me.

"We just got home last night," she says.

"I thought it was quiet down there. I almost texted you."

"It was so crazy. We wouldn't have answered." Thora brushes loose bangs away from her forehead.

"Did you take a cab?" They don't drive in the States. "I would've driven you."

"Oh, no, Marie. It was so late. And it happened fast."

So Per and Thora had slipped out in the middle of the night while I slept beside Patrick. I stoop down and look at the two girls and their milky blue eyes. The sidewalk is damp from an earlier rain. Against the stones the infants look as soft as silk and assaulted by the porch light. Thora tells me their names: Bolette and Hilma.

"Bolette. Pretty. Hilma, too." I look up at Thora. "How are you planning to get that stroller with those babies up the stoop?"

"To be honest," Thora says, "I was hoping Per would get home soon. I just had to take them for a walk. There wasn't enough oxygen in the house. Is this what they call 'mommy brain'?"

"I think it's just called tired brain."

"Good," Thora says. "Reminds me I'm still a human."

"Very human," I say, and together we take the babies inside.

The next day I wake up early to the sound of the 6:00 a.m. flights taking off from Newark Liberty, and I've been sitting in the window since, watching traffic gear up with coffee steaming under my nose. I'm supposed to be writing, but Patrick is sleeping in my bed, and I've made up this rule as an excuse not to write: that I can't write with someone else in the house. When I try, and Patrick asks me what I'm doing, I tell him I'm online shopping. No packages ever arrive, and when he notes this, I say I'm online window shopping.

Patrick sleeps through the early morning. He stayed out late last night with friends from class. I slip quietly from the bedroom and crack the front door open to listen to the babies shrieking downstairs. They've been up for hours, too.

I ease the door shut. I listen to the new sounds—cooing, crying—until it's almost time for work. My boss represents the people with the money, the studios and the producers, not the artists, and the contracts we prepare make every project seem boring.

Patrick is stirring. He has summer classes, and I live much closer to the Business School than he does, so he stays with me most nights. In fact, for a month we've spent almost every night drinking together. Sometimes just a glass or two, sometimes so much we drown in it, fall into sleep and curl up in the rocky bottoms of our drunkenness.

He emerges from the bedroom looking sleepy. He wraps me in his arms. I tell him there's coffee in the pot.

In the bathroom I rub the line between my eyes that has become permanent, the one from squinting and scowling. An uncomfortable feeling descends on me: sickness, hangover. I woke up so early this morning because my body was breaking down the sugar in the wine, and I couldn't get back to sleep. Patrick and I are helping each other talk about the things that have happened, but we're drinking too much, and now I wake up each day feeling ill. I don't know how much longer I can live with this never-ending hangover.

But then again it's nice to be with someone who understands.

I splash cold water on my face and do my best to cover the dark circles beneath my eyes. I put dry shampoo in my hair and fluff it around. Patrick eats cereal as I stuff my things in my bag. I leave him at the kitchen table to finish his reading for his class later on.

"Oh," I say, stopping at the door. "The babies were born, so take care to be quiet in the hallway."

Sitting next to me on the train is a woman with a baby strapped to her chest. I offer to hold her takeout coffee while she digs through her diaper bag in search of something. I smile at the baby, but he stares skeptically back at me.

The train swoops into the tunnel, the light disappears like a curtain falling, and the baby looks around in surprise. The sudden absence and appearance of light is new to him, lights flipping on and off, scenery appearing and disappearing from windows. Years ago I went to Iceland with Ralph. It was summer, and we camped beneath the midnight sun. We never stayed in a place with blackout curtains, so it was light all the time until the day we drove through a long tunnel and the darkness felt like a new discovery.

Absently, because I'm in that tunnel in Iceland, I take a sip of the woman's coffee.

"Thank you," she says to me, reaching for her cup. She didn't see. I'm ashamed as I hand the coffee back to her and avoid her eyes as we pull into Penn Station. I should say something, she deserves to know, but I don't, and though maybe it's a small thing, I'm pretty sure I'll remember it every so often and feel badly whenever I do.

"You've been hiding something," my friend Aamina tells me on the phone. She's the one who wrote the book I read aloud to Patrick. She teaches poetry at Rutgers–Newark, and I met her last year at a reading put on by the Creative Writing Department.

"That's true," I say.

I lean against a pillar in Penn Station. I missed my train and have to wait for the next.

"Spit it out," Aamina says, exasperated.

"I'm seeing someone."

"*What?*"

Unlike Thora, Aamina doesn't put up with my bullshit.

"I have to meet him," she says. "I'm coming over tomorrow. For dinner."

"Aamina," I say, "I'm not ready for company. My house is a mess."

"Your house is never a mess. You just don't want me to meet this guy."

A track announcement echoes in the corridor, drowning out Aamina. I pull the phone away from my ear until it passes.

"Okay," I say. "Tomorrow. Seven thirty."

"Where did you meet him?" Aamina asks.

I can hear her moving around her kitchen. A knife striking a cutting board. A voice—cool, female—calls my track from overhead, and I drift with the crowd of people toward the track entrance.

"Look, I'll tell you everything tomorrow. I'm about to go through the tunnel."

Patrick has to cancel plans with his friends because of the dinner, and he's annoyed.

"One time," I say.

"It feels a little soon." He looks down at the beer he's holding.

"She's a friend," I say. "She's not my mother."

Aamina arrives wearing a silk shawl wrapped over her yoga clothes. She teaches free community classes in Military Park. Her curly black hair reaches her shoulders, appears weightless, and is electrified by a streak of gray. She pushes her glasses up the bridge of her nose as she shakes Patrick's hand.

I made lamb meatballs and a feta salad, and we sip the wine Aamina brought. All evening I worried Patrick or I would say something stupid, something that would make Aamina think I'm making a mistake, but in fact we can't think of anything to say at all. Patrick's description of the MBA program is boring, and he can't quite articulate what he wants to do after he graduates. Nor can I articulate anything about where I am with my book. At one point, Aamina sighs, and looks at me like I might be an alien, and I ask her about her next book of poems. As she pulls up the cover art on her phone, Patrick disappears into the bedroom.

"Beautiful," I say, spreading my fingers over the screen to expand the shadowy reflection of a woman in a mirror.

She scrutinizes her screen, smiles a distant smile, lost for a moment in the question of whether or not the cover is right. When she looks up, her eyes fall on Patrick's empty chair.

"Where'd he go?" she asks.

I shrug. "I guess our shoptalk wasn't interesting for him."

Later, after Aamina and I share one of her cigarettes on the fire escape, she asks me to walk her out. We lean against the stoop railings, one of us on either side, and look up. The stars fight to be seen in the brightly lit sky, tinged blue by the office building down the street that recently added blue perimeter lights to its roof. Aamina folds her arms over her chest. She went to Harvard, and in the moments when she intimidates me, I always remember that, as though her degree is a detective badge.

"So, what's going on with that?"

"With what? Patrick?"

She looks at me. She knows I know what she means.

"It's just, you know."

"Is he a mature twenty-three?" she asks.

"He's almost twenty-four."

"That does not answer my question."

"Okay!" I hold up my hands. "It's new. I don't know what I'm doing. He's a . . . you know, he's a project."

"I liked Ralph."

"I know you liked Ralph. Everyone liked Ralph. He could charm a brick off a fucking wall."

"Not your brick, apparently."

"Aamina."

"I'm sorry," she says. "I know it was complicated. Just try to remember what you want, okay? Like, long term. And work on your book."

I smile. "I know. I'm one of those writers who doesn't write."

Aamina rolls her eyes. "Self-fulfilling prophecy."

She's one of those writers who sits down, does the work, revises the work, and produces something beautiful. A career writer. She hugs me and pushes hair off my shoulders.

"Be in touch more," she says. "I'm in Newark the whole summer."

The dinner and Aamina's skepticism hang over me the next day in the waiting room at my doctor's office.

I liked Ralph.

For a moment, I allow myself to miss him. I do every day, of course, but I bury it with movie-template faux feminism: I'm stronger on my own, etcetera. He was there when my father died and there when I got sick. I see him in the chair by the hospital bed, sleeping, his legs tucked into his chest. His coarse reddish blond hair falling into his eyes.

My name gets called. I return the unopened glossy magazine I've been holding in my lap to its stack on the table.

I'm seeing a new doctor this time. My old one, who told me I shouldn't get pregnant, moved to Chicago in the spring. I got a postcard in the mail letting me know. Even though my medical history is in the computer, I go in ready to give the new doctor my whole story. It's like this every time. They want you to explain yourself. They want you to prove you're not making it up.

It began with blood clots, I say.

Then my joints swelled. My red blood cells disappeared. My organs became inflamed. I couldn't breathe. My heart almost stopped. My GI system almost failed. Sepsis, blood transfusion, IV antibiotics, steroids. I was in the ICU for five days.

Except, really, it began with my father's death. The body blaming itself as much as I blame myself. But I don't tell doctors this part.

In the same exam room, my new doctor listens and asks questions occasionally. She nods, makes notes, and, as every doctor I've had since I was diagnosed has done, she asks, "Any family plans?"

I hesitate. Isn't she here to disabuse me of any such notions?

"Is it possible?" I ask.

She looks at my chart. "It's not *im*possible," she says. "There are some things that would be issues. You're already at risk for blood clots and pregnancy increases that risk. You'd have to stop most of the medications you're on, and it's hard to say if you're in remission on your own or if the medications are keeping you in remission."

"But I could? In theory."

"Possibly. You'd have to talk to a high-risk ob-gyn. The risks might end up being too great."

"Okay," I say.

"So you *do* have family plans?" She looks up, trying to get on with things.

"No," I say.

But throughout the rest of the exam—as she feels my joints and glands and checks my eyes and mouth—I think of a baby in my arms. I still don't know if I want it, but I imagine it there anyway. I imagine the possibility of it being there.

The thought of that particular happiness carries me home, as the sadness had when I was here last. In the hallway, I run into

Thora, who's taking garbage out to the curb. I take the bag from her. She accepts my help with relief because she left the babies in the apartment, Per's at work, and as she rushes back through her door she tells me to come inside on my way back in.

I put the garbage on the curb and rub hand sanitizer between my palms. Inside, Thora sits on the couch, a baby lying on either side of her, and I tell her to put me to work.

"I'll just close my eyes a minute," she says. "If a babe cries, will you wake me?"

I sit on the floor while Thora naps. The babies fall in and out of sleep.

"You're perfect," I tell them.

Their blue eyes search the ceiling. Their mouths gum the air. If my father were alive, and if I had a baby, well, that baby would be someone we would both love. Tears fill my eyes. One of the babies—I can't tell them apart, according to Thora one is a little bigger, but they look the same to me—catches hold of one of my fingers and doesn't let go.

Thora wakes up. We have a glass of wine. She roasts vegetables and tofu for her and Per's dinner, and then I go upstairs.

Patrick sits at the table with wine and a textbook. I didn't hear him come in when I was with Thora, and he looks up and says he was wondering where I was.

"Downstairs," I say. "With Thora and the babies."

I hang my bag on the back of the chair next to Patrick's. Bottles chime as I open the fridge door. "Oh," I sigh. "What's for dinner?"

It seems like I only have carrots and yogurt. I sent the leftovers home with Aamina last night.

"Takeout?" I ask.

Patrick shrugs. Something is annoying him, but I'm too tired to ask, and in any case, I don't really want to know. I search for my phone in my bag, pulling out my wallet, keys, the visit summary from the doctor, my hand sanitizer, my book. "I know I had it when

I got home," I say. "Aha." I find it buried beneath a bill for my health insurance. "What do you think? Thai food?"

Patrick doesn't reply, and when I look at him, he's holding the visit summary, reading.

"Systemic lupus?" he asks.

"Oh," I say. "That. It's nothing. I had an appointment today."

I hold out my hand for the papers. Patrick doesn't give them back. He scans the notes, my vitals, the long list of medications.

"When do you take these pills? I've never seen you take pills."

"At lunch," I say. "At work. I have to take them with food."

Patrick's scowl deepens. He keeps reading, and the longer he holds the summary the more uncomfortable I feel. He's prying. I didn't tell him about my health for a reason, because it ruined everything with Ralph, because I have to think about it all the time as it is, and because I'm just so tired of it all.

"Give it back," I say. "Ask me questions if you want, but give it back."

Patrick ignores my outstretched hand.

"Why didn't you tell me?" His eyes darken; his voice turns bitter. "You have this huge thing, and you didn't tell me."

"It's not that big of a deal."

"It looks like a big deal to me!" Patrick brandishes the health summary. "Four medications. Blood clots. Hospitalization. A blood transfusion? I mean, what the fuck, Marie? Why would you hide this?"

"I didn't hide anything," I say. "It just didn't come up. I've had it a long time."

"Nice spin," Patrick says, tossing the papers on the table. "Why? I mean, that's not really what we're doing here, is it?"

Patrick twists the stem of his wineglass. "What's that supposed to mean?"

"Just—look, it's not that I didn't tell you for a reason. It just didn't come up."

"Bullshit," he says. "I guess, what, it didn't fit into your project?"

"My project?"

"I overheard what you said to Aamina."

"Jesus Christ." I push the skin on my forehead away from my eyes. Patrick stands up. I can sense his energy rising.

"You're just taking from this what you want, is that it?" He pulls open the fridge door, searches. "Just phoning it in."

"Wine is on the table," I say. "If that's what you're looking for."

"Fuck you," he says.

"Hey. Don't do that."

"Do you think this is a transaction, what we're doing?"

"That's not fair. You were the one who said it, remember? You believe me, I believe you."

"You know that's not what I meant."

"Well, Patrick, what do you mean? What do you want?"

"Nothing," he mutters, sitting back down, deflated. "I don't want anything from you."

I laugh. "That's not true."

"Fuck you," he says again, and I laugh again because I can't help but find it funny when he says it, and he smiles a little.

"I'm sorry," I say. "I don't think you're a transaction."

"It's just, like, take me seriously," he says.

"Okay," I say, trying to look at him seriously, but a laugh bursts through my closed lips.

"What?" he exclaims, but he laughs a little, too.

The silence that comes whenever we talk ourselves into a corner wraps itself around our necks like scarves, and I refill our glasses.

"Okay, I'll tell you about the doctor today," I say. "It was a new one. She seems good. The last one said to me, 'Someone like you should never be pregnant,' and I was like, Wow, good bedside manner. This one isn't so sure. I mean, I don't even know if I want a baby, but whenever I see a baby or think of babies I think of my father in a good way—like he would be a part of that baby and I would have a new chance to get it right, to be a good parent because I wasn't a good daughter. It feels like it could be right somehow."

I keep going with my thoughts—the wine has given them buoyancy and they float right out of my mouth. I tell Patrick about the empty parts of me, parts that are empty because I haven't loved people the way I should. My father and then Ralph. I've been self-interested and my illness has made me obsessed with myself.

"That enough info for you?" I say, smiling.

I was looking into my wine as I spoke, not at Patrick, and now I see he's looking away, eyes cast down at a diagonal. He finishes his wine and reaches for the bottle, but we've emptied it.

"It sounds like you only want a baby because you were told you shouldn't have one," he says.

Harsh and fast like a slap. "That's an awful thing to say."

"Well, you're making me feel really uncomfortable, talking about children."

"This isn't about you."

"How?" he says miserably. "How is it not also about me? We're sleeping together."

I stand up, exasperated, swing open the fridge door in case we missed a bottle of wine. "This is ridiculous," I say. "A second ago you were saying I don't take you seriously, and now you're angry that I'm talking about the future?"

"We'd be fucked-up parents," he says bitterly.

"Me! This is about me!" I yell, loudly, and then hold my breath and listen for a baby crying downstairs—but everything is quiet. Softer, I add, "This is not about you."

"Why didn't you go with Ralph to California if you wanted a baby? Seems like you two were at that point."

"Seriously," I say. "What do you want me to say?"

"I'm not mad that you're talking about the future," he says. "I'm mad that you've already decided I'm not in it."

"Come *on*. Don't tell me you weren't planning on ending this if I didn't do it first."

"From the beginning for you this was over." Patrick looks into his empty wineglass. "You're just cold. Frigid. No wonder you can't write. You have zero imagination."

I burst into laughter—what he said is truly funny, and my fuse is short: scream, laugh, cry. One of them has to happen.

"That's great," I say. "I love that."

"This isn't funny."

"Yes, it is. It's ridiculous. Why are we even fighting? We have nothing to fight about." I reach over to put my hand over his. "Maybe we're not helping each other anymore. Maybe being sad is all we have in common."

"I'm leaving." He pulls his hand away, knocks back his chair and grabs his coat roughly from the hook by the door. "You're right. I'll end it if you don't. I won't be back."

When he's gone, I rest my elbows on the counter, my head over the sink, and push back my hair. A wave of nausea rolls over me, and I try not to throw up. It's hard to believe that when I walked in the door not long ago I thought we were going to have a normal evening.

Later, very late, my phone rings. It's Patrick, but when I answer the voice isn't his—it's someone telling me he needs to be picked up from the bar. I've come down, but I'm a little drunk still, so I walk there and find Patrick sitting outside the bar with his head between his knees. I sit down next to him, push his chin up with my finger. He has a bloody nose.

"I'm not even going to ask," I say.

"Thank you," he mutters.

"Come on," I say. "Time to walk."

I hoist him up, pull his arm over my shoulder. It's only a few blocks, but the air is moist, Patrick's weight is heavy, and I start to sweat.

"You're okay," I say when he dry heaves.

We're almost to my stoop when the gunshot rings out in the night. It sounds close, but maybe it's just the echo that's close. It pings against my heart, I hope it missed whoever it was for, and then I get Patrick inside.

In the morning we read that a student was shot during a botched burglary. He lived in a frat house just down the street. We both knew him in our own small ways. He'd helped me dig my car out during a blizzard last year. And Patrick had been a TA for the boy's economics class the semester before.

I walk to the train the next morning and the air feels thick, as though it's heavier with one less person breathing it.

Patrick and I slept eventually last night and parted ways in silence this morning, and I'm clumsy with everything at work because I can't stop thinking I should end things with him before they get any worse. For a few minutes the night before they were over, but then I'd helped him home.

I hand deliver a contract without the appendixes and am scolded for it.

"It makes me look bad," my boss says.

The frat boy creeps into my thoughts as I finish the day, and I hide my tears in the bathroom. The paramedics tried to save him, but he was dead by the time they got to the hospital. I have no business being broken up about him, but I am, and I keep checking the internet to see the comments on the articles about him, the condolences and stories of how nice the boy had been, what a good student and good neighbor he was. The articles note the fact he was in a fraternity almost as an apology. The fraternities aren't well liked by townies, but this boy was an exception.

My father's body rested for days in his apartment before anyone knew he was dead, before a friend called the police to do a well-being check. I think of the paramedics arriving and having nothing to do except confirm he was dead.

I stay late finishing work I was too sad to do earlier in the day, and then I take my time getting home. I don't run through Penn Station to catch the 7:18. I lean against a pillar and wait for the 7:56. When I get off at Newark Broad Street I walk slowly down the steps, past the light-rail station, and down Essex, past the Audible building and onto my cobblestone street. Tree roots have disturbed the bricks and made the sidewalks jagged. The peonies my landlord planted are dollops of color in the window boxes. I stand outside in the dark, breathing the air, watching a plane glide overhead, and finally go inside. I know Patrick is there. The light is on.

We say kind things to each other. I tell him we'll only make things worse if we keep doing this, and he agrees. We hug. The hug becomes a kiss, which turns into sex. Patrick leaves when we're finished. He hangs the key I gave him on the hook. It was Ralph's key once.

When the police tape has been removed from outside the fraternity house and the reporters have trickled out of the neighborhood, my landlord emails me to see if I'd like to have lunch. He takes his tenants out for long lunches sometimes. Ralph used to join when he still lived here. Yuejin is always worrying about whether his tenants are happy, and the shooting probably brought about a resurgence of his worries. He imagines we could leave our brownstone and move to Brooklyn, but I always reassure him that I love Newark.

Life here is the subject of my landlord's email.

I wait for Yuejin outside my building. In our mailboxes, the neighborhood association has left flyers advertising a meeting that will address the recent shootings. The frat boy was the second student to be killed in Newark this year; the first was involved in a drug robbery. I scan the flyer as Yuejin crosses the street. He drives us to a Portuguese restaurant in the Ironbound. Behind the wheel, he presses his palms together in apology when he turns in front of a woman in a blue pickup truck.

We eat garlic shrimp and talk about the upcoming neighborhood association meeting. By now people have begun to feel bold enough to ask questions about the murder. What *was* the boy doing outside so late? The story was the burglars had followed him home from the twenty-four-hour minimart down the street. Why did he fight back instead of putting his hands up and letting them have what they wanted? What really went on inside that frat house?

I grimace at these questions. Prodding at a death, picking apart someone's final hour, never brings answers.

"I'm not going to the meeting," my landlord says. "In my experience almost nothing can be learned from isolated incidents like this. And I don't want to hear what the police have to say, whose livelihood depends on crime."

I've decided not to go, either. These things happen everywhere in America. They're not what I think of when I think of Newark. Instead I think of the first few weeks of April when spring bursts in and the cherry trees blossom and they make the air fragrant until the blossoms fall and a verdant canopy overtakes the parks and the backyards. I think of the very blue sky of Newark in the summer, and the night that's only dark enough for the brightest stars, and summer weddings in the yard of the Newark Museum. I think of free yoga in Riverfront Park, planes coming in so low for landing at Newark Liberty that I can see into their windows. They're big international flights, British Airways and Lufthansa jets, their shadows rippling over our bodies as I struggle through even the basic yoga poses, pausing to massage my aching joints. The river smells bad on hot days. There's also yoga at the southern tip of Military Park, the class Aamina teaches, beneath the bust of JFK, planes taking off on this side of the city and American flags snapping on the tops of buildings above us as we lie on the mats. Once a man riding by on his bike yelled, "What's this, the fat bitch roly-poly club?" I wasn't offended, though maybe I should've been. Mostly I couldn't help but admire how quickly he'd come up with the insult, how the words *roly poly* had been so readily retrievable for him, and I liked that he saw us as a club.

But these aren't the things one talks about at neighborhood meetings.

Yuejin takes a sip of his water and clears his throat.

"Have you heard from Ralph?" he asks.

Yuejin rented the apartment to both of us, and he was concerned when Ralph left. He also knows everything that goes on in the neighborhood, so I'm sure he's seen Patrick come and go, unlocking the front door on his own, then moments later the light coming on in my apartment.

"He posts on social media. His new job is good, I think. I don't really see us talking again anytime soon."

Yuejin shrugs. He's a fatalist.

"If it's meant to happen," he says, "there's nothing you can do to stop it."

I let my gaze escape through the window. There are tears in my eyes because for a moment I imagine my father sitting across from me instead of my landlord. He was a fatalist, too, my father. I'm not—I don't like to think that that boy had to die. I don't like the thought that Patrick and I were supposed to hurt each other, or that Ralph and I were before that. If that was fate, then I'm the common denominator in a lot of pain, and it's hard to see that pattern changing. But I'd like for it to change.

Yuejin changes the subject to the abandoned lot near the train station.

"Soon we'll have our garden," he says.

Every day he sneaks under the fence to scatter and water the seeds he bought for the empty lot. Sunflowers, grass, Queen Anne's lace, and bleeding hearts. Sometimes I go with him to help. He tried to get approval from the owner of the lot, a New York businessman who is never in Newark, but once the businessman saw the design for the garden, he said no. It would be too beautiful, he said. People don't care about abandoned lots, but they get attached to gardens. He doesn't want trouble when he mows it down. He doesn't want to be accused of taking something good away from the people. When property values in Newark have skyrocketed, he's going to make a fortune off that lot by building condominiums.

Water Burial

Before Dee left California for a long-awaited reunion with her sister, she'd gone to a party thrown by her boyfriend's work. Linus had been with this company almost as long as he'd been with Dee—two years, and though he'd started out hating the job, she suspected he now felt settled in it. Dee wondered if their relationship had taken an opposite course: comfortable in the beginning, it was starting to shock and prick them in unexpected and annoying ways.

The work party had ended dramatically, she and Linus had fought, and now, with Dee away in Boston, they were still on sour terms.

On her third day in Boston, she and Emily went to the Charles River to sit on a bench and watch the sailboats billow across the water. Dee finally had the courage to tell her sister about the fight. Emily spent more time studying lemurs in Madagascar than she did with people and didn't always understand the way Dee caused trouble with others in her life.

"I didn't want to fight with Linus that night," Dee said to Emily. "I don't even know why it started."

In truth, Dee had begun to realize why the fight had been brewing in her, why the mix of woes inside of her had turned frothy that night and foamed over. Simply, she just didn't feel well. In fact, she felt very ill. Her joints were swollen and painful and she sometimes woke feeling as though her insides were swollen, too, ready to burst through her skin. She had an appointment with a specialist, but he was booked for the next month and on the phone she hadn't expressed how serious she felt her condition was, and because she'd never learned to self-advocate—but was passive aggressive instead—she didn't think to ask they make room for her somehow.

Emily looked out at the river as Dee spoke.

"I agreed to meet Linus there," Dee said. "At the restaurant his work had picked. Even though I wasn't feeling well."

The night had started well enough; the party was at a restaurant on the Sacramento River, with a porch that swung far out over the water. The sky was partly cloudy and turning pink and gold just as Dee arrived. The delta breezes burned off the heat of the day, leaving a cool silk residue. Downriver the city rose up, its short buildings glimmering in the fading light, and though Dee had never intended to stay in Sacramento after she graduated from college, the place had begun to feel like home.

Dee walked slowly from her car to the restaurant. Her knees had swollen even though she'd kept her legs up and wrapped in heating pads all day. Her fingers were as stiff as pencils and she'd driven to the restaurant with her palms flat on the steering wheel because she couldn't bend her joints to grip it.

The party, for the company's five-year anniversary, was not where she wanted to be. Home in bed was where she wanted to be. But Linus wanted her to come. She never felt like doing anything anymore, he said, so she dragged herself there even though each step caused her pain. To her sister she clarified that she hadn't been honest with Linus about the pain—in fact she'd been hiding her symptoms from him. Even still, she hoped Linus would ask her how she was feeling. But she'd been secretive since the beginning of their relationship, and Linus had adapted to her nature.

Dee imagined she and Linus looked ill matched to outsiders. She was sure their friends talked about how she needed someone more independent and he needed someone more reliable, but in their private spaces Dee and Linus sank into an easy world where they shared a comfortable togetherness. Once the outside world interrupted them, though, they couldn't translate what worked for them alone into something they could present to others.

Dee found Linus at the restaurant. He was standing across the porch, near the railing, with a coworker named Martha. Their elbows were propped up on the splintered wood and their bodies leaned over the water. Dee caught Linus's eye and waved to him. He returned the wave, and Dee expected him to excuse himself to Martha and come to her, but he didn't—he was waiting for her to come to him.

A cloud parted and a rope of sunlight fell on Martha's hair. She spread her fingers through her hair and shook big clumps of it, as though to spread the light around. Linus appeared rapt, his eyes unbroken from Martha.

Dee fell sullen. She and Linus only treated each other as a priority when they were alone. As though if they appeared too much in love others would be disgusted, or would find them inauthentic. As though as young people they should be looking to hurt each other. Their friends seemed to think there was nothing to be learned from happiness.

Dee was offered a margarita by a passing waiter, which she took. The salt on the rim stung her hands. The swollen joints had cracked her skin open, leaving paper-cut-size slits on her palms and fingers. Dee sipped and pretended to look around for someone she knew, but she had already found her someone, and he was absorbed in someone else.

She remembered when she'd met a woman who was tall and tattooed, with a severe expression, at a party a few months ago. She had intimidated Dee. Her name was Renée, and Dee had assumed she didn't allow men to give her any nonsense, that maybe she was a ballbuster, but at one point Renée turned to Dee and asked why the men at the party were gripping her hand so tightly when introducing themselves. "They're about to break my fingers," Renée had said. "Are they doing that to you, too?" And Dee had realized that she, like the men around her, had assumed certain things about Renée all because of her leather jacket, her stature, and a few tattoos.

Now, Dee felt something like what Renée might have felt. Because she needed her independence, Linus sometimes ignored her. But that wasn't what she wanted when she said *independence*, not quite. But maybe it was asking too much of a person to detect the more sensitive tremors of need that run inside another person—especially when she didn't know how to say what she wanted. When asking felt like whining. When needing to begin with felt like a betrayal of her independence.

Dee was inching across the patio because she couldn't find anywhere else to go. She wanted a chair, but saw none, so she moved among the tables that were laid out with neat rows of canapés and fanned clusters of napkins. Finally, she was so close to her boyfriend that she could hover no more and simply had to approach him. That she couldn't approach Linus comfortably spelled trouble, but at the same time she felt there was something special and complicated about their relationship, even if they repelled each other sometimes, even if they had shifting ions of desire inside of them.

But Linus smiled warmly at Dee and reached his arm out to pull her into a hug. He was happy to see her. Dee and Martha shook hands, and Dee tried to ward off the gloom that often followed her relief when she was proven wrong about a feeling that, if only briefly, had trapped her heart so tightly.

"We were just talking about you," Martha said.

Dee, instead of feeling flattered, felt persecuted.

Dee paused her story and looked at her sister, who was still staring out at the Charles River. The wind had forced the sailboats sideway at forty-five degrees and their bright sails skimmed the frothy whitecaps.

"Everything okay?" Emily asked, because Dee had stopped speaking.

"The next part of the story doesn't show me in the best light," Dee said.

"That's okay," Emily said. "That's why you're telling me."

Dee had smiled at Martha, she told her sister. Dee said, "Oh really?" and glanced at Linus who smiled a tight-lipped smile, as though he'd known this wouldn't go over well.

But Martha went on.

"He was just saying that you sometimes make him eat freegan— that is, when you don't finish your own meal—"

"Yes," Dee interrupted. "I know what *freegan* means."

Since they'd met, Linus had followed a vegan diet. Dee had briefly been vegetarian, but her protein levels had sunk so low she had to give it up. When she told Linus what her doctor said (that she needed to eat a serving of meat the size of a deck of cards each day), she felt he didn't believe her, that he thought she hadn't tried hard enough to replace the protein in her diet and was using her weight as an excuse.

Lately, even though she was eating meat again, Dee was still losing weight. It simply evaporated like fog burning off from her body. Her ribs appeared, thin tributaries running over her abdomen. When she swallowed food, the food passed through a balloon of pain near her lungs. Even a portion the size of a deck of cards was too much; she just had no appetite these days.

Even more than Linus hated eating meat, he hated wasting food. If her nonvegan meal was going to get thrown away, he would finish it, citing freeganism. Lately, Dee was simply unable to clear a plate, no matter how badly she needed the calories. Nor could she bring herself not to take any food at all, as if that would mean giving in to whatever was going wrong inside of her.

Linus had never complained about finishing her food. Until now she had thought it was one way they were secretly intimate, breaking the rules of Linus's diet together.

Linus looked away from her and Martha, at the slowly moving

river, brown and murky. A hanging vine reached one tendril into the river and the water parted around it.

Dee's veins went icy with self-pity. She hadn't known she was upsetting Linus, trespassing on his life choices by making him feel obligated to finish her servings of meat. But she also understood the pleasure of telling your friends how an important person in your life is harassing you, the attention it garners, the cachet of having difficulties with one's partner.

Martha, with her calm smile, seemed to expect an answer. So Dee said, "I don't make him. He can say no."

"Anyway," Martha said, "we were just discussing the different ways you can be vegan. I'm thinking of going vegan, too."

"Very good," Dee said.

To try to put a stop to the conversation, she leaned between Martha and Linus and rested her elbows on the porch railing. Her skin soaked up the warmth the wood had absorbed from the day's sunshine. A waiter passed by with a tray of sausages speared with toothpicks, and Dee took two. She couldn't resist trying to eat.

"Is one of those for Linus?" Martha asked.

"Will you lay the fuck off?" Dee snapped.

She threw the sausages into the river.

Martha went pale. Her eyes darted toward Linus, and they exchanged a look that Dee couldn't decipher. Maybe pity, mixed with something else, something private.

"I'll just be over there," Martha said, gesturing toward the bar.

When she'd gone, Linus said, "Jesus, Dee, I have to work with her."

"Well, I would appreciate it if you didn't talk about me behind my back."

Linus rolled his eyes. "We were just talking about stupid shit. I wasn't even talking about you at all, I was talking about food."

"And you could've stood up for me," Dee said.

"Stand up for you? You were the one being mean."

Linus rubbed his eyes. He had tired eyes, which Dee loved, and a rush of regret plummeted inside of her and landed in the pit of her stomach.

"I have to go fix this." Linus left before Dee could reach out and touch his arm.

Her sinuses seized up with the feeling that she might cry. She cleared her throat, faced the water, and gulped what was left in her drink. She looked around for another, swiped a glass of sparkling wine from a passing tray. Quickly, the alcohol made her head float. She was on blood thinners because of clots she'd had in her leg last year. Just a fluke, she'd thought at the time.

Dee sulked beside the river while her brain filled with bitter thoughts. She and Linus couldn't always recognize what they loved about each other—but the problem had gotten worse with Dee's illness, the pains and feelings she could barely describe to doctors, who prompted her with all their knowledge of how the body works, much less to Linus. And she no longer recognized herself in her new body, with its frozen joints and 8 percent body fat, and how after a certain amount of walking she couldn't move any longer. She didn't understand, either, how this new body had changed her relationship with food, how people mistook her inability to eat with refusal, how some said she looked good and others thought she was anorexic. She knew Linus didn't love her new gaunt body, and when she looked in the mirror she didn't either, but when people praised her for being thin she felt good about herself. It was something to hold on to—something about her body some people believed to be good—and though she knew she was unhealthy she appreciated it all the same.

She couldn't express this to Linus. She would sound crazy. So she just hadn't said anything to him, and now he believed she was shutting herself farther away from him, burrowing deeper inside of herself. Like many sick people, though, she wanted to be taken care of.

A few tears fell from her eyes into the river. Then she steeled herself. She didn't want to make more of a scene, not here. She lifted her champagne glass and watched the bubbles rocket to the surface. Clumps of clouds wafted through the sky above her—she could smell the clean rain inside of them, and she took a few deep replenishing breaths. She watched the party behind her through its reflection in her wineglass. The chilled glass felt nice against her swollen palm, and she smiled when a clown appeared with an air pump and a handful of balloons. This was the type of thing Linus's company found whimsical, an ironic throwback to childhood that they could make hip again. Start-up culture.

There was laughter, either of approval, or people just being good sports. The clown inflated a few balloons into long snakes and twisted them into a crown. He handed the crown to Linus's boss with a flourish.

Dee turned, leaned her back against the rail. She searched for Linus and found him with Martha, in conversation again near the bar. They seemed not to have noticed the clown, who offered dogs and giraffes as he made his way through the crowd. He neared Linus and Martha and, without warning, put a crown on Martha's head, then began to inflate another one for Linus.

Martha's hands flew to her head. She grabbed the crown and threw it to the ground; it wafted lazily down. She spun toward the clown, a look of distress and anger on her face. Dee moved closer.

"Stop it," Martha said to the clown. "Get away from me!"

Her voice was thin. Dee wondered if she was afraid of clowns, but then Martha clasped her throat; she began to gag and cough. She bent forward and her glass of wine spilled onto the ground in a burgundy arc. Dee, puzzled, walked toward her; maybe Martha was having some kind of episode, but her eyes caught Linus's, and he motioned for her to stop. His face was twisted with concern, and then Dee saw the concern loosen into understanding.

"Latex," he said quickly. "Latex allergy."

He grabbed the purse she'd dropped on the ground. Martha grabbed his arm, one hand still clutching her throat as her breath came in heavy gasps. Linus rooted around inside her purse until he produced an EpiPen. With his arm around Martha, holding her up, he uncapped the auto-injector and drove it into her thigh.

"We got into a big fight later that night," Dee told Emily. "I accused him of sleeping with her. Knowing where her EpiPen was just felt so intimate to me."

"Is he?" Emily asked. "Sleeping with her?"

Dee shook her head. "I don't think so. He's just a caring guy."

Dee hesitated. What she didn't tell her sister was that she'd felt betrayed by the way Linus had leaped, without hesitation, to save Martha, how he'd intuited so quickly what was wrong with her when he couldn't seem to see that Dee's body was becoming an uninhabitable place for her. She took a breath, and she thought she would follow the breath with an explanation of these feelings to Emily, but she felt so ashamed that a sense of competition had sparked in her that night on the Sacramento River. She'd wanted Linus to abandon the suffocating Martha and come to her instead.

The wind was getting so fierce that the boats on the Charles River were tipping over, wind tangled up in their sails, though the day was still warm and beautiful and the sun beamed abundantly. When a boat overturned, its sailors flipped it back over and hoisted themselves in, dripping wet and laughing, but there was a boat in the middle of the river that floated on its side with no one near it.

Dee pointed to it.

"Do you see that?" she asked Emily.

Emily shaded her eyes. "I wonder what happened."

Dee bunched her hair nervously; it was coarse and windswept and dirt from the park was caught in it. The stranded boat bobbed in the water. The current seemed too fierce for someone to have swum ashore, but maybe they'd climbed into another boat. For a moment Dee imagined herself neck deep in the river, her boat unmanageable, and it wasn't hard to imagine because her body made her feel like she was drowning on land.

"Oh, good," Emily said, pointing. "It's the coast guard."

They'd arrived in a rubber inflatable with a motor attached. Dee was relieved she didn't have to do anything.

"Do you want to work things out with Linus?" Emily asked.

"Yes," Dee replied. There were a lot of reasons why she wanted to work things out, but in part she just didn't know who else would want her. She worried she would never feel well again. Linus would inherit her illness, but it would be a different thing to ask someone new to adopt it.

She also missed the feeling of lying so close to him their breath touched, and the electricity that their skin exchanged. Each moment when they were alone together was patient and slow and felt meant to be. At least in her old body it had been—and as much as she loved Linus, she also loved the memory of the healthy young woman she'd been when she met him.

Linus had driven Martha home from the restaurant in Sacramento, leaving Dee there by herself. It had been their plan to drive separately, but the blood thinners had carried the alcohol swiftly through Dee's body, and she was drunk. She sat alone while she sobered up. Linus's coworkers filtered out, some of them no doubt wondering who she was. She clutched a warm cup of coffee in her hands and watched a pontoon putter to a stop in the middle of the river. From its deck flowed the slow drawl of someone playing taps. Each note stabbed her with its blunt edge. A persistent sad throb was all that song was. Ashes were being scattered—a water burial. Dee closed her eyes and imagined the billow of ash beneath the surface. The release, the dispersal of atoms, the end.

Before Emily and Dee left the park they walked slowly to the bank of the river to feel the cold spray of water on their faces. Dee had to leave soon to go to the airport to catch her flight. She thanked Emily for listening, and Emily said she was happy to, and there seemed to be more Emily wanted to say but she didn't say it.

At the airport, each step with her luggage left Dee feeling more and more breathless. By the time she reached Salt Lake City for her connection, she had to use all her energy not to faint as she went up the gangway and trudged to her new gate. On the second flight, her breath was as thin as tissue paper. Her heart rushed against the thin walls of her chest, hit her rib cage, retreated. She felt her heart might burst, or fail just because she could not provide it enough oxygen. She breathed as hard as she could without wheezing.

The plane's wheels thudded on the ground in Sacramento, and Dee was relieved to still be alive. A few weeks later she would be admitted to the ICU in hemorrhagic shock, her cardiovascular system shutting down because she was severely anemic. This is what she'd been feeling on the plane, in the thin air of the high altitude, but by the time she was kissing solid ground she wasn't thinking about a doctor, she thought only of Linus. He was waiting for her in their car outside baggage claim, and when she saw him she dissolved in tears and into his arms. She told him she'd thought she was having a pulmonary embolism on the plane and was going to die—but now she was safe on the ground, safe with him.

He wrapped his arms around her and only let go when the airport police flashed their lights at them.

He would stay by her side in the hospital, too, and the fight they'd had blew away, an empty boat on water. After three blood transfusions, Dee began to stabilize, and Linus held her face in his hands and without saying anything, they started over.

They didn't talk about the night on the Sacramento River, but if things had gone differently, if she hadn't almost died, Dee thought that Linus might've ended up with Martha. She wasn't jealous anymore, about the idea of it. Martha just might have been the natural choice for him. If her near death hadn't revived their love,

Martha's attack might have been the beginning of new love, hers and Linus's, although Dee couldn't claim to know what Martha would have wanted. Sometimes Martha's name came up in conversation about work, but Linus always steered them away from that rocky shore. Once he added, casually, that Martha had gotten engaged, as though it would reassure Dee.

Dee didn't need reassuring. Even when she began treatment for her autoimmune disease, even when her healthy body more or less returned, she would sometimes wonder what Martha and Linus had said to each other during that car ride home from the river. Dee couldn't help but notice that Linus had stopped bringing her to his work functions after that, had in fact stopped going to them himself.

Aerosol

I built a fire in the backyard using lint from the dryer as kindling. It curled up and disappeared almost instantly, but after I added enough of it, the twigs caught and the flame committed itself to eating the logs. Everything was bright and contained in the pit I made out of cinder blocks, which I dragged from the neighbors' backyard where a pile of construction garbage sat from their stalled addition. Money problems, I guess. We had them, too.

My sister, Sarah, was supposed to be staying with me that week. She went to school in Ann Arbor, but it was her spring break now and she had some time off. Spending the week bonding with Sarah was the deal I had made with my mom, who'd gone to Florida with her boyfriend and had wanted me to go, too. They were sailing on his boat; they'd started in Daytona Beach and were winding all the way around the southern tip then up the gulf coast to Sarasota. Hours and hours of sitting on a boat as the hull slapped the water repeatedly. I'd Google Earthed the route, zoomed in so I could see the gulf coast sand beneath the blue glass of shallow water. It looked pretty, but Ken hated me and would probably toss me overboard midvoyage. "I'd rather die," I said to my mom—which had started another fight, of course. She did that thing where she pushed her fingers into her temples to let me know I was giving her a headache. She was angry, but also tired, and her thin lips trembled and I wondered what she really wanted to say.

We didn't speak much the day before she left. She explained the numbers on the fridge, reminded me it was *really important* that I answer the phone when the realtor called because she might want to set up a showing, told me again how to thaw a chicken breast, that sort of thing. We hugged goodbye. Her shoulder blades were two sharp stones in my hands. I didn't get her, and she didn't get me.

"So," I said, when Sarah and I were sprawled on the couch watching the *Daily Show* on Thursday night. "What are you going to do all next week while I'm at school?"

"Actually," she said. "As long as you're okay here, I was thinking of staying at Chris's apartment. I can stop home a few times, if you want."

"Sure." I'd already driven my mom's car to the store to buy deli turkey and cheese and a jar of pickles. I didn't want to touch raw chicken. "I'm a survivor," I said.

Sarah laughed at me.

So that was how I ended up alone.

I built the fire because it seemed fun, and because I was entering a time in my life when I would have to fend for myself, and because I was working on a novel in which the heroine will probably need to build a fire. She's going to fall into a pond, and her foot is going to get caught on the root of a water lily, and just as she's about to pass out, the light above her will change and the sky will spin and the weed will disappear and she'll be able to kick her way to the surface because she won't be in her world anymore. She'll be somewhere else, somewhere unknown.

So the fire was research.

In shorts and a T-shirt, I lay on the grass by the flames I'd coaxed into existence and thought of names for my character. Jamie. Matilda. Elsbeth. And names for the brooding but beautiful guy she meets, the archer in the rebel army: Hayden or Harrison. Or maybe Parker.

Imagine just how strange the world will feel when Jamie emerges from the pond, the sky above her not the blue she's used to but violet with black clouds. The trees will blow in a thicker wind than her wind and the birds will be singing in different tones. She'll be confused at first, because that's how it always is in books—even though if I'm ever transported in space and time I'll think *Yes, finally*.

But then, gradually, she'll realize the change has enhanced her life. She's trading in the boring details for the wild ones. She has a purpose, suddenly; she's emerged from the pond baptized, the old pains and boredom cleansed from her body. Emerging as someone new, but also realizing she was that new person all along. Love, war, valor—in fantasy books, they're all a disguise for the simple feeling of wanting to be someone a little bit special. A little bit worth remembering. Her fears vaporize as her clothes dry beneath some bright faraway sun that looks bigger than her sun at home. All her raw courage is reforged into a sword.

My idea was good. I just had to get the words on paper.

The light faded and my eyes tricked me into thinking the fire had gotten brighter. Our house backed up to a thick patch of forest—a good selling point, according to the realtor who'd stuck in our front yard a big sign with her face on it. She'd hung a little box on our doorknob with a combination lock, and nestled inside was a key so she could get in anytime. It was like the house already wasn't ours.

Overhead, a hawk swooped gracefully into its nest. The stars popped out one at a time, like giant fiery mosquitoes. If I stared long enough without blinking, they began to vibrate. It was peaceful. I would miss this house. I didn't know where we'd go when it sold— probably with Ken, who rented an apartment here in Michigan but had his boat docked in Florida.

I felt the pain piercing my thigh before I heard the pop of exploding metal and a hiss of air released. I didn't scream, but all my breath rushed out of me. I could almost see it, the way you can see air get sucked out of astronauts' mouths in movies when they go out in space without their suits. A rusty aerosol can, tucked into one of the cinder blocks: I hadn't noticed it before, but the heat from the fire had made it explode. I froze as I looked down at my thigh, at the shard of metal as wide as my big toe embedded two inches deep in my flesh. I didn't breathe, not until I couldn't stand it any longer.

My mom met Ken in AA, where she'd met all of her boyfriends, including my dad twenty years before. I'd told her the AA pool was too small and that she needed to meet someone from somewhere else. Or she could look on the internet. But instead she'd brought home Ken, then kept bringing him home. He had thick gray hair that fell to his shoulders and he walked around with his hands in his pocket, shaking loose change. He was tall, and he slouched because of it.

Mostly I wanted her to let my dad move back. Since she'd tossed him out, he'd stopped calling her, stopped begging her, and he'd also stopped calling me from Minnesota, where he'd gone to rehab, and where he now rented an apartment since my mom had decided he couldn't come back. He had a roommate. Fathers weren't supposed to have roommates; they were supposed to live with you.

My mom feels like she's wasted time. And there's nothing scarier than adults who feel like they've wasted time, with the ends of their lives burning their heels like hot coals, like death is something that starts happening the minute you reach a certain age. At least, that *must* be why she's into Ken: she's afraid of dying alone. He has a job and his sobriety—things my dad doesn't have—but he also has a pathological need to be right and he expects us to clean up after him. He came into our house ready to assume the position of the patriarch. And my mom expected me to immediately adjust. I tried to tell her how I feel—I didn't have the same anger against my dad as she did, and what I thought we needed was a little bit of time because she and I were a team—but she didn't want to hear it. She asked me if I expected her to be alone for the rest of her life and then she called me spoiled. And maybe I was. I was the baby of the family, and I hadn't grown up as quickly as my sister. I still liked fantasy books. But none of this changed the fact that Ken grossed me out. And that's what hurt the most: my mom didn't think my opinion mattered. She didn't think I was anything but an immature teenage girl.

I finally breathed, quick inhalations of air that hit my lungs like a staple gun. I stared at the shard of metal for a second, completely bewildered. I reached for it, but my hand hesitated like my fingers didn't have the muscles to pinch it and pull it out. Then I did it. Quickly, but it still seemed to take forever—metal separating from flesh. There was a pause, everything was still and it seemed like even the flames stopped flickering. Then the blood flowed out and I rushed at the wound with everything I could find: my math homework from my back pocket, leaves from the ground, my T-shirt pulled down to cover my thigh.

"Oh no," I said. "No, no."

Wasn't there an important vein in your thigh? I'd never seen so much blood; it seeped through my fingers and ran down my wrists. I stood and almost fell into the fire. Droplets of blood went flying and sizzled in the flames. I left a trail of blood that dotted the grass like dewdrops as I limped inside.

In the bathroom, the fan sputtered and one of the light bulbs flickered. I propped my leg on the counter and lifted my hand and my math homework to look at the cut. It was a gouge, really, my skin completely opened in a bloody trench. I tried to press the pieces back together, but the pain hit me even harder. I leaned over and threw up on the floor.

Another moment passed, and then a few more. I had no idea what I was supposed to be doing.

Then I tore through the cabinets, leaving bloody handprints on everything. I found small Band-Aids and hydrogen peroxide. I couldn't wedge my thigh under the faucet so I limped upstairs to the bathroom with the shower, still trailing blood—God, the house was going to look like a crime scene—and upstairs I stood under cold water without even taking off my clothes.

This was Saturday, day two of being alone, and I was watching bloody water swirl down the drain.

Two questions I have about the fantasy novel: Why does the character get transported from her home in the first place, and does she ever come back? These questions are more important than whether or not she falls in love with the brooding archer boy. Also, let's face it, she definitely falls in love with the brooding archer boy. Who could resist?

There will be a section where she gets wounded, because she'll take naturally to a bow and arrow and join the army against the dark lord. She might get separated from her company, stumble into a forest, delirious, with beasts roaming among the trees and their yellow eyes gleaming hungrily. But she'll mix a salve, she'll use her wits, because girls in fantasy novels always have hidden talents.

When I was out of the shower, I poured the hydrogen peroxide over the cut and watched it fizz as it cleaned the wound. The bleeding had slowed a little. I wrapped half a roll of paper towels around my leg and taped them with masking tape. I needed stitches. I needed a wound evaluation. I should call Sarah and have her take me to the hospital.

But our insurance had been my dad's insurance, and we'd lost it when he'd gotten fired. An ER bill would cost thousands of dollars. I didn't know how much my mom had in the bank. I had three hundred dollars saved from birthdays and my irregular babysitting gigs. More than anything, I didn't want to have to ask Ken to pay. He'd demand a repayment plan from me. He'd take credit for saving my life.

The morning, I thought. I'll see how it is in the morning. I was very tired, and I felt very woozy, and so I limped to my bedroom and wrapped myself up into a burrito with my blankets and fell into a really deep sleep.

There was this one time a few months ago when Ken and my mom were fighting. It was about my father. Ken didn't think my mom was being aggressive enough with him, and he was threatening to answer the phone himself the next time my dad called.

Maybe it was the thought of Ken trying to intimidate my dad, who was weak right now and drug addled and desperate to have his family back. It made me sick. Ken and my mom were fighting in the kitchen, and when I couldn't take it anymore I burst in and told him to stop yelling at her. I told him he better not dare talk to my father.

"Your mom and I are trying to have a conversation," Ken said.

I raised my palms up. *So what?*

Ken only needed to take one step to close most of the gap between us, like he was using his size to intimidate me. I turned to my mom and said, "God, can this idiot please just leave for two seconds?"

Ken took another step. He glanced at my mom, then at me. "When are you going to learn to respect people's privacy?"

He was close enough that his spittle landed on my cheek; his breath smelled like coffee. I'd never felt tense in this way before, like I might have to deflect a blow. My mom was saying "Whoa, whoa," and pulling Ken back a little. But it was too late—she'd brought him into our house, and for the first time ever I felt unsafe there.

It was a nightmare, what happened next. Three-way screaming. Everyone was red in the face. My mom was crying. I stormed upstairs because I'd be damned if I was going to let Ken see me cry.

I woke up late the next morning. The same old sun blazed above the house, except that now there were spots in my vision that made the sunlight look moldy. One empty-headed minute went by before

I remembered everything that had happened: the fire, the aerosol can, the deep cut on my leg. I rolled over and my skin tore away from the sheet. I felt a new oozing. The blood had dried and now the cut was wide open again.

In the bathroom, a repeat of the procedure: hydrogen peroxide, new paper towels. The cut was seeping, but not gushing blood. Maybe it would scab today. I just had to keep it clean. Keep paper towels on it. Everything would be fine.

The house, though—the house was a wreck. The blood would be easy enough to clean off the hardwood stairs and hallways, but there were drops of it on my mom's rugs in the living room. The vomit had dried on the bathroom floor, and blood was on everything I'd touched.

I started cleaning, but I felt so tired. My leg hurt and too much movement made the cut split open. So I cleaned up the vomit and sprayed carpet cleaner on the rug. I had all week to clean the rest.

The phone rang. I was lying on the floor next to the rug and didn't think I could reach it in time, crawling, but I did. It was Sarah, telling me she was coming over for dinner.

"No!" I said, though no one was there to hear me; she'd already hung up.

I waited for her on the front stoop. I had to keep her from going inside. The wind blew cherry blossoms from the trees and the blossoms spun twister-like and landed on our blacktop driveway. Little blushes of color. I toed them with my good leg. The other leg I'd wrapped in more paper towels and duct tape before putting on loose pants. The vein throbbed beneath the bandage, as though it was trying to bust loose. I compulsively pinched the fabric and shook it out, checking for blood.

I leaned all my weight on my good leg, slung my messenger bag over my shoulder, slipped my thumbs into my pockets. The thing with real life is that you have to do something to make yourself less miserable. You can't just fall into ponds and emerge a warrior.

A big gust made all the leaves talk over one another and brought my sister's car swooshing around the corner and up the driveway. Chris was in the passenger seat. He rolled down the window and said, "I thought you were going to cook us chicken breasts."

"Let's go to Olga's," I said. "I'll buy us those bread things with the cheese dip."

I took small quick steps to the car, hoping they wouldn't notice that I was limping. But as I slid into the back seat, Sarah said, "Are you limping?"

"Just twisted my ankle," I said. "No big deal."

Sarah looked at me in the rearview mirror. I smiled really wide because I thought that would let her know I was okay. But instead she snorted. "You're grinning like a maniac," she said and put the car in gear.

Sarah made a quick turn out of our neighborhood. The motion made me dizzy. The houses and stores and billboards passed in a blur as we glided through every yellow light. I thought about how important timing is—how it decides everything. Sarah got out of the house at just the right time. Jamie falls into the pond at just the right time. Hayden hears the splash because he's nearby at just the right time. Then the clock resets, and everyone who wasn't there at the right time is stuck.

Monday, I had to go to school. I packed the hydrogen peroxide and extra paper towels for the midday wound cleaning. As I drove there I thought about what might happen to the girl in my book if she slipped back into her real life. Maybe she gets struck by an arrow, and dying in her new world means returning to her old one. Would she go back to school? Would she try to get back to Hayden, or whatever his name is, to continue fighting for the cause? And why does she feel so attached to a cause she just found out about, when she never really did anything to help any cause in her old world? Maybe it's because suddenly everything that makes her comfortable is gone, her whole system of social support gone, with no one around who remembers it. That sort of thing would rattle a person, would maybe make a person see things she'd ignored before.

I parked the car. I limped into precalculus late because I couldn't race the bell. A few people looked at me as I slid into my seat, but no one said anything—I was too quiet in school for people to take much notice of me—and Mr. Simon was oblivious as usual. All day I was dragging behind, walking slowly so it wouldn't look like I was limping. At lunch I started sweating. "Is it hot in here?" I asked my friends, who shook their heads and said they were cold.

In the bathroom, I propped my foot on the toilet seat and gagged as I peeled away the paper towel and saw the congealed blood. The skin around the cut had gotten puffy. I could feel my pulse beating in the wound. More hydrogen peroxide, more paper towels. On the way home, I decided, I would get proper bandages.

By third period I was feeling dizzy again. By fourth period I was flushed and feverish and I thought I might pass out if I tried to play my flute. The idea of all that air rushing out of me, air I needed, air that would be hard to get back, made me feel even sicker. I didn't have anyone to call me out of class, though. My mom had only listed herself on the form the school sent home. So I stood by the front entrance for a second, considering. The parking lot monitor had parked his suv at the curb and was chatting with the ladies in the main office.

The engine of my mom's car whined brightly when I turned it on. I didn't look in the rearview mirror as I drove away from the school. Maybe Jamie would try to return to the other world, so that she could finish the fight and be with her love—only to find that she couldn't return because she'd already died in that world. There was only this world, her home, and the only option was to find a way for Hayden to get here.

At home, I rolled pickles up in deli turkey and dipped them in mayo. I wasn't that hungry but hadn't eaten much the last few days.

I got cold again, wrapped myself in the throw blanket and shivered while reruns of *Gilmore Girls* played. I watched with glazed eyes, one episode after another, the bubbly music rising and falling over me. I'd seen them all before but the show was comforting.

My mom called a little while later. I tried to be polite, told her everything was fine, and she told me she was having the time of her life. She'd held a hose over the dock at the last marina so she could give fresh water to the manatees that had swum up out of curiosity. Ken's idea, she said, as though to prove he was gentle or something.

She sounded happier than she'd been in weeks, and I thought it was probably because she was away from me. I should've let it go but I couldn't help it. "You know, it's illegal to interact with manatees," I said. "You're not supposed to give them water. You're supposed to just watch them."

My mother sighed.

"I'm just saying, if Ken claims to be so knowledgeable about sailing, he should know this."

"Erica, please."

"Tell him to stop messing with the manatees or I'll report him!"

My mom's voice got really low; it was almost a growl. "If you ruin this for me," she said, "I'll never forgive you."

There was silence. It beat in my ears like it had wings. Never— such a big, lasting word, a word that keeps expanding and never stops, never gives up. It's its own universe, that word. She'd already decided he was more important than I was. And maybe I shouldn't have been so aggressive about the manatees—I mean, what's really so bad about giving them fresh water?—but my gut reaction was to find something wrong with whatever Ken did because he was wrong for us, and it wasn't fair, and my mom was going to uproot us and make me move like it was no big deal.

I'm not sure which of us hung up first. We'd already left the call, was the thing.

I fell asleep. I woke up sweating, kicked off the blanket, limped to the freezer and got an ice pack to put on my forehead. I turned on the light above the stove, rolled up my pajama shorts. The wound was sticky and inflamed; the veins surrounding it were like a map, the blue lines creeping farther and farther up and down my leg. I thought of Jamie shaking through a fever in the woods and waking up having made it through. She wouldn't need help. I found a Tylenol and went back to the couch.

The hours crossed the border into night slowly, on foot, and I moved in and out of sleep like my brain was a pendulum—one side sleep, one side restlessness. When I woke it was maybe to raccoons knocking over trash cans outside or night-bruised headlights slicing through the windows. Time felt loopy. The clock on the wall ticked but didn't tock. Water didn't help my dry mouth. What if I was getting too sick, getting past the point of being able to make rational decisions? I wondered if there were any leftover antibiotics in the medicine cabinet. It was possible, but I couldn't muster the energy to get up and look.

If Jamie were back in her home world, back in school, would she be distracted and uncertain? Would she think her time in the other world had all been a dream? She couldn't tell any grown-ups; they'd make her go to therapy, or worse. She'd stay quiet, burdened with a secret and heartbroken and not equipped to deal with any of it, but she'd get through it. At night she'd go to the pond where she'd fallen in and sit and breathe in the muddy smell of the water, tear up blades of grass and roll them between her fingers. She'd write messages on rocks and throw them into the pond, but they'd go unanswered. *Fall in*, her messages would say. Or *I'm waiting*. Or maybe she'll realize that even though she can't go back to the other world as a human, she can go back as a ghost. And she'll fall in and emerge shimmering, floating, a specter gliding across the blood-soaked fields of war. She'll find Hayden in a field tent, injured and dying, and she'll cloak him in her invisibility and guide him back to the pond where for the last time they'll look upon his world and understand that they'll never be able to return because she's dead and he's dying and the war is almost lost. So they'll sink into the pool together, the water a silk cloth around them, the other world breaking into smaller and smaller pieces until it disappears. They'll emerge gasping for air on the banks of the pond near Jamie's house. Hayden will be fading, like a filament in a light bulb starting to pop, and in Jamie's world she'll give him antibiotics and vitamins and clean water. And he'll recover.

I woke up hours later. The clock radio in my room had been sounding its alarm for a long time. School had started; first period was almost over, in fact. The phone rang and I let the answering machine get it. It was the attendance office, inquiring about my whereabouts since no one had called in to excuse me.

I looked at the cut and saw it had started to ooze yellow pus. I tried to stand but the ceiling started spinning, and I collapsed back onto the couch and put my head between my knees. I wasn't breathing very well. I got the phone and dialed my dad's number. It rang and rang and he never answered. All the anger I'd been wrestling with before now just felt like sadness. My mom just wanted love, and yet for some reason we couldn't figure out how she could have that without tearing everything apart.

If you ruin this for me, I'll never forgive you.

I wondered if Jamie would begin to feel like she'd made the wrong choice after bringing Hayden back with her. They might have fun at first—go boating on a lake, and he'll never have experienced speed so fast, and it will take his breath away, and he'll associate all those good highs with Jamie. He'll eat pizza for the first time and feel the tickling cool of air conditioning. But then depression will sink in because his friends and family back home have been destroyed, and he wasn't able to help them, and he won't feel like he belongs in this new place (even though somehow everyone speaks English in the book). He'll be homeless, because there's no way Jamie's parents will let a boy move into her room with her. He won't be vaccinated against the diseases of this world. He won't understand the politics. His past will be a fiction to everyone in this new world. He and Jamie will look at each other and think what a bad idea their being together had been.

"Oh my God."

I opened my eyes. The realtor stood across the room. I hadn't heard her open the door. The little box with the key—I'd forgotten about it. Usually she called before she brought people over, but maybe she had and I'd been sleeping, or maybe she called my mom's cell.

Behind the realtor stood a man and a woman. Their hands covered their mouths as they looked at me and at the blood on the floor and on the back door. The tangle of blankets and the blood that had leaked from my wound onto the couch. They looked horrified.

"Are you okay?" the man asked.

Nausea swelled inside me and I got up and tried to limp to the kitchen sink but threw up on the living room floor instead.

"Oh, honey," the realtor said. She dropped the folder she was carrying onto the coffee table and knelt beside me.

Without saying anything, I rolled up my shorts and showed her the cut. A horrified look darkened her face. She looked at the cut, then looked at me like I was a stranger, though we'd met before and she'd told me she'd played the flute in high school, too.

"Where's your mom?"

"I thought it would get better." I watched her dig her phone out of her purse. "Wait—don't call my mom!"

She wasn't. She was calling an ambulance. I wondered if a doctor would think I was crazy. I prodded the cut. It did look a lot worse.

I sort of knew then that the damage had already been done. It would be a long time before anyone would trust me again. This— this was what my mom would never forgive me for ruining.

Antibiotics dripped from an iv bag into the inner fold of my elbow. Machines beeped out my vitals. A psych evaluation was in the works, though I insisted I wasn't crazy. The hospital had called Sarah, who had called my mom, who was waiting on standby to get home.

Maybe Jamie and Hayden will run away and try to start a new life. Maybe they'll go back to the other world and live as ghosts, floating around for eternity like eerie balls of incandescence. It sounds good but probably won't be that much fun after a few days. All the things they love have to do with being alive.

I was stuck. I didn't know how to make the book something that wasn't depressing. I didn't know how to end it. It all seemed so small and senseless now, all my ideas, my book, my quest to get my mom to realize Ken's a jerk. Maybe one day I'll think bigger. Two years from now I'll graduate. Maybe then I'll be on my way to college, or I'll save up for my own car and drive to a place where people are just waiting for a stranger to come to town.

V

Skin

A theater company comes to Newark in midsummer to perform a production of *Romeo and Juliet* in Military Park. All day the sky looks thunderous. The dark bellies of the clouds sag toward the ground, and the air seems to sulk through the city, brooding. I check Military Park's Twitter feed to make sure the performance is still happening, and whoever is tweeting reassures us that it is, that rain or shine the show will go on. So at 7:00 p.m., I text Aamina to see if she wants to meet me there, and I leave the apartment and walk alone toward the expansive green lawn of the park.

I come upon a small set, just a backdrop of a medieval town and a few chairs pushed together to serve as Juliet's balcony. There are rows of folding chairs set up for the audience, and they're mostly empty. I sit in one on the end of a row and look around the park, which was revitalized last year and is now manicured, with gorgeous bushes of purple hydrangeas along the walkways. A Japanese maple burns red behind the set. Beyond, the Gutzon Borglum statue of American wars towers over the grass: Revolutionary War soldiers morph into Civil War soldiers who become the soldiers of the twentieth century. From above, the park takes the shape of a sword, and the statue is its hilt. The blade, once a reflecting pool, is now a vibrant bed for two thousand red pansies.

I read about the revitalization on the Military Park website, and I've spent my summer days since Patrick left reading here.

The park manager walks among the chairs with a clipboard, asking people to sign up for the mailing list. She has a big smile and beautiful blue braids twisted into a pile on her head. "I'm already on it," I say, and then she recognizes me and says it's good to see me again.

Aamina dashes across the park lawn late, just as the men are roaring through the streets of Verona in their billowy white shirts.

"What did I miss?" she says, laughing, as she slips breathless into the chair next to mine.

"Well, there are these two families," I say. "Believe it or not they cut out the chorus in the beginning. How are we supposed to know what the 'two hours' traffic of our stage' will be?"

"Two hours?" Aamina checks her watch. "Really?"

"One," I whisper. "They abridged it."

Someone shushes us. Romeo sulks over Rosaline. Juliet ponders marriage. The actors are young, students at a musical theater school somewhere in New Jersey. Even though they've abridged the play, they seem to be hitting all the main points. They're earnest, but a few of them hit the lines just right. I lean my chin on my fist, watching.

The weather in Newark builds a tension of its own. A quiet wind turns into a sharp one that blows dirt in our faces from a construction site across the street. They're building a Whole Foods, and a little way down Broad Street they're raising the new Prudential Tower. A woman sitting near me wraps a scarf around her head. When we get to the part where "parting is such sweet sorrow," the backdrop falls forward, revealing the costume rack and the offstage actors behind it, and everyone laughs. The company takes five to reset the stage, and my eyes wander around the park. That's when I see Patrick walking nearby. His head is bowed against the wind and he's wearing his red spring jacket.

I stand up. I almost go to him, but a fierce gust of wind blows dust in my eyes. The dust blinds me and forces me back into my seat. When I've wiped my eyes clear, Patrick is gone.

"What?" Aamina asks, looking over her shoulder.

"Nothing," I say. "I thought I saw . . ."

"Oh no," she says, taking my hand. "You're staying here."

The actors can't get the backdrop to stay upright in this wind. We hear a ripping sound nearby. Atop the skeleton of the new Prudential Tower a construction tarp has torn free and spins above the skyline. An unoccupied chair topples. A low rumble of thunder takes the whole evening in its grasp and shakes it. The park manager hurries to talk to the director of the play, and as the first fat drops of rain are falling they call off the rest of the production.

The small audience scatters. Most of Military Park has emptied; a few people are huddled under the bus shelter on Broad Street. The rain is picking up, but Aamina and I walk slowly toward the fancy cocktail bar on Halsey Street, the one where we know I won't run into Patrick.

"That was cute," Aamina says. "The play."

Two martinis appear before us. Dirty gin for me, dirty vodka for Aamina.

"That doesn't sound like a compliment."

"*Cute* is a compliment."

"What if someone called your poetry cute?"

"My poetry isn't cute."

"See?"

We laugh. Aamina suggests another drink when we finish our first.

"You sure?" I ask. "One is good, two is too many, and three's not enough."

"Stop it," Aamina says, signaling the waiter. "Tell me you wrote something down today."

"You know, Aamina," I say. "I think I'm going to write a book about a woman who drinks a magic martini and is bestowed with the superpower of never spilling a drop when she carries her drink from the bar to her table."

"I'm not going to hang out with you anymore if you keep this up."

"Come on, though, isn't that a pretty good superpower? You'd take it if offered. You don't have to trade anything for it. I would take it."

"Of course you would," Aamina says—and it makes me blush, it makes me think I really shouldn't order that third drink.

Later, we part ways, and the wind and rain force me homeward. I cut through Washington Park, the scraggly cousin to Military Park. I haven't read yet if they'll revitalize it or not. Even though it's July, the city hasn't undecorated a squat pine tree strung with lights and ribbons for the winter holidays. The grass grows anemically, but the John Massey Rhind statue of George Washington and his horse still holds forth at the corner of Broad and Washington Place. I pay attention to the history of places because my father loved history.

When I was a child I always kept a close eye on my father because he made me curious, he was so quiet and removed and I felt he needed protection. I would see him hide his canisters of pills around the house. Vicodin, Oxy, Xanax, that sort of thing—those were his favorites. I turned the bottles over in my hands, examined the labels, and then returned them to their hiding places. Because I loved him, and because I believed he had a reason for hiding these things, I didn't tell my mother. Mostly I could forget that I'd seen him tucking pills behind books on the shelf or in garment bags in his closet, but I knew, too, that there was something to hide, and that if I told my mother then she would divorce him.

Across Washington Street, the symmetrical face of the Ballantine mansion is dark, stately. I wait for the light to change even though there are no cars coming. Once I grew into a teenager, and I could see more clearly the ways my dad was hurting our family, I shunned him. Shut him out. Didn't help him through his illness. I didn't even think of him as sick, just as someone who couldn't help himself. When I was sixteen, and he left to go to rehab just as my mom was finally divorcing him, I told him I never wanted to see him again.

We did see each other again, but not very many times. For my mother, his death was the closure to her grief. For me it was just the beginning.

I come up to my house and am happy to see Per outside. I need someone to lift me from my memories. I accept eagerly when he invites me inside for a drink. When Patrick was staying with me I saw Per and Thora less frequently, and now that he's gone I hope they'll welcome me back.

The babies are asleep in the front room of the downstairs apartment, and the door to the back room is closed to keep noise from a museum wedding out. I try not to stumble or trip on the toys scattered on the floor. There are no windows in the middle room, with the small kitchen and an open space for the table, but Thora has lit candles, and a soft yellow bulb glows in a lamp on a shelf stacked with books and houseplants. We need more oxygen in the house, Thora had said when she brought the plants home. The very first time I met her, she was on the stoop repotting a zz plant. Ralph and I had just moved in.

There's the lovely sound of wine splashing into the bottom of a glass. I look up to see Thora's filled three. I love the feeling I get being in their kitchen with them at night. The only light is soft and artificial—we're tucked in the middle of a row of brownstones, tucked in the middle of the house. We're safe.

We clink glasses. I tell my neighbors about the show, how it had gotten canceled, but next time the company performs—at the end of August—we should go together and they can bring the babies.

Per and Thora exchange a glance. I take an uncomfortable sip of wine and comb over my words, worried I said something stupid or offensive.

"We have some news," Thora says. "We're going back to Denmark."

It's gotten too hard to live in America, they say. They'd like more space than what our brownstone offers, but instead of finding a new apartment they'll return to Copenhagen, where they're from, and where they'll have free health care and where the quality of life is much higher.

"We loved our New York party days," Per says. "But they're over."

We laugh, and I agree with them about everything—if given the option of free health care, I would take it. "It's cold there, right?" I ask. It's the only negative thing I can think of.

"It is," Thora says, but she tells me that in Denmark, snow is cleared with large brushes, and she can't believe Americans still tear up their roads with plows.

"What will you do in Denmark?" I ask. "Besides paint."

Per shrugs. "There are a lot of unknowns, Marie."

I smile, because he seems fine with the unknowns, and I'm impressed that Per isn't catastrophizing. He sips calmly and puts his hand on Thora's hand absently. Their daughters sleeping in the other room make the unknowns something to be conquered, not surrendered to.

"Well," I say. "I'll never find neighbors as good as you."

"Oh, not true," Thora says. "You'll be happy not to have babes crying in the night."

I insist that they've never once woken me. In fact, I love hearing them squeal in the mornings.

Their news has made it difficult to shift to a new topic; we find ourselves circling back to their preparations, their timeline, getting the EU passports for the babies at the embassy in New York. After a while the bottle of wine is gone, and as Thora takes her last sip, one of the babies starts to cry. "What timing," she says, and she starts to clear away the glasses but I tell her I'll do the dishes. She disappears into the babies' bedroom while I wash the glasses and Per searches in the dish rack for the pacifiers. We hug, and though they're not moving until later in the summer, it feels like we're saying goodbye.

I visit Thora in the evenings, and we talk about the plans they've made, each of us holding a baby. She tells me what belongings they're leaving here and what they're taking with them. She gestures vaguely in the direction of a storage unit a few miles away and complains that it's full of Per's unsold paintings. It would cost a fortune to ship them to Denmark.

I tell her I'll be their U.S.-based art dealer. Just bring them upstairs, I say.

She asks if I'm serious. "Of course," I say. "No one uses the second bedroom. It was Ralph's office, but I like to work at the kitchen table."

Thora looks startled. I haven't mentioned Ralph casually since he left. Then she shrugs. "I'll talk to Per about it."

One day Per shows up with a U-Haul and brings a dozen large canvases into my apartment. I choose one for him to hang on the wall. It's a depressing scene of a cemetery next to a baseball diamond, but in the right corner is a patch of bright blue sky where the clouds have parted.

The next day, walking home from the train, I'm thinking about how the painting looks on my wall. Before I left that morning, I stood before it for several minutes just taking it in. Learning its specifics. When I reach my house, I come upon Patrick sitting on my stoop.

"Hello," I say.

"Hi," he says.

My hand twitches toward my keys in my pocket, I'm itching to let him in.

I sit down next to him instead of opening the door. I snake my arm through his and lean my head on his shoulder. I tell him the truth, which is that I miss him. There are no visible stars, the lights are too bright, but I search the hazy dark sky for something to focus on. Each minute that passes is another minute that I don't let him into my apartment. I think of my mother, who worries that I've inherited her and my father's addictive traits. I squeeze his arm harder.

"Maybe we need each other," he says.

"I don't know," I reply.

The night gets old this way. When he throws up what he's been drinking, I care too much for him not to let him inside. I bring him in and get him settled on the couch. I return to the stoop with a pitcher of water to clean the sidewalk, my beautiful brick sidewalk on my quiet, beloved street.

I measure the waning of summer by the movies that play in Military Park on Tuesday nights. Each week the movie begins when the sky is completely dark, earlier and earlier until soon I'm not home from work in time to catch the beginning of the film.

I haven't let Patrick back in since the night I found him on my stoop, though he texts me, and I sometimes text him back, and then I have to convince myself all over again that it's best just to let things go.

August comes to an end, and it brings the departure of Per and Thora. I help them pack the last of their things and see them off the day they leave for the airport. I hold one of the babies as Per loads the cab. I watch the car turn the corner, and when it's gone I go inside and look into the spare bedroom that's so packed with Per's paintings I can barely maneuver around them.

I pull out a few storage tubs that are filled with things I took from my father's apartment after he died. I finally feel intrepid enough to sort through which things to keep and which to discard.

I find a case of burned DVDs, labeled with the names of songs. My laptop is old and has a DVD drive so I pop in the first disk. On the DVD my father recorded himself playing his guitar and singing, and since I haven't seen him or heard his voice in almost four years, the tears come without warning. "Next," he says, "Gordon Lightfoot's 'Did She Mention My Name?'"

He looks at the camera before he starts playing. "A little bit of trivia—Marie, this is the first song you ever heard, in the hospital, the night you were born. I don't know why your mom allowed it. She was probably in too much pain to care."

I watch the video again and again because he's talking to me. We're talking, or as close as we'll ever come again to talking. At the end of the video he recounts also having played the song to my mother on the second night of their honeymoon.

"A bad idea," he says, shaking his head and looking away from the camera. "Bad, bad idea."

The first time my dad met Ralph, we were at the lake house in Michigan, the house we later sold, but the three of us spent the weekend there—we were awkward at first, but then comfortable around each other.

He came into the house from the porch where he'd been smoking as we were readying to leave on the last day.

"The verdict is in," he says. "I like Ralph."

Hearing those words had made me so happy then. I'm about to text Patrick to ask him to come over when the doorbell rings. It's the mail carrier. She extends a package for Thora my way, and I'm about to tell her they've moved, but a letter from my insurance company distracts me. It's thick and is stamped Urgent. I put the package on the hallway table, I'll have to forward it later, and I tear open the letter.

The company is bankrupt, the letter says. I'll have coverage through the end of September, but afterward the company will be liquidated.

"Oh, fuck," I say, because they'd just approved an expensive infusion drug, the first drug I've tried that has helped my joint dysfunction and my fatigue.

I forget about Patrick. I look for a new plan on the internet, but most carriers seem to have left the New Jersey marketplace, and none of the remaining options covers the drug. I could buy a plan from a different carrier off the marketplace, but my search makes it clear I need the government subsidy. I don't know what to search for next. Google stares back at me. I wish Thora were here. We could at least talk about universal health care in Denmark and agree that it makes much more sense.

"Why don't you move to Brooklyn?" my mother says on the phone. "You work in the city."

I always call her when I already know the answer to a question but don't want to listen to myself. I look out my window. Pink evening light falls on the brick buildings across the street.

"It's so expensive there," I say.

"Well," she says, "you'll have to weigh the difference in cost. The difference between paying for the drug and paying more in rent."

"I mean, it's not a *lifesaving* drug," I say. "It just improves my quality of life."

My mom laughs.

"What's funny?"

"Can I ask what you see is the difference?"

I don't want to leave Newark, but I find a health insurance plan on the New York marketplace, which will start January 1. I look for an apartment. My mom has to cosign, which makes me feel ashamed, but once I have an address, I can lock in the plan. I'll have a gap of three months between my old insurance ending and the new insurance beginning, so I refill my medications and see all my doctors and suck every last dime from the insurance company before they turn out the lights.

I could leave Newark without ever telling Patrick. I could block his number and when he next shows up at my apartment, he'll find it empty. But since finding my dad's DVDs I've become obsessed with closure, so I text him and ask to meet for a drink at the cocktail bar on Halsey Street, where Aamina and I go together. It has a leafy patio strung with bare white light bulbs. It's different from our old haunt, the dive bar, so maybe that will encourage us to behave. He's standing outside when I get there, his thumb caressing his phone screen, and when he sees me approaching he gives me a thumbs up, which makes me laugh.

We get a table outside and wait a long time for our drinks, but I'm okay with the wait. There are wet leaves pressed to the brick patio and the air is cool, damp, and clean.

Patrick sighs and looks at me with a sad smile when I tell him I'm leaving. He picks up the coaster and taps it against the table.

"It's only ten miles away," I say.

"Ten miles, with eight million people in between."

Then he says, with some love in his voice, that I'm going to become boring like all the other people our age moving to Brooklyn.

"You might not be wrong," I say. "But I was boring here, too."

"No, you weren't." He brandishes his pint glass. "Perish the thought."

Our server comes to place a flickering tea light on the table and clear our empty glasses. Against my better judgment I agree to a second round. The light rain from earlier in the day returns, and Patrick raises the table umbrella so the droplets bead down the fabric. It gets dark, but we're the only ones outside and no one from the restaurant has plugged in the string lights yet. I can barely see Patrick's face across the table. I want to end things the way we began them, by bringing the people we've lost to the table, except this time I want to prove to Patrick—and to myself—that if his friend and my father were still alive, we'd all be ready to be happy with one another.

"What do you miss the most about Sam?" I ask. "I mean good things about him."

Patrick rubs his neck so hard it turns red. "I don't know," he says.

"Come on. One good thing."

Patrick sighs. "He laughed easily. Even when things weren't that funny. That made me feel good about myself."

"That's good," I say. "When we met, would you've been able to come up with that?"

Patrick shrugs. I can tell he doesn't want to talk about the night we met. I ask him what's wrong, and he says, "When you leave, there won't be any chance of running into me again."

"We were good at that. Running into each other. More often than not, though, I think we orchestrated it. Time to stop living a lie, Patrick."

I mean to be funny, but his smile fades.

"I get it," he says. "I'm a fuckup."

"You're young enough that it's okay to be a fuckup. I can't keep living my life like this. I have things I should be doing."

"And I don't?" He looks offended. "I don't have things I should be doing?"

"You do. You just have more time to do them. I've only had one type of job my whole life, and I'm tired of being an assistant to power-hungry men." I narrow my eyes. "Like the type you're going to be when you finish business school."

Patrick chortles. "Remind me of this conversation when I have an assistant someday. If I have an assistant."

What he says implies a future in which we'll still be in touch. I think of Yuejin, my landlord, and his fatalism. If it's going to happen then it's going to happen.

When I don't respond, Patrick clears his throat and goes on. "But you're writing here. That's something."

"I'm not really writing here."

Patrick tilts his beer so the meniscus slides up the glass. "I wonder what Sam and your dad would say about us. Us together."

"I think they'd be happy we weren't alone," I say. "For this time, I mean."

"I think they'd think it was weird. Meeting at a bar in a sushi restaurant."

I smile. "Maybe."

"You know," he says, brightened by having just realized something. "If Sam hadn't died I probably wouldn't have talked to you at the bar. I probably wouldn't have been in that bar. But look what happened, I got to meet you."

I laugh into my drink. It's an exciting thing to realize when you're twenty-three, that one thing leads to another. You may know this to be true earlier, but experiencing it comes with age. I want to poke fun at him but I don't want to leave a cynical impression on him. "You're right," I say. "If not for Per and Thora almost getting hurt the night at the party, I probably wouldn't have taken you home."

Patrick suggests a third drink, but I decline.

We hug for a long time on the sidewalk. Cars swoosh through puddles in the road, shooting up soft ferns of water. The humidity lays a black velvet cloak over our shoulders. In a year or two, the Whole Foods across the street—we're looking at it from the back now, and through the building is Military Park—will be finished, the gentrification of Halsey Street underway. This block used to be where you went to find methadone, Yuejin told me once. Now there's scaffolding and Coming Soon signs.

"I'm going to miss it here," I say, wiping tears from my eyes.

"You'll get over it," Patrick says. "It's getting bougie here."

Our hands meet without meaning to. They entwine. Maybe I'm already a few sips past making a mistake.

I'm leaving next week. What's one more night?

During my last lunch with Yuejin, I tell him to let me know if he ever decides to sell the brownstone. If I could scrape together a down payment, I'd snap it up without hesitation.

Yuejin waves the thought away and tells me I don't want anything to do with the property. "It's a mess," he says. "The heater is the original oil heater from the 1920s. There's no one alive who fixes those types of heaters anymore, so it's a pain when it breaks, and it costs me eight hundred per month to heat that building."

"Why didn't you charge me for utilities?" I ask, incredulous.

Yuejin shrugs. "It was too much, you wouldn't have stayed."

"Still," I say. "I'll put in a new heater. Natural gas or something."

"It's not up to code, the wiring. It needs sprinklers installed if you want to rent it out. Every time I return home I'm surprised to see it hasn't burned down."

"I'm glad you didn't tell me this before," I say. "I was very at peace in that brownstone."

"You'll like living in the thick of things," Yuejin says, smiling.

"But I'll miss you," I say. "And Laura and the kids."

My new apartment in Brooklyn doesn't have the quiet of Newark, but it has a garden where I spend the last nice days of fall, winter about to descend like a cold kiss on the city. There's no spare bedroom like there was in Newark, and I regret agreeing to store all of Per's paintings—they're crowding me out, stacked everywhere, and my cat tried to scratch the paint off one of them the other day. But at least, in a way, they remind me of home.

Though I've been here for more than a month, I haven't finished unpacking yet, so once the pregnancy test delivers the news that a hunch I had was right, that I am in fact pregnant, I sit among the boxes of books, knees tucked to my chest, and worry I've already ruined this baby's chances. For weeks I've been pregnant, and also taking blood thinners and an antirejection drug that can cause birth defects. I signed a form at the doctor's office when I started taking the drug, agreeing to stay on two forms of birth control—except I was lying, I only ever used one. And drinking, too. Drinking less than when I was with Patrick, at dinner when water hits my tongue it's not the taste I expect, but still, I've been drinking. And now I have to make the decision I was always threatening to make—a hard thing to do when you don't feel at home, because instead of staying in the place I did know, I did love, I had to cross state lines for health insurance, to live in the thick of things.

Tough Beauty

Greta's always got my back at parties, even last week when I cried about the tuba player in band who doesn't love me back. She put a breath strip in my mouth before I walked home so my mom wouldn't find out I was drinking. That's the difference between us: I'm more likely to fall apart, but Greta's tough. Sometimes I try to act like Greta but it's always clear I'm copying, like this one time midparty when Greta took someone's macaw from its cage and let it sit on her shoulder. Later I coaxed the same parrot onto my arm, but it bit me right next to my eye.

I took it too far that night with the parrot. Earlier Greta had caught me diluting her drink with club soda—I was worried she was getting drunk too fast—and shame burned in my cheeks as I watched her expression darken. After that I took shots, which I hate doing, just to prove I was fun.

What I like more than the parties is just being alone with Greta, taking breaks from acting boy crazy and drinking. Greta and I like to spend time together reading, or Greta will lay down her tarot cards and we'll decide what our lives are going to look like. This is what it used to be like all the time—the two of us together, not really needing anyone else—but then sophomore year came around and Greta started hanging out with popular kids. I've been trying to fit in ever since.

Sometimes I think I'd be happier hanging out with kids from band, but Greta's my best friend. I can't just leave her behind, even if the other day, when we were reading the tarot, she said she felt more special than our town, Hollis Hills, would let her be.

For a minute the silence between us was sad, because she didn't say I was special, too. I like Hollis Hills. I like taking lonely walks around town. But the sadness passed because we still have two years left of high school, two years that seem endless. It's summer, and school's out, and next year we're going to be upperclassmen. We have coveted jobs at the swim club—me in the Snack Shack, Greta as a lifeguard.

One day at work Greta points out this new guy while we're both on our break, sharing an armchair and a can of Coke. He's been around the pool this past week, painting the buildings. He looks older, and everyone knows it's hot to be older.

"His name's Ian," Greta says. "He just moved back in with his mom last spring. She's my neighbor."

"Have you talked to him?" I ask.

"Barely," she says.

Ian's wearing cargo shorts and a holey, paint-stained T-shirt. His muscles flex as he paints the eaves, and his eyes are hidden behind sunglasses. He must feel my gaze because he turns and catches it. I look away but not quickly enough. When I look back, he's on his way over. My heart pounds because I think he's coming over for *me*, but when he's standing in front of us, he stares at Greta.

He holds out his hand for me to shake, and I shake it even though it's crusty with dried paint. He keeps his eyes on Greta, though. He says, "I saw you outside your house this morning."

"Oh," Greta says. "I didn't see you."

The feeling in the air has changed now that he's here. I avert my eyes to give him and Greta some privacy, unsure of whether or not I should just slink away without saying anything.

The pool spreads gelatinously before us, mostly full of bobbing children. One boy splashes another—a big wave of water right in the face—and Greta blows her whistle. "No horseplay!" she yells.

"No horseplay?" Ian says. "That's a shame."

The pool is closed the next day because of thunderstorms, and I'm grateful for the break, not from work but from drinking. Every night after the pool closes we drink, and I'm starting to feel ill all the time from trying to keep up with Greta.

During a pause in the rain, Greta comes to pick me up, and she takes me back to her house. The sky looks like the skin of a watermelon: green swirls of angry clouds. Once we're there, Greta showers. I tell her she could get struck by lightning in there, but she says that's an urban myth.

It's early afternoon but the gloom outside darkens Greta's bedroom; shadows accumulate in the corners, cottony and comforting. I curl up on her bed and listen to the shower compete with the rain. We feel at home in each other's houses. Our moms are gone a lot, so no matter whose house we're at, we have the run of the place.

Ingrid (Greta's mom) and Mary-Anne (mine) are both single moms with jobs and Yahoo! Singles profiles. Ingrid's an attorney, and my mom works as a secretary and is taking night classes to become a paralegal. Sometimes I think the best my mom could do is work for Greta's mom. When it comes to men, though, they both married duds. Greta and I hardly ever see our dads.

We used to just do homework or lounge in Greta's room after school, but then Greta got her license and an ancient Honda Civic, and we started going places, just driving and talking. I'm a good listener. Greta says she doesn't know a better one.

Ian's been bobbing up in my mind since yesterday. He won't stay out of it, and trying not to think of him is like trying to keep a plastic bottle submerged in water. It's not that I'm interested in him; it's just that I wonder why I can't captivate attention the way Greta can.

I grab a book from Greta's nightstand in a feeble attempt to think of something else. When Greta comes in with a towel wrapped around her head she snaps on the overhead light. "You'll wear out your eyes reading in the dark," she says.

Greta sits cross-legged on the floor and rubs lotion on her face, her palms pulling her cheeks taut. She has red hair the color of wet bricks, and one crooked incisor that makes her smile lively. Her cutoffs are always just a little bit shorter than mine. As she brushes her hair, she says, "Can I tell you a secret?"

I put the book down to let her know I'm listening.

"Well," she says. "Ian and I are sort of seeing each other."

"What? You told me yesterday you hadn't even met him."

Greta gives me a look like I'm slow to catch on. "We're neighbors. We see each other all the time. I just didn't want it to get out at the pool, you know?"

The book falls shut in my hands. My thoughts dart around, all in turmoil.

Greta sees it, the hurt in my expression. "Don't get all wounded," she says.

"Why didn't you tell me sooner?"

"Because I didn't want you to mother me." Greta's voice is like a sharpened pencil. She scowls even as she dabs lavender eye shadow into the creases of her eyelids.

I must look stricken, because Greta softens. "There's nothing for you to worry about, E."

"Totally," I say, trying to recover. "But he's so old."

"He's twenty-one. It's not that weird."

I let the idea of it sink in. I'm dying to know more, but I don't know how to pick up the threads of the conversation.

"Do you want to lay out the cards?" Greta says finally. She traps strands of her hair between her fingers and twists them into a braid. In just a few minutes she'll have gathered a crown of hair around her head, and she'll look ready for anything. It takes me an hour at least to interrogate my hair with a straightener until it confesses. I put in so much effort with so little payoff. I hope Greta interprets something good in the cards.

"Yes," I say. "Outside? The cards are always better when you read them outside."

Greta shrugs. She doesn't believe me, that I get better results with the cards outside, but we gather ourselves and leave her bedroom. Her porch is a long slab of concrete with a high, second-story pavilion held up by wooden pillars. It's raining all around us, but the porch is dry. The raindrops, big as eyes, give us privacy. We sit cross-legged. I get the chills when I lay out the cards in a Celtic cross and flip over the first one, as though there's real magic in them. Greta won't touch the cards, because she wants the reading to be about my energy. Sometimes I try to read the cards for Greta, but I need *Learning the Tarot* open in my lap and it takes too long. Greta gets bored.

"Oh," Greta says, pointing to a card. "The chariot. This is an interesting one to get for the center card."

She's about to explain when Ian steps out onto his porch. Greta's attention snags, and the cards turn lifeless on the cement. I go where her attention is and watch Ian as he snaps a lighter in the breeze. Of course he smokes, and even though it's a cliché, I'm sort of into it.

"He looks so melancholy," Greta says, and I can tell she loves it. She stands and calls his name. A smile lights his face immediately. He runs through the garden with just a few springs and then he soars, he's actually in the air for a moment, and his boots land hard on the porch. He looks proud, as though he's just cleared a row of burning cars on a motorcycle. He envelops Greta in a soggy hug.

"Stop, stop!" She folds her arms over her chest, where he's gotten her tank top wet, but her voice glimmers with laughter.

"Elizabeth!" he says, and he hugs me, too. I'm surprised by the genuine affection in his voice. How can he be happy to see me when I've only met him once?

The tarot cards are forgotten. Ian settles into one of Greta's cushioned rocking chairs.

"So, where did you move here from?" I ask.

"I was in Chicago a few years."

"How could you stand to leave Chicago for Hollis Hills?" Greta asks. "This place stunts your growth."

"Hollis Hills isn't that bad," I say.

I regret saying it, because Greta rolls her eyes.

"I'm serious," she says. "They put something in the water that kills brain cells."

"Chicago kind of chewed me up and spit me out," Ian says. "Cities are hard."

Greta nods sympathetically. She seems to like him, and I usually agree with Greta about people. Ian's been nothing but nice to me, but I still feel outcast, and the feeling pits me against him, and I don't know why.

"How did Chicago chew you up?" I ask.

"It's complicated." Ian waves a hand as though to clear away the conversation.

I think about asking for more information—complicated how?—but he and Greta have sunk into a private conversation, like they did at work yesterday. I go inside for Cokes and chips just so I don't feel so useless.

The next day at the pool, it's like the storm never happened. The sun tractor beams all the puddles from the glass tables and lounge chairs. I wipe away the last of the moisture from the Snack Shack counter, then set out the ketchup and napkin dispensers, the salt and pepper, the cup full of straws. Ian's back again, and he starts painting the Snack Shack. I retreat from the order window, wash the floor and clean the ice cream cooler. I change the oil in the deep fryer. Ian starts singing "Ruby Tuesday" and I know he's singing to get my attention. At first I roll my eyes, but there's something about it, something sweet, and I feel like he knows to give attention when someone wants it. I think the word is *charisma*. Greta has it. Ingrid has it, smiling and showing some leg in her Yahoo! Singles photo. Sometimes I glimpse it in myself, but as soon as I see it, it dies, like a glow bug caught in a jar.

Ian sticks his head through the order window. "You seem blue," he says.

The truth is I've been agonizing over what Greta said, about how I mother her. I feel the urge to renew my efforts to ignore my worries and be more like her.

"I'm fine," I say.

He smiles at me. He's being kind. I think I should reciprocate, so I take out an ice cream bar and hand it to him.

The day becomes so hot and humid that most people choose to stay inside in the air conditioning. A fan in the Snack Shack bears oscillating witness to my boredom. Ian moves his paint buckets and ladder from the Snack Shack to the clubhouse, though he takes frequent breaks to linger under Greta's lifeguard stand, or to dare me to say something vulgar over the PA system. I pick up the handset once, ready to curse, but I chicken out. As the day goes on, I start to look forward to his visits to my window. It's not personal, I tell myself. It's just that getting attention is nice.

Everyone complains and sweats, but this is Michigan in the summer: the rain yesterday brought a chilly gloom, only to be swiped away by heat today. I love how curious the weather is, how desperate for attention it seems.

Finally, the pool closes. The gates swing shut, the assistant manager roars off in her car, and the party starts. Every night, after hours, we party. Someone puts music over the PA. I'm handed my first drink and I gulp it down. Everyone else is kissing, swimming, laughing. We all have a sun-worn look: hair washed in pool water, late nights, work in the morning, red sunburns. Those of us who drink often have had so many bad hangovers already that the miserable mornings combine to form one big everlasting summer hangover.

Just thinking of alcohol tonight, of the thick liquid sliding down my throat, turns my stomach. I've just had a little too much lately, have spent one too many nights this summer clutching the toilet, with the fan on and the water running, trying to throw up quietly so my mom won't hear. It would be so nice to take a long, lonely walk home, with the chirps of crickets leaping all around me, the sound of a car passing and the brief, second-long thrill I get thinking the car might stop, and I'll meet a stranger who might change my life. And then the relief I feel when the car passes. Night is full of rushes like this, rushes that renew you—but I only feel these rushes when I'm alone. I'm too nervous around other people to feel anything but anxiety.

I see Greta across the pool. She's on her lifeguard stand. Ian's standing beneath her, holding one of her feet in his hand. People are eyeing them. It's a gossip-worthy sight, but platonic enough to pass as Greta being just plain cool.

I want to stand near her but there's no room for me when she's with Ian. That much is clear even though it's only been a few days since I've met him. I have nowhere else to go, though. My body is awkward and gangly and takes up too much space. I realize I'm clutching my left forearm with my right hand, as though the police are questioning me. How is it that no one else here looks like me—no one else's brain is signaling their bodies to be terrified by all the ways things could go wrong, all the ways you could embarrass yourself for good, the final embarrassment that makes you a social Typhoid Mary.

I inch closer to Greta, just to make it look like I'm headed somewhere. I wish I had my phone to look at but it's in my locker. I've already damaged it twice from pool water, and my mom has said no more repairs.

My toe catches the leg of a pool lounger and I stumble forward;

my knees and palms meet concrete and I feel the burn of tiny rocks getting pushed into my skin. Laughter seeps into the air behind me. I look over my shoulder and see some of Greta's friends—Wendy and Ryan—just sitting there smirking, hiding their laughter behind their hands.

"Had too much to drink?" Ryan asks.

I've had hardly anything, but I immediately react the way I think he wants me to: I throw my hair back and try to look loose limbed. I say, "I am *so* wasted."

Their smirks deepen.

"He was kidding," Wendy says. "We know you're not drunk."

Shame takes my breath away. My eyes dart to where Greta is sitting. I see she's watching. She'll say something to help me, to chide her friends.

But then she looks away.

My heart fades in my chest, like the moon when it's out during the day. It's there, but barely visible.

I pull myself up. My knees and palms sting. Little bits of cement cling to my skin. I dust off slowly and move away. I hear Ryan whisper that I'm a poser.

The stinging I feel is from tears now. Greta still isn't looking at me so I walk past her. It's too late, but I look for something to drink anyway. Poser or not, what else is there for me to do?

I swallow one shot, then another. After the third, the world tilts a little and my mind is wrapped in a cozy blanket. I sit alone on the far side of the pool and watch Ian; he blurs in and out of focus. He's surrounded by Greta and her friends, gesturing as he speaks, occasionally making the group erupt in laughter.

He's the one who doesn't belong here, so why am I the one sitting by myself?

I look sullenly at the sky. I'm sitting beneath my precinct of stars but the constellations make no picture for me, not without Greta to point out the mythical figures and tell me their stories.

I look for more to drink. The drinks find their way to me like bugs to light. I'm the light. Or maybe the bug. I might be getting drunk faster because I'm alone. When you're with someone, talking, you drink more slowly, you expel some alcohol through your breath. Not so with me right now.

Cheers catch my attention. Greta climbs up the ladder to the diving board. When she's up there, she curtsies, then dives in—a smooth, long-limbed, graceful dive. People clap. *Whatever*, I think. I could do that.

I could do more than that.

Greta glides through the pool underwater and emerges on the shallow end. She hoists herself up, and by the time she turns my way I'm already halfway up the ladder to the high dive. The ground beneath me falls away, and sometimes it feels like I'm climbing sideways rather than up. My fingers sweat, and with each rung I climb I get less giddy, my idea seems less good, but I have no choice but to keep going: first rule of the diving boards is once you're up, you can't climb back down.

I'm up. I walk the plank. Below, necks crane, people murmur, and I put my feet in fourth position, shoot up on one toe, and do a pirouette with my arms over my hand.

I almost keep my balance at the end, but I tumble off the board. My forehead catches the rough edge and all the way down I spin my arms to try to keep from landing flat on my back in the water.

I hit the water hard; a muscle in my shoulder pulls loose from its tendon. Dazed, drunk, my heard hurt and spinning, I float beneath the surface for a few moments, like I'm just a ghost, or a memory, and the weightlessness makes me feel at ease.

Later I'll think that I didn't *need* saving; it's just that I'd had a shock and didn't quite realize, at first, I needed to kick, needed to breathe.

The surface of the water breaks again, and I feel the rush of a moving current. Two hands grab me beneath my arms and I'm suddenly above the surface, gasping for air. When I've wiped my eyes clear I'm looking right at Greta, her dark wet hair clinging to her face. Her eyes blaze—angry, annoyed. I see no trace of concern. For the first time, I look around at the people surrounding the pool. Maybe I'm being dramatic, but I swear no one looked worried.

She grabs my arm, pulls me kicking to the ladder.

When I'm out, she wraps a towel around me, leads me to a lounge chair, and pushes me gently into it. She gets close to my face. "Get your shit together," she hisses.

I wake up the next morning and in my sleepy haze, I have no idea where I am. There's something crunchy in my mouth, and when I spit frantically into my palm I see it's a leaf. I blink and the world straightens. I'm outside, lying in the lounge chair where Greta left me last night. My head throbs; I bring my fingers to the tender, blood-filled bruise on my forehead. I pull myself up, my shoulder aches, too, and I go about examining my body for all the drunken injuries I sustained. My raw knees and palms, my aching ankle.

It's early. I've never been here this early and the sunlight lands like netting on top of the water. A soft breeze sends calm ripples through the leaves, across the empty, shade-soaked concrete pool deck.

I try to summon memories of last night, but they're hazy. I remember the fall, I remember Greta wrapping me up in a towel, but not much else.

A thought trips into my mind: my mother. I search for my phone, but it's not on me, so I limp to the locker room and dig for it. I find it, finally. Its battery is about to die.

Are you coming home soon, love?

A few minutes later:

Never mind, Greta called and said your phone died. Have fun my love.

My heart sinks. I picture my mom in bed with the covers pulled over her legs, papers and textbooks fanned around her, plus emails from work chiming in, and then I don't respond, and she has to figure out what to do, if anything, about her daughter, drunk and loose in the night.

Good morning, Mom! I text now, so she knows I'm not dead.

I leave the pool wearing my bathing suit, with the towel wrapped around my waist, my flip-flops slapping the parking lot pavement wetly. I take them off; they're annoying. Before I've even decided where I'm going, I head in the direction of Greta's house, which is a short walk from here. The wooded road that leads away from the pool opens up to the wider country road that, if followed, brings you to town. Greta lives in a neighborhood on the town's outskirts. Insects engage in small skirmishes midair. Birds swoop into the fields, making big parabolas. The road is dirt but I don't put my shoes back on. If I bend over I feel like I might fall over and never be able to get up.

With Greta's house in sight, my heart starts to pound. Her words have slipped back into my memory: *Get your shit together*.

I'm walking up to her door when Ingrid steps outside, her head bowed to her phone. When she sees me, she jumps. She's dressed for work, carrying her car keys. She says, "Elizabeth, sweetie, are you all right?"

"Yes," I say, brushing hair over my face to cover the bruise. "I had to work really early, to clean the pool. Is Greta here?"

Ingrid inspects me. She looks at her watch, at the car, at Greta's window. She sighs.

"She's asleep inside, hon."

Just like my mom, she's always too busy, always wishing she had more time, always a little too ready to believe we're telling the truth. She inches toward her car.

"Have a good one!" I say, trying to sound cheerful, but my hangover is like a wood chipper and I spit the words out in an unused, choppy voice. Ingrid waves, then drives away.

Just as I'm about to slide open the glass door that's always unlocked, Greta emerges from the house next door. Ian's house. She walks slowly and cranes her neck toward the road, maybe checking for her mom's car. Strands of her hair are airborne in the wind. When she sees me, she stops. She looks me up and down. Her face is serious, but then she yawns, and the yawn collapses into laughter.

"You look like shit," she says.

"Speak for yourself," I say, but it's not true, she looks terrific, a little tired maybe, but beautiful all the same.

"Come inside," she says, "we'll have breakfast."

I follow Greta inside, and as I walk behind her I keep opening my mouth to say something, then closing it, then opening it again. I must look like a fish, my mouth pumping water. Before I've always been relieved that Greta forgets the ways she was annoyed with me, but this morning I don't feel ready to forget what she's said. She insults me and then applies the remedy of her attention, but small deposits of ridicule have been gathering in me ever since Greta started changing. She left me last night, and I was passed out and hurt, and now she's pretending it didn't happen. That's what hurts the most—that she carries no memory of me from day to day. Of course she *remembers* me, but it's not the same thing as mattering to someone.

She shakes cereal into a bowl in her kitchen. She asks what I want to eat, but I tell her I'm not hungry, so she shrugs and leans her elbows on the counter, shoveling big spoonfuls of cereal into her mouth.

So she's not going to talk first.

It takes all of my self-control not to start off by apologizing to her. I do owe her a thank you, though, so I say, "Thank you for helping me last night. Helping me out of the pool."

Greta rolls her eyes. "That was *torture* to watch, E. What were you thinking?"

I try to keep an even face, but there's a scowl inside of me, deepening.

"I was drunk," I say timidly.

"You were only drunk because Wendy and Ryan accused you of not being drunk."

"Not true," I say, my voice heating up. "I was drunk because I didn't have anything else to do. You were ignoring me and I'm not close with anyone else."

"You don't know them well because you never talk to them," Greta says. "They wonder why you're just standing around looking sullen."

"They're just not very nice," I say.

Greta drops her spoon into her bowl. "You're not my charge, you know. You have to learn to fend for yourself without doing stupid shit. You could've gone home if you were bored. If you don't like the people at the pool."

"They're not really the problem, though," I say. "It's Ian. Ian who's everywhere, who's changing things. He's so annoying—and so old. There's just something gross about him."

I don't mean it—not all of it, anyway. But I know it will get Greta's attention.

"Spare me," Greta says. Milk runs down her chin and she wipes it away angrily. "I don't need boy advice from you."

"He's not a boy," I mutter. "Old man is more like it."

"Shut up," Greta says. "Just stop talking."

"Look," I say, frightened a little by how angry Greta is—finding myself, as I always find myself, desperate for her not to stray too far from being happy with me. "I just want to help you. I don't want you to get hurt by this guy—he's clearly taking advantage of you. It's barely not illegal, what he's doing to you."

Greta turns cold. She dumps her cereal bowl in the sink, where it lands with a spin and a clatter. "You don't know anything about what we're doing together because I haven't told you, and am not ever going to. You don't own me. You're not my husband."

"First I'm your mother, now I'm your husband?" I say. "You're crazy. You just don't give a shit about me anymore and you don't want to be my friend but you're trying to find a way to make it my fault."

The self-pity that has always been so much a part of my everyday life swirls like a double helix inside of me, but this time, I can't let Greta see it. What she said—she's trying to hurt me, I realize. Maybe she doesn't realize it. Maybe she'll regret it. But if I back down, she'll only want to ridicule me more.

"I saved your life last night," she says. "Jesus Christ, what more do you want from me?"

"Uh, for you to not be the worst friend ever," I say snidely.

"You've been annoying the shit out of me. It's just not worth it anymore."

"I'm trying to help you."

"Well, you're not." She throws her hair up into a messy bun and grabs her keys from the counter. "I'm going for a drive. Be gone when I get back."

The door slams shut behind her. The house makes all the noises of a quiet house, the ticking and creaking and sighing of the foundation. I feel wronged, but also guilty, like I messed up big time, too. I look around desperately, like I could find the pieces of our friendship on the floor and put them back together, but there's nothing but the usual mess of Greta's house, the piles of mail and loose shoes and her lifeguard suit hanging to dry over the back of a chair.

Panic settles in: it's really over between us. My best friend doesn't want me anymore.

I find it strange that I don't feel empty inside. Instead I feel so energized I might burst. I want to do something that will leave a mark on Greta, but all I can think of is cleaning up the kitchen so she'll feel bad that I had to clean up after her—but she probably wouldn't even notice. I think about leaving her a note to tell her how much she'll regret taking me for granted, but I can already see the photos of the note pinging from phone to phone at the pool. The rumors that will spread about my attempt to make her miss me.

There's nothing left for me to do but leave. I put on one of her shirts and a pair of her gym shorts. I leave her towel, the one she wrapped me in, in the laundry room for Ingrid to wash. Cool morning air meets me when I open the door. I start down the road to walk the three miles home, feeling like I'm about to embark on the second phase of my life, the sad phase, the one without Greta, when a voice calls after me.

It's Ian, jogging down the road.

He looks completely jovial. A cigarette sits between his fingers. He's wearing a T-shirt with the sleeves rolled up; a tattoo of a sword pierces his bicep.

"You had a rough night last night!" There's laughter in his voice, but it's not cruel laughter. He nudges my hurt shoulder. I grimace. "Oh, shit!" he says. "Sorry!"

"Yeah," I say. "Last night was a real doozy."

As friendly as he's being, I'm ashamed of the way I look—bruised and dirty—and the fight with Greta is still echoing in my ears. I excuse myself, say I have to head home to clean up, when Ian pulls his car keys from his pocket.

"Let me drive you," he says. "You look like you could use the break."

I almost turn him down, but he's already walking backward toward where his car is parked on the street. I'm aching all over. My leg is bruised from where it hit the water. So I walk with him and climb in.

Greta's somewhere not too far away, tearing up the roads, her aviator sunglasses perched on her nose. The windows rolled down and the music up. Ian doesn't know anything about the fight, about what Greta said about me or what I said about him. Soon he'll know, but for now he doesn't. He's casually flipping through the radio stations, frowning at the offerings, finally reaching under my seat for a book of CDs. His arm brushes my leg, his face is near my knee, and when he straightens, I catch his forearm. I kiss him.

I'm smarter than this, better than this, less petty than this: but I want it this way anyway.

And the thing is: Ian doesn't pull away. I know it's nothing special about me; he's confirming what I thought all along, that he'll hook up with anyone. The fact that he kisses me back feeds my desire—not for him, but for some glimpse of attention, of affection. I know that later I'll feel sad about Greta, and I won't feel good that I was right about Ian, but right now I just feel like I want something, anything, and I don't know what it is so I'll just try everything.

Ian pulls me into his lap.

"This is an E. I haven't seen before," he says, his voice breathy, and I think he's stupid for saying it, but I kiss him again.

I know that, soon, Greta will return home, and she'll see us. Word will get out. Maybe I'll be praised for what I'm doing, maybe I'll be as cool as Greta, or maybe I'll be ridiculed. A slut, a backstabber. It could really go either way.

As I kiss Ian, Greta's tarot cards fan open in my mind. The chariot card—she said it was an interesting one to get for the center card, but she never told me why. I want to know badly all of a sudden. Maybe, if I'd asked her sooner, I would've known what to do today—I would know what it was I wanted.

Ian's hand crawls up my shirt.

I could look the chariot card up online, but the answer from the internet wouldn't be as good as if Greta told me herself.

Higher Power

Although Harris's ex-wife, Ella, had divorced him six years before, and it was bad at first, they'd grown friendlier over time. When Harris found out he needed quadruple bypass surgery and that the recovery would be long and painful, Ella flew from Michigan to South Dakota to help him out.

He'd called his daughter first, not asking her to come but hoping she might pick up on his hints and offer to fly out for a week. Lindsey sounded worried for him on the phone but also distracted. She was a college student. One day she would know what it was like to be sick but not now. But even so, he'd been hopeful his impending surgery would have had more of an effect on her. Maybe that was asking too much. They'd only just begun talking to each other again. He hadn't even seen her since the divorce. He'd tried, but for a long time she'd been too angry with him. He was sober now but hadn't been for much of her childhood. He often wondered what it would take for them to be friends again, or if they would ever be.

So he called Ella. She heard the question in his voice. She came to him even though travel was hard for her. Her ms had debilitated her in recent years. She needed a walker to get around, and trips to airports required that she be pushed in wheelchairs by underpaid airport staff.

Still, she came even though it was winter and bitter cold. She slept by his bed while he was in the hospital. The night before the surgery found Harris tangled in sleeplessness. iv bags of liquid medication were strung above them like mistletoe. Machines coughed out numbers. The blood pressure pump inflated around his arm automatically once every hour, but Ella dozed through all of this. Earlier that day, when his hospital gown had slipped off his shoulder and exposed his bare ass, she was a good sport. She said, "It's nothing I haven't seen before," and good memories of their old life together flooded back to him. But as the nurses wheeled Harris into the OR, and as the mask was fitted over his face, the memories became sad. He thought of the days when he and Ella shared prosperity if not happiness, when their togetherness had felt natural and perpetual, and how those days were gone forever, and then the anesthesia massaged his brain to sleep.

When he came out of sedation after the surgery, the pain was so great and the world pulsed in a disorienting way that made him believe he was dying. His heart rate soared and Ella held his hand as they put him back under—to give him a little more time to rest.

She stayed for two weeks. When he went home to his one-bedroom apartment (Ella had gotten the house all those years ago, but had lost it to the bank during the housing crisis, and now lived in a similar apartment herself), they watched movies together. The break from loneliness did his recovering heart a lot of good. He had someone to talk to. He told Ella about the good news he'd had right before the surgery: the advertising agency where he used to work before he'd been fired (for being drunk too often) had hidden pension funds from their employees. A retirement account with a hundred thousand dollars in it was to be set up in Harris's name. This came just in time: his savings were dwindling. He hadn't worked in a couple years, though for a while he'd worked for a small agency in Sioux Falls. Then the recession hit, and he was let go in a last-one-hired / first-one-fired sort of situation. Luckily, he was allowed to keep his old health insurance and pay for it himself. He had a vague idea that Obama was to thank for this, and he was indeed thankful.

Before the surgery, he'd flung hundreds of applications into the void of the internet. He had a profile on every job site there was.

He'd even flown to Missouri for an interview, though he could tell as soon as he sat down that they had no real intention of hiring him.

Ella congratulated him when he told her about the money. "You worked hard at that agency," she said, "up until the end, at least."

It was true. He'd won awards. He'd had a corner office. It had all collapsed around him, but for years his creativity flowed and he made money for the company by snapping his fingers. He'd made his and Ella's money disappear by snapping his fingers, too. There'd always been another paycheck, until the day the severance ran out.

Ella left Sioux Falls and Harris kept going to physical therapy. A month passed. Harris and Ella talked at first, but then Ella stopped calling. She was distracted by her own life. Lindsey didn't call much either, but that wasn't unusual. The last time they had spoken, she had made a comment about always being tired, and Harris worried she was depressed—he was sometimes depressed and had spent years feeling overlooked until he finally started taking drugs for it—but she didn't sound sad. Harris told her to call him if she needed anything. Another month passed and Harris felt a dark cloud engulf him once again.

He emailed Lindsey and told her how he was feeling.

I'm lonely out here, he wrote. *Send me a note when you have time and tell me how you are.*

Lindsey didn't respond. Harris's sadness sharpened into anger and roared through him like a motorcycle alone on the road in the middle of the night. Lindsey was a cold girl. But then the bad feelings deflated. His contempt for his unhappy angel never lasted long.

Then the money came in, gloriously six figured, and the money worked alchemy on his feelings, mixing them until they were golden and happy.

Harris turned fifty-six, another year having come and gone. He started dating a woman from AA named Claudia—a lifelong South Dakotan who wore camouflage and never cut her hair. She inspected wastewater treatment plants for the state but was planning to retire soon. Harris newly had a job as a copywriter for another agency. He'd had the same title in his twenties—he was a senior copywriter before he'd even turned thirty—but these were different times. He would have taken anything that came his way.

Things got serious with Claudia quickly. They both thought, What the hell? After a few months, they decided to move in together. After looking for rentals was unsatisfactory, they put a down payment on a house together, a small ranch with a big yard right on the edge of Sioux Falls, where the city met the prairie. Harris stood in the front yard as Claudia wrestled the big wooden For Sale sign out of the ground (the realtor was taking too long to come and get it, she said) and he thought it was nice to have one's own front yard.

They hadn't finished unpacking when Ella called, just a few weeks later. She said she'd done some thinking. She said it broke her heart to do this, but she felt she had no other choice.

"Half that money is mine," she said. "It's from a job you had when we were married."

Harris got a lawyer, who said there was no use fighting it because Ella was right. It wasn't so simple as just giving her half, so Harris still had to pay the lawyer, even though all the lawyer had done was tell Harris he'd lost. Harris's lawyer talked to Ella's lawyer to hammer out the details of Harris's losing. He charged five hundred dollars for each hour it took him to figure out how best to give Ella half the money.

Then the lawyer asked if Harris had a will, and Harris said he might as well make one, so they did that too, and he made it so everything would go to Lindsey. The two of them, Ella and Lindsey, had punted him out of their lives, and here he was giving them all his money.

He calmed down quickly. He was always getting angry and then calming down.

He left his lawyer's office after signing the paperwork and climbed into the Ford Escape he'd bought after the money had come in. He was still driving around with the temporary license plate taped to the back window. He wondered if they would buy it back, and how much of a hit he would take just for having driven it around for a month. He'd taken pretty good care of it. There was a stale muffin crumbling on the passenger-side floor, but he could vacuum that up with the car vac outside the Sinclair. It cost twenty-five cents for the car vac to run for a few minutes, which was all the time he needed.

Maybe he was getting ahead of himself. He rolled down the windows, adjusted the mirrors, and eased his way into the light Sioux Falls traffic. Maybe he wouldn't need to sell the car.

The bigger problem was that he hadn't told Claudia about Ella or the lawyers, maybe hoping Ella would change her mind. Now money that should be going toward the house was in Ella's pocket, and he hadn't put a brake on expenses he should have put a brake on.

He'd just had a pool guy over, and the pool guy had marked off the dimensions for a pool with posts and spray paint. There probably wouldn't be a pool now, just paint on the grass and posts with plastic flags flapping in the wind until Harris mowed everything away.

He tried to do calculations in his head but the numbers were recalcitrant to his efforts. He could only hold one figure at a time. It was like choosing fruit at the grocery store, only to have the whole pile topple because you picked the wrong apple from the middle, an apple that was really crucial to holding everything up.

Instead of going home, he drove to the DMV to get the plates for his car. It had taken him long enough. It was a thirty-minute drive to the DMV. Summer was upon them, and the neat rows of fields scrambled together, meeting at a point in the distance, then blew apart as Harris sped down the country road. Involuntarily Harris felt himself brighten. This gorgeous day spread before him, ready for him to fill it. Irrigation pivots snapped their heads back and forth in the fields. The first hint of green cabbages appeared.

Harris would've died without the surgery. He wasn't out of the woods, though. He needed to be careful. He'd had a cigarette the other day. The urge to smoke had felt like such a brilliant solution to all his problems, so he'd lit one up. It hadn't solved anything, just made him worry Claudia would smell it on him.

He approached the little city that held the county seat. Harris had to drive all this way because he lived in the part of Sioux Falls that crept into Lincoln County. It was a small town, its streets tree lined and quiet. At a stop sign he fiddled with the glove compartment until the latch popped open and his amber canister of Chantix appeared, the pills rattling, practically promising they would help him quit smoking. He took one. The tiny pill felt heavy on his tongue.

He waited in lines, took numbers, approached windows, filled out forms, and finally he left with his license plates. He would put them on right away. He kept tools in the trunk. He tore the temporary plate from the back window, crumpled it up, and tossed it in a garbage can at the edge of the parking lot.

Then he realized he only had a flathead screwdriver. He walked across the street, where there was a small hardware store, but they were sold out of Phillips-heads. Harris asked how that had happened, wasn't that something they always had, given its popularity?

The cashier shrugged.

He went back inside the DMV, but they had no tools he could use. He looked for his paper plate in the trash, but someone had dumped coffee out on top of it.

He stood by his car for a few minutes, thinking of what to do. A school bell rang. It was one of those bells you actually had to ring manually. Harris could see the schoolyard, kitty corner to the DMV. There was a kid in an orange safety vest pulling the rope and making the clapper swing. Harris decided he would just drive home without the plates on.

He got pulled over halfway. The state trooper approached his car, unhurried. Harris was ready with the window down.

"Where are your plates?" the trooper asked.

Harris explained the situation. He held up the plates in their plastic package.

"You'll have to put them on before driving any further," the trooper said.

"Do you have a Phillips-head screwdriver?" Harris asked.

The trooper seemed to be deciding whether or not it was reasonable for Harris not to have the right screwdriver with him. He stared off into distance, drummed his fingers on Harris's car door, and eventually sighed and wrote him a ticket.

"Go right away to the nearest hardware store and get a screwdriver." The trooper tore away the ticket and gave it to Harris.

Harris agreed, but instead he just went home, where he knew where he already had the right screwdriver.

Claudia asked him where he'd been. She was sitting in their new breakfast nook with its half-moon table. A mug of tea before her sent spirals of steam into the air. The sun came strongly between them, the light level with their faces. Her eyes squinted and captured him suspiciously as he stood with his hands in his pockets, rattling change.

He broke down and told her everything, finishing with the story about the screwdriver and how he really hadn't meant to drive without plates.

"Did you realize half that money was Ella's when you started spending it?"

Harris shook his head. "I was just glad it had come to me. I didn't think about whether or not anyone else had a claim to it."

"You've been divorced for a long time," Claudia said. "It's reasonable that you wouldn't remember."

She looked out of the window, just stared, like the trooper had done earlier, and Harris wondered what it was people were looking for when they stared off like that.

"It sounds like Ella needs it," Claudia continued. "From what you say about her."

"It's true. Illness and debt."

"And she's basically a good person?"

"Yes, she's good, more or less. The way anyone is good."

"Okay," Claudia said. "I suppose I'm not upset, but you should have told me."

"I guess we need to look at finances," Harris said.

"I guess so."

They put it off, though. They said they would talk about it over the weekend, but they didn't. They put the pool guy off, too, though Claudia didn't want to take down the stakes—not yet. The grass grew long. Harris mowed around the stakes. One day when he was mowing Claudia came out onto the patio, waving the cordless phone. Harris killed the engine and it went out sputtering.

It was Ella.

"Claudia almost wouldn't give me the phone," Ella said. "She said she didn't know if you wanted to talk to me."

"What did you say?" Harris asked, full of dread that Ella had called spitting fire.

"I told her it concerned *our* daughter, whom she's never met and didn't raise."

"What about her, Ella?"

She said Lindsey was in the hospital.

Harris bought a plane ticket that night. He called his supervisor at work and explained that his daughter was sick. "She's in the icu at the University of Michigan hospital," he said, to prove things were serious.

He was sure to get a window seat. He searched for the window seat because that's what he always did, and then wondered if he shouldn't have cared about what seat he got, if he should have just picked whichever one the mouse landed on, or not even have asked to pick one at all, because it was an emergency and in emergencies you don't care where you sit. The window seat had been chosen, though, and there was no point in thinking about it further.

The ground fell away as the plane took off, and after a few tips of the wings the plane straightened and they roared east. He'd been surprised to learn, upon getting sober, that he loved flying. He always used to be drunk for flights. But today the plane couldn't keep his attention.

When the flight attendant stalked the aisle with the beverage cart, he almost ordered a scotch and soda, his old drink. The impulse bewildered and unsettled him; it reminded him of the haunted feeling he got whenever he had a dream he was drinking.

Lindsey had no diagnosis but was in the hospital, having things done like blood transfusions and emergency surgery to remove a kidney. What were the doctors doing removing kidneys when they didn't even know what was wrong? He felt a lot of built-up emotion rush through him as he sat on the plane. He was thrown back into the years of suffering he and Ella had put each other through. And now he was seeing Lindsey for the first time in six years. All those years had just vanished, and how could he have let them disappear? Maybe Lindsey didn't want to see him, but he could have insisted. And he was only seeing her now because she'd almost died.

Tears filled his eyes and he pressed the heels of his hands into his sockets. His seatmate shifted uncomfortably. Harris wanted to tell this stranger everything, but he didn't.

It was easy to forget that Ella was an addict, too, because she'd gotten clean and stayed clean, whereas Harris had relapsed time and again until the divorce. That was when Lindsey stopped liking him. She'd written him a letter right after he moved out, saying she never wanted to see him again. Her letter had finally brought him to a place where he knew he only had two choices: get clean and scrape together the remains of a life, or die.

Things would never be the same, but he was on this plane trying to make things right, or as right as could be. The loss of his family was mostly his fault, if not entirely. Even though he and Ella had met in rehab—even though their whole relationship had grown from that demented seed—he was the one who hadn't recovered soon enough.

Harris found the hospital to be labyrinthine when he got to it. He asked many people for directions but still wandered the long echoing corridors whose overhead fluorescents made rectangular puddles of light on the floor. He found himself on a breezeway overlooking Ann Arbor. He briefly wondered if he was even in the hospital anymore. Maybe the hospital was connected to a mall or something.

He remembered the first time he'd met Ella. It hadn't been that far from here. They were both in rehab in the early 1980s, a dank facility their parents were paying for. It was understaffed and full of shaking junkies. Ella was detoxing from a mix of stuff, and Harris heard her cry for help from the hallway. There were no nurses around, so Harris went in himself. She told him the room was filling with Ping-Pong balls. Her eyes were blue and wild and long blond hair fanned her pillow. She'd been tied to the bed with restraints.

"I'm going to suffocate," she'd said.

Later, when she was a little better, they decided they looked familiar to each other. They listed mutual friends until they realized they must have seen each other before at parties in Ann Arbor, thrown by a cocaine dealer who'd been Ella's boyfriend at the time.

Harris stood on the sixteenth floor of the hospital, thinking of all this. He could see above the tree line. In every direction he could see trees. South Dakota didn't have as many trees. Mostly just prairies and political billboards with Photoshopped fetuses on them. He'd ended up in South Dakota by accident. He'd gone to a fancy rehab in Minnesota after the divorce, and there he met a guy who knew a guy in advertising in Sioux Falls.

If someone had told him, when he was in his twenties, that he was going to end up in Sioux Falls, that younger version of himself would have said there'd been a mistake. But then again, Harris thought, your former self was always turning into your current self, and the former self didn't have much say in the matter of how all that went down.

Finally, he found Lindsey in her bed. She had a little curtained cubicle that was crowded with machines and IV poles. One IV pushed thick red blood into her veins. It was someone else's blood, but whose blood, and could they trust this person? An oxygen tube lined her cheekbones, sending oxygen into her nostrils. She was so thin. She looked like a pile of bones covered in a sheet; he couldn't believe there was flesh beneath the blanket, but there was.

She didn't see him at first. She had her head turned away and her eyes closed. Outside her window, a construction crew was building a new parking garage. A big crane swung a metal beam around. It looked like whoever was operating the crane didn't quite know where to put the beam.

Lindsey held a plastic cup of water to her chest. The surface quaked with the beating of her heart. She'd had a brush with death, Ella had said on the phone. If Ella hadn't stopped by Lindsey's apartment to check in on her, her heart might have stopped. It was beating at 150 beats per minute. It bothered Harris that Lindsey had just been sitting in her apartment not doing anything about her heartbeat. That wasn't a normal heartbeat; everyone knew that.

As though Lindsey could feel his thoughts turn to her, she opened her eyes and looked his way.

"My girl," Harris said.

"Dad," she said.

She smiled. It was a smile he hadn't seen in years. All the other smiles he saw every day didn't seem to matter compared to the one small crooked smile of his daughter, whose lip was draped with an oxygen tube.

The smile disappeared, though, and Harris felt himself panic as Lindsey threw her head back against the pillow and began to cry. At first it was mostly silent sobbing, but she picked up steam. Harris wouldn't have guessed such a loud sound could come out of someone so thin and sick.

A nurse rushed through the curtain. "What's going on?" he demanded.

Harris put his hands up, guilty of he didn't know what.

Then he heard the scrape of a walker, and Ella poked her head through the curtain. "What did you do, Harris?" she said as she pushed her way inside. It was crowded and dark in the cubicle now. The metal beam still swung uncertainly outside. Harris noticed that there were two additional ivs stuck in Lindsey's veins. Unknown fluids maintained a steady drip.

"He didn't do anything," Lindsey said, but she didn't stop crying.

Still, the nurse asked him to leave for a minute because anxiety wasn't good for her body right now.

Not knowing what else to do, he went to the cafeteria and got a coffee. It burned his tongue when he took a sip, and he went back up to Lindsey's floor with his tongue feeling bald.

There were still tears in her eyes, but she didn't seem as upset anymore.

"I'm sorry," she said.

There had been many times over the past six years when Harris had been angry with Lindsey for shunning him. He'd wondered if she was cruel, or had no empathy, or was just so self-centered she couldn't see he'd struggled every day not to be the addict he was. In a way, he'd wished this illness on her by thinking she didn't understand how lonely it was to be sick. Now he wanted to tell her she'd done everything right in her life and that she never had to be sorry about anything.

But instead of saying any of this he gave a strange and formal nod.

Ella eyed him. They'd only spoken through lawyers since the call about the money. But none of that money stuff seemed to matter right now, with the three of them tucked away in this small cubicle in the large hospital, a place where it seemed they could hide forever and never be found.

Harris left the hospital late, and while Ella offered to drive him to a motel, she didn't say he could sleep on her couch. For some reason, he'd expected to sleep on her couch. He'd never seen her apartment but could envision himself stretched on the sofa under a blanket, the light above the stove on, as she'd always left it on when they lived together.

Instead he checked into a Days Inn. He sunk into the bed, too soft, and flipped through the channels. He suddenly remembered to call Claudia and was surprised he'd forgotten. It was like his life with her was a parrot in a cage and now that he was here he'd put a white sheet over it to keep it quiet.

He told Claudia what the doctors had said. The tests they'd done were inconclusive. They'd ruled out certain infections and cancer. There were other things they'd ruled out, and Harris wondered how many things they were going to rule out before they found the right thing. That could take a long time. He didn't have a return ticket booked. Claudia asked what he was thinking about that.

"About what?" Harris asked.

"Coming home. When will you?"

He put her off, like he'd put off the pool guy.

They hung up and Harris thought back to the first few weeks after Ella had kicked him out of the house. He'd almost given up hope, and the memory of that feeling haunted him. He'd been in a motel room not unlike this one. He was empty, bereft. No feelings had crashed down around him or flooded him or made him cry. There had just been silence, and it had been heavy, and he'd held it in his arms.

Back then, he drank to feel better, or at least to fall asleep. Now he got up and got dressed again and walked down the block to the CVS to buy cigarettes. He shouldn't be smoking, but he could be doing something worse, which made smoking seem okay.

He got to the hospital early and found Lindsey alone in her room. They chatted. She wasn't unhappy, and she said she was feeling a little better. She fidgeted uncomfortably and a mortified look fell on her face when the nurse popped his head in and said they would still be using the bedpan today but would bring in a toilet tomorrow.

"Jesus," she said. She got this look on her face like she didn't know what kind of person she'd become.

She looked a lot like Harris. Their baby pictures were identical, separated by thirty-five years but otherwise identical. Sometimes Harris thought about how there was this woman who looked like him walking around. Not a girl anymore, but the last time he'd seen her, she'd been fifteen. He could feel all that time taking up space in the room. All the questions he could ask got lost because of the sheer number of them.

Lindsey took the burden of speaking first. "How are you feeling after your surgery?" she asked.

"Good," he said. "But that's old news. They took veins from my leg and put them in my chest. Good as new."

Lindsey looked stricken. At first Harris thought she was concerned about the surgery, but then he realized she was looking at his breast pocket.

"Dad, are those cigarettes?"

They were. He'd meant to leave them at the hotel.

"Give them to me," Lindsey demanded. She spoke urgently. She reached out her hand, causing her IV tubes to sway.

Harris gave them to her.

"I'm flushing these down the bedpan," she said, smiling.

Harris started laughing. It overtook him, the laughter. He felt they were both waking up after a long sleep.

Lindsey laughed too, her oxygen tubes twitching as she did. But then clutched her chest. "Ow," she said. "Laughing hurts. There's fluid around my lungs."

Harris stopped short. "Want me to put the bed back?" he said. "Where's the remote thing? I'll put the bed back."

"I'm okay."

They were quiet for a while. The parking garage had grown bigger since yesterday. The crane operator must have decided where to put that beam. In a month or so, whoever was in this room wouldn't be able to see anything out of the window other than the parking garage.

"I'm sorry about yesterday," Lindsey said. "About crying."

"Shh," Harris said. "No need."

"I was worried you weren't going to come." Her voice grew hoarse. "I didn't even call you after your surgery."

He sat with her and told her to breathe, but he was also panicking a little. He didn't want Lindsey to feel the guilt he'd felt, the guilt of not being there for someone.

"I feel like we both almost died," she said. "And we would never have gotten to fix things."

"Don't say that." Harris didn't want to hear her talk that way.

"No," Lindsey said. "Let me finish."

But she didn't finish. She looked like she didn't know how to phrase what she wanted to say. She would know when she was older, Harris thought. He had an idea of what it was. They had another chance, but there was still the possibility they'd blow that chance, too.

Harris sat there, holding her hand and promising himself he wouldn't blow it. But as the day went on he didn't know how to keep that promise. He sat in the cafeteria with another coffee—and another burn on his tongue, he didn't seem able to learn—and as the coffee cooled he realized that even if he saw Lindsey once a year, he'd only see her twenty or thirty more times before he died—if that. It didn't seem fair that the number was so small, and whatever he filled the rest of the years with would never make up for what he was missing.

He thought of the house in Sioux Falls, and the pool. He thought about whether or not he and Claudia would get married. They'd talked about it, but also talked about how there wasn't much of a point at their ages. In any case, Lindsey was the one in Harris's will, not Claudia.

Nothing in Sioux Falls felt as strong as the desire he felt to stay here with his girls. He swirled his coffee in its cup. But what could he do about it?

Ella arrived and the three of them fell easily into conversation. Lindsey was weak but getting better. Then she spiked a fever, and the nurses made Harris and Ella put on smocks and masks. "She might have a methicillin-resistant bacteria," a doctor said.

They put Lindsey in theoretical isolation, but all that separated her from the rest of the floor was the curtain that fluttered in the ambient air.

"I'll be honest," one doctor said. "I was hoping your blood work would look better by now."

No one had an answer, but there was always forward momentum in the hospital. Another few days passed. When Lindsey's fever came down, doctors came by and said they would release Lindsey when she was stable enough, and continue searching for the answer through outpatient care.

"Wait a minute," Harris said, but no one waited a minute.

"They're just going to let her out in the world?"

Lindsey shrugged. "Better than being in here. In case you didn't notice, Dad, it's fucking awful here."

Ella snorted. "It's a good sign that she's swearing again. Harris, you might not know it, but your daughter has a foul mouth."

"Takes after her fucking dad," Harris muttered. But the thought of Lindsey getting swallowed by endless tests and doctor's appointment, plus the looming threat of something like this happening again, filled Harris with agony.

Some kind of excitement through the curtain interrupted Harris's pain. A machine beeped wildly, and there were the sounds of a crash cart hurtling through the hall and through a curtain. From the hurried voices of the doctors and the nurses, Harris understood that the man next door—who was there because he'd tried to kill himself, Harris had heard earlier—had just bitten clear through his breathing tube.

Calls of *clear* rang like crystal bells through the ward.

When it was over and the time of death was noted, one doctor defended himself to another one: "I wanted to save what was left of his brain, so I took him out of sedation. I had no idea he was going to suffocate himself."

Ella, Lindsey, and Harris listened but didn't speak. Though they couldn't see through the curtain, they still looked at it when they heard the man getting wheeled away.

"Please," Lindsey said. "If I ever want to go that badly, just let me. Just drive me someplace and set me free."

"Don't be morbid," Ella said.

Lindsey was moved from the ICU to a regular room, and then she started walking again. The steroids they gave her were dangerous magic—they'd ruin her body, the doctor said, but for now they saved her life. The nurses freed her one by one from her IVs. Harris saw his daughter start to emerge.

"We'll talk on the phone," Lindsey said, when Harris admitted that he had to leave soon—he'd been gone almost a week already—but that he didn't want to.

Lindsey, feeling better, did not feel so desperate to connect with him, as she had when she was in isolation, bound to IVs with fluid cushioning her lungs.

"She's young," a doctor said. "She'll bounce right back."

Harris didn't want her to bounce back to the way she'd been. Ignoring him at every turn. Hating him. He cornered Ella in the hallway later and said the thing that had been lurking in his mind for days now.

"What if I came back? To be close to you and Lindsey."

After all, he and Ella had made it through so much together. From that very first stay in rehab, when they'd teamed up and decided to get better and get out of there, to his bypass surgery in Sioux Falls, to Lindsey's troubles now, they'd stuck it out, elbowed their way to safety. They'd figured it out. They made a good team. In Sioux Falls he never seemed able to figure anything out. Nothing was whole. Even the settlement he'd gotten from his old company was split in half now. If they were together it would be whole again.

"Oh, Harris," Ella said.

Harris looked for a reflection of what he felt in her eyes, but he didn't see it.

"We tried that, remember? We didn't do so well together."

"So much time has passed, Ella. I don't want to live so far away anymore."

"You can move wherever you want. But things aren't going to be the same again. That's not such a bad thing. We just have to adjust. We never adjusted."

Harris couldn't look away from her. She'd been his higher power. Looking at her now, he wondered if she still was, so strong was the feeling of despair that ravaged him at the memory of the feelings he'd had for her. He remembered what he'd done when she told him the room was filling with Ping-Pong balls: he mimed shoveling them out the window.

He went back to Sioux Falls the day Lindsey was released. Harris wheeled her to the pick-up zone, where Ella waited with the car, and then they parted ways so Harris could catch a cab. Lindsey hugged him, but now that she had her body back, she seemed distracted. Matters of the heart once again took a back seat.

"It was a good trip," Harris told Claudia when she picked him up from the airport. "Lindsey and I will be better friends now."

"Do they know what's wrong with her?"

"No," Harris said. "But they'll figure it out. They always do."

"Tomorrow," Claudia said, "we should probably look at finances and figure out the pool."

"Let's," Harris said.

They rode the rest of the way in silence. He'd tried to fix things with Ella, but she'd turned him down, and now he was back here with Claudia, who didn't know anything about it.

He pulled out his phone and texted Lindsey. *I love you*, he wrote.

She texted back a picture of a heart followed by an exclamation point. He wondered if her enthusiasm was real or empty. Enthusiasm meant you either really did care or really didn't care, and it was hard to tell the difference sometimes.

They pulled into the short, wide driveway. He saw Claudia had planted a garden while he was gone.

"Hey, that's nice."

"It's a butterfly garden," Claudia said.

"So it attracts butterflies?"

"Obviously."

"Good," Harris said. "It's good to be home."

He brought his things inside. Everything was the same as he'd left it.

"Do you mind if I mow the grass?" Harris asked. He felt the need to keep moving. He worried about what would happen if he stopped moving. Maybe if he never stopped moving, his body would never have a chance to quit. Maybe he could share that idea with Lindsey, and they could laugh about it.

"When you want to mow the grass is your decision," Claudia said.

So Harris circled the lawn on the riding mower. It was soothing, methodic, like pretending to shovel those Ping-Pong balls had been. He could have shoveled those Ping-Pong balls forever.

It was too windy to be riding the mower, but he kept going anyway. He hadn't done a sweep of the yard first, so the blade kicked up rocks. Harris made smaller and smaller circles, until he came to the spot for the pool. The stakes had grown weatherworn and splintered. Their little plastic flags had frayed. Only a faint trace of spray paint remained on the grass. He took care to avoid the plot, even though he knew there would never be a pool.

VI

Skeleton

After many years of silence between us, I called my friend from college, Octavia, the one I had bought Pedialyte for that night at the grocery store. I find myself recalling the phone conversation at a reading I give in the city, not long after I publish my book.

The story comes out as a response to a question asked by an audience member. "What feelings went into writing this book?" she said, and as I stare at her serious face I realize she's not joking. She really wants to know. I can't recall all my feelings, and the longer the silence extends the more I think I may have never had a feeling before in my life. That was when I stuttered my way into the anecdote.

The story gets too long and the audience looks as though they regret not slipping out of the bookstore before the start of the Q & A. Each passing moment is an opportunity for me to stop talking, an opportunity I glide right past.

"Octavia's the real name of the character called Maille in the book," I say. "I mean, the character is real; the story's not. But you know what I mean. Anyway, for a long time we were very close. I'd heard bits of news about Octavia here and there, but I found her contact information right after I got pregnant and decided to end the pregnancy."

Aamina is sitting in the front row. Her eyes widen. She presses her fist to her mouth and shakes her head nearly imperceptibly.

When I called Octavia, her voice sounded far away. She'd gotten off social media for good years ago, so she hadn't heard anything about my life since we last spoke, which was when Ralph and I still lived in Michigan and she'd just moved to California to teach in San Francisco. She hadn't heard that I'd also gotten sick with an autoimmune disorder, like hers, and she hadn't heard my father had died. She said she felt like we'd been living parallel lives three thousand miles apart.

I stumble through backstory so the conversation will make sense to the audience in the bookstore. I say Octavia and I talked about how we weren't the first people in the world who've gotten sick and whose fathers have died. But sometimes it feels like our loneliness is unparalleled, and so we try to make connections, to turn coincidence into fate, in order to fill the empty spaces, but instead of feeling a sense of understanding, the empty spaces just grow the more we try to connect and analyze them.

"Until you find the right person to help you through, that is," I say.

For Octavia that person was her husband, who introduced her to Jesus. She says she's found peace that way.

"I'm telling the truth when I say I wish I was a believer the way she is," I tell the audience, and for some reason they laugh.

"No, I mean it."

And they laugh more.

"Anyway," I go on, "I told Octavia about how I decided not to tell the father. I knew what I wanted."

As we spoke, I imagined Octavia in the apartment she shared with her husband and son. They're in Los Angeles now. I don't know what the apartment looks like, but I can see citrus trees in the yard—the lemons sunning themselves, round grapefruits almost the size of basketballs, and baby-blue curtains billowing above the windows.

She'd known Ralph—she and I were roommates when I met him—and she asked me if I thought I could work things out with him.

"No," I said to her on the phone. "That was years ago. He married someone else."

"So anyway," I say to the audience. "I told Octavia about the baby, and I wish I could've told my father."

As an afterthought, I add, "My father would have been a good grandfather."

"So that was it," I say to the audience in the bookstore. "That was one of the feelings that made me write this book. It's the feeling that life is always on the brink of never being the same again, and sometimes pieces of our lives fall off the edge, but some things, good and bad, we carry with us after the crash. And those things make us who we are. And then you find something or someone that helps you survive and persevere. For me it was trying to write this book with hope.

"I mean," I add, "there is friendship and hope in this book. Right? I mean, did you get that? If you read it?"

I sound desperate by now. I know I should stop talking, let the audience go, release their attention before they're forced to stumble through the rows of chairs, coats in hand, trying to sneak out quietly while pretending they had to leave early all along.

"Does that answer your question?" I ask.

The woman who asked the question nods. Silence inflates in the room, a giant suffocating balloon. No one has any other questions, and it's time for me to thank the audience for coming and let them disperse to bars to laugh about how awkward I was, how I used the reading as an excuse to share my emotions. Or to forget about the reading entirely and immediately. But I hold on to the silence. There's a feeling I was hoping for, one I didn't get tonight. I'm searching faces for someone who might give it to me. Tonight is a night my father would've been proud of me. I'm yearning to glimpse the glow of that pride in someone's eyes. I can't find it anywhere, and it's not because the people here despise me, as I worry they do, but simply because none of them is my father. And the longer I look the less likely it seems that I'll find him.

ACKNOWLEDGMENTS

To my agent, Maria Massie, for treating my work so carefully and for advocating for this book, and to Lexi Wangler for pulling me out of the slush: thank you. This book wouldn't be here without you. How lucky I am to be a part of the MMQ family.

I want to thank Kwame Dawes, Ashley Strosnider, Courtney Ochsner, Timothy Schaffert, Xu Xi, Haley Mendlik, Anna Weir, and everyone at *Prairie Schooner* and the University of Nebraska Press for taking a chance on me. Thank you, Anne McPeak, for your extraordinary copyediting. I'm grateful I can say my first book found its perfect home.

John Lescroart and the Maurice Prize at UC Davis gave early support to this project: thank you for the encouragement when I needed it most.

To my teachers, whether from long ago or very recently, thank you: Joe Cislo, Chris Cronin, and Thisbe Nissen, who introduced me to short stories; Warren Hecht and Julie Orringer, who read my work early on; Lucy Corin and Pam Houston at UC Davis, a superb creative writing program in a beautiful place; Jayne Anne Phillips, who built more than an MFA but a community, too, at Rutgers–Newark, as well as Akhil Sharma, Jim Goodman, and Tayari Jones. And Elizabeth Gaffney for all her support.

Especially among my teachers I would like to thank Yiyun Li for her belief in my work during and after my time at UC Davis; Laura Kasischke, whose early and continuing support in both life and writing has meant more than I can say; and Alice Elliott Dark for her friendship, wisdom, and for pushing me at a time when I needed to be pushed.

I'm very grateful to the editors who have published my work: Victoria Barrett and Andrew Scott; Patrick Ryan, Kyle Lucia Wu, Sadye Teiser, Hillary Brenhouse, Jonathan Lee; and especially Brigid Hughes: a more brilliant mentor I could never find.

My friends, from both the writing and the regular worlds, thank you, and you add to the joy of living: Hanna Ketai, Janice Karr, Daniel J. Saleh, Rachel Bourgault, Lena Valencia, Laura Preston, Megha Majumdar, Maria Kuznetsova, Daniel Grace, David Owen, Ellen Kamoe, Ashley Clarke, Aaron Fai, Josh Brown, Kiik Araki-Kawaguchi, Nick Falgout, Melissa Murphy, Kelley McKinney, Masaki Matsuo, Jonathan Hoffer, Brett Fletcher Lauer, Jamel Brinkley, Kristen Radtke, Sidik Fofana, Laura Spence-Ash, Safia Jama, Andrés Cerpa, Nick Fuller Googins, Drew Ciccolo, Tony Cirilo, Michelle Hart, Mel King, Kanika Punwani, Elena Schilder, Olvard Smith, Caitlin Ferguson, Jesse Shuman, and Zach Webb.

Thank you, Sarah Blakley-Cartwright, for your best friendship, your spirit, and for always being my last-minute editor on everything I do; and Nicolas Party for your art and your kind soul.

My family has supported me from the beginning and never wavered, and I know how lucky I am to have that. Thank you: my mother, Lynne Cummins, who read the stories I wrote as a child, sent me to writing camp, and who, incredibly, was happy when I chose to study creative writing; my sister, Emily Ross, who has always been equal parts friend and sister, and my new brother, Jonathan Ross; as well as: Kathleen and Dave Devereaux, Joe Cummins and Dede Kinerk, Carson Cummins, Jill Priebe, Jean Priebe, Gail Prohaska Cosgriff, Marty Cosgriff, Abigail Cosgriff and John McKinnon, Charlie and Tarina Cosgriff, and Kenna Hauser. Though we all live great distances from each another, every day you're with me.

And most of all, to my husband, Francis Cosgriff: thank you. Every day with you is a day well spent on this earth.

To order or obtain more information on these or other University of Nebraska Press titles, visit nebraskapress.unl.edu.